ROMANTIC INTERLUDES

Tales of Love and Marriage

ABOUT THE AUTHOR

———

Among the many great novelists who emerged in 19th-century England, Anthony Trollope (1815–1882) is known today as one of the most enduring and beloved.

Though Trollope's father, Thomas, had come from landed gentry, the family was miserably poor during much of Anthony's childhood. His mother, Fanny, became a successful writer while Anthony was in his teens, and largely supported the family with her novels and travel writing.

Trollope is known chiefly for his novels, particularly those in the "Chronicles of Barsetshire" series (*The Warden,* 1855; *Barchester Towers,* 1857; *Doctor Thorne,* 1858; *Framley Parsonage,* 1861; *The Small House at Allington,* 1864; and *The Last Chronicle of Barset,* 1867), and those in the "Palliser" series (*Can You Forgive Her?* 1865; *Phineas Finn,* 1869; *The Eustace Diamonds,* 1873; *Phineas Redux,* 1874; *The Prime Minister,* 1876; and *The Duke's Children,* 1880).

Many of his novels were first published in serial form in popular magazines of the day. He also supplemented the income from his novels and from his career in the postal service by selling short stories to magazines. The stories collected here were published in the popular press between 1860 and 1878.

ROMANTIC INTERLUDES

Tales of Love and Marriage

ANTHONY TROLLOPE

RUSHWATER PRESS

RUSHWATER PRESS
P.O. Box 50151
Sarasota, FL 34232, USA

Includes editors' note and biographical sketch.

PUBLISHER'S CATALOGING-IN-PUBLICATION DATA
Names: Trollope, Anthony, 1815–1882.
Title: Romantic interludes : tales of love and marriage /
Anthony Trollope.
Description: Sarasota, FL: Rushwater Press, 2017.
Identifiers: ISBN 978-0-9801-5324-8
Subjects: Marriage—Fiction. | Great Britain—Social life and
customs—19th century—Fiction. | BISAC FICTION/Short stories
(single author)
Classification: LCC PR5682 .R66 2017 | DDC 823/.8—dc23

Printed in the United States of America
www.rushwaterpress.com
10 9 8 7 6 5 4 3 2 1

FIRST EDITION

Book design by Simon M. Sullivan

Cover illustration and photo: Shutterstock.

EDITORS' NOTE

––––––

These stories by Anthony Trollope have never before been collected in this form. The text, edited by Patricia T. O'Conner and Stewart Kellerman for Rushwater Press, is published here under the title *Romantic Interludes: Tales of Love and Marriage*.

"The Lady of Launay" was first published in serial form in *Light*, a short-lived periodical, in the spring of 1878.

"The Courtship of Susan Bell" first appeared in print in *Harper's New Monthly Magazine* in August 1860.

"The Parson's Daughter of Oxney Colne" was first published in *The London Review* in March 1861.

"Malachi's Cove" originally appeared in the periodical *Good Words* in December 1864.

"Miss Ophelia Gledd" first appeared as part of a book, *A Welcome: Original Contributions in Poetry and Prose,* an 1863 collection of original works by prominent literary figures.

"The O'Conors of Castle Conor, County Mayo" was first printed in *Harper's New Monthly Magazine* in May 1860.

CONTENTS

THE LADY OF LAUNAY

Chapter I

How Bessy Pryor Became a Young Lady of Importance

HOW great is the difference between doing our duty and desiring to do it; between doing our duty and a conscientious struggle to do it; between duty really done and that satisfactory state of mind which comes from a conviction that it has been performed. Mrs. Miles was a lady who through her whole life had thought of little else than duty. Though she was possessed of wealth and social position, though she had been a beautiful woman, though all phases of self-indulgent life had been open to her, she had always adhered to her own idea of duty. Many delights had tempted her. She would fain have travelled, so as to see the loveliness of the world; but she had always remained at home. She could have enjoyed the society of intelligent sojourners in capitals; but she had confined herself to that of her country neighbours. In early youth she had felt herself to be influenced by a taste for dress; she had consequently compelled herself to use raiment of extreme simplicity. She would buy no pictures, no gems, no china, because when young she found that she liked such things too well. She would not leave the parish church to hear a good sermon elsewhere, because even a sermon might be a snare. In the early days of her widowed life it became, she thought, her duty to adopt one of two little motherless, fatherless girls, who had been left altogether unprovided for in the world; and having the choice between the two, she took the plain one, who had weak eyes and a downcast, unhappy look, because it was her duty to deny herself. It was not her fault that the child, who was so unattractive at six, had become beautiful at sixteen, with sweet soft eyes, still downcast occasionally, as though ashamed of their own loveliness; nor was it her fault that Bessy Pryor had so ministered to her in her advancing years as almost to force upon her the delights of self-indulgence. Mrs. Miles had struggled manfully against these wiles, and, in the performance of her duty, had fought with them, even to an attempt to make herself generally disagreeable to the young child. The child, however, had conquered, having wound herself into the old woman's heart of hearts. When Bessy at fifteen was like to die, Mrs. Miles for awhile broke down altogether. She lingered by the bedside, caressed the thin hands, stroked the soft locks, and prayed to the Lord to stay his hand, and to alter his purpose. But when Bessy was strong again she strove to return to her wonted duties. But Bessy, through it all, was quite aware that she was loved.

Looking back at her own past life, and looking also at her days as they were passing, Mrs. Miles thought that she did her duty as well as it is given to frail man or frail woman to perform it. There had been lapses, but still she was conscious of great strength. She did believe of herself that should a great temptation come in her way she would stand strong against it. A great temptation did come in her way, and it is the purport of this little story to tell how far she stood and how far she fell.

Something must be communicated to the reader of her condition in life, and of Bessy's; something, but not much. Mrs. Miles had been a Miss Launay, and, by the death of four brothers almost in their infancy, had become heiress to a large property in Somersetshire. At twenty-five she was married to Mr. Miles, who had a property of his own in the next county, and who at the time of their marriage represented that county in Parliament. When she had been married a dozen years she was left a widow, with two sons, the younger of whom was then about three years old. Her own property, which was much the larger of the two, was absolutely her own; but was intended for Philip, who was her younger boy. Frank Miles, who was eight years older, inherited the other. Circumstances took him much away from his mother's wings. There were troubles among trustees and executors; and the father's heir, after he came of age, saw but little of his mother.

She did her duty, but what she suffered in doing it may be imagined.

Philip was brought up by his mother, who, perhaps, had some consolation in remembering that the younger boy, who was always good to her, would become a man of higher standing in the world than his brother. He was called Philip Launay, the family name having passed on through the mother to the intended heir of the Launay property. He was thirteen when Bessy Pryor was brought home to Launay Park, and, as a schoolboy, had been good to the poor little creature, who for the first year or two had hardly dared to think her life her own amidst the strange huge spaces of the great house. He had despised her, of course; but had not been boyishly cruel to her, and had given her his old playthings. Everybody at Launay had at first despised Bessy Pryor; though the mistress of the house had been thoroughly good to her. There was no real link between her and Launay. Mrs. Pryor had, as a humble friend, been under great obligations to Mrs. Launay, and these obligations, as is their wont, had produced deep love in the heart of the person conferring them. Then both Mr. and Mrs. Pryor had died, and Mrs. Miles had declared that she would take one of the children. She fully intended to bring the girl up sternly and well, with hard belongings, such as might suit her condition. But there had been lapses, occasioned by those unfortunate female prettinesses, and by that equally unfortunate sickness. Bessy never rebelled, and gave, therefore, no scope to an exhibition of extreme duty; and she had a way of kissing her adopted mamma which Mrs. Miles knew to be dangerous. She struggled not to he kissed, but ineffectually. She preached to herself, in the solitude of her own room, sharp sermons against the sweet softness of the girl's caresses; but she could not put a stop to them. "Yes; I will," the girl would say, so softly, but so persistently! Then there would be a great embrace, which Mrs. Miles felt to be as dangerous as a diamond, as bad as a box at the opera.

Bessy had been despised at first all around Launay. Unattractive children are despised, especially when, as in this case, they are nobodies. Bessy Pryor was quite nobody. And certainly there had never been a child more powerless to assert herself. She was for a year or two inferior to the parson's children, and was not thought much of by the farmers' wives. The servants called her Miss Bessy, of course; but it was not till after that illness that there existed among them any of that reverence which is generally felt in the servants' hall for the young ladies of the house. It was then, too, that the parson's daughters found that Bessy was nice to walk with, and that the tenants began to make much of her when she called. The old lady's secret manifestations in the sick bedroom had, perhaps, been seen. The respect paid to Mrs. Miles in that and the next parish was of the most reverential kind. Had she chosen that a dog should be treated as one of the Launays, the dog would have received all the family honours. It must be acknowledged of her that in the performance of her duty she had become a rural tyrant. She gave away many petticoats; but they all had to be stitched according to her idea of stitching a petticoat. She administered physic gratis to the entire estate; but the estate had to take the doses as she chose to have them mixed. It was because she had fallen something short of her acknowledged duty in regard to Bessy Pryor that the parson's daughters were soon even proud of an intimacy with the girl, and that the old butler, when she once went away for a week in the winter, was so careful to wrap her feet up warm in the carriage.

In this way, during the two years subsequent to Bessy's illness, there had gradually come up an altered condition of life at Launay. It could not have been said before that Bessy, though she had been Miss Bessy, was as a daughter in the house. But now a daughter's privileges were accorded to her. When the old squiress was driven out about the county, Bessy was expected, but was asked rather than ordered to accompany her. She always went; but went because she decided on going, not because she was told. And she had a horse to ride; and she was allowed to arrange flowers for the drawing-room; and the gardener did what she told him. What daughter could have more extensive privileges? But poor Mrs. Miles had her misgivings, often asking herself what would come of it all.

When Bessy had been recovering from her illness, Philip, who was seven years her senior, was making a grand tour about the world. He had determined to see, not Paris, Vienna, and Rome, which used to make a grand tour, but Japan, Patagonia, and the South Sea Islands. He had gone in such a way as to ensure the consent of his mother. Two other well-minded young men of fortune had accompanied him, and they had been intent on botany, the social condition of natives, and the progress of the world generally. There had been no harum-scarum rushing about without an object. Philip had been away for more than two years, and had seen all there was to be seen in Japan, Patagonia, and the South Sea Islands. Between them, the young men had written a book, and the critics had been unanimous in observing how improved in those days were the aspirations of young men. On his return he came to Launay for a week or two, and then went up to London. When, after four months, he returned to his mother's house, he was twenty-seven years of age; and Bessy was just twenty. Mrs. Miles knew that there was cause for fear; but she had already taken steps to prevent the danger which she had foreseen.

Chapter II

How Bessy Pryor Wouldn't Marry the Parson

OF course there would be danger. Mrs. Miles had been aware of that from the commencement of things. There had been to her a sort of pleasure in feeling that she had undertaken a duty which might possibly lead to circumstances which would be altogether heartbreaking. The duty of mothering Bessy was so much more a duty because, even when the little girl was blear-eyed and thin, there was present to her mind all the horror of a love affair between her son and the little girl. The Mileses had always been much, and the Launays very much in the west of England. Bessy had not a single belonging that was anything. Then she had become beautiful and attractive, and worse than that, so much of a person about the house that Philip himself might be tempted to think that she was fit to be his wife!

Among the duties prescribed to herself by Mrs. Miles was none stronger than that of maintaining the family position of the Launays. She was one of those who not only think that blue blood should remain blue, but that blood not blue should be allowed no azure mixture. The proper severance of classes was a religion to her. Bessy was a gentlewoman, so much had been admitted, and therefore she had been brought into the drawing-room instead of being relegated among the servants, and had thus grown up to be, oh, so dangerous! She was a gentlewoman, and fit to be a gentleman's wife, but not fit to be the wife of the heir of the Launays. The reader will understand, perhaps, that I, the writer of this little history, think her to have been fit to become the wife of any man who might have been happy enough to win her young heart, however blue his blood. But Mrs. Miles had felt that precautions and remedies and arrangements were necessary.

Mrs. Miles had altogether approved of the journey to Japan. That had been a preventive, and might probably afford time for an arrangement. She had even used her influence to prolong the travelling till the arrangements should be complete; but in this she had failed. She had written to her son, saying that, as his sojourn in strange lands would so certainly tend to the amelioration of the human races generally—for she had heard of the philanthropic inquiries, of the book, and the botany—she would by no means press upon him her own natural longings. If another year was required, the necessary remittances should be made with a liberal hand. But Philip, who had chosen to go because he liked it, came back when he liked it, and there he was at Launay before a certain portion of the arrangements had been completed, as to which Mrs. Miles had been urgent during the last six months of his absence.

A good-looking young clergyman in the neighbourhood, with a living of £400 a year, and a fortune of £6,000 of his own, had during the time been proposed to Bessy by Mrs. Miles. Mr. Morrison, the Rev. Alexander Morrison, was an excellent young man; but it may be doubted whether

the patronage by which he was put into the living of Budcombe at an early age, over the head of many senior cu-
rates, had been exercised with sound clerical motives. Mrs.
Miles was herself the patroness, and, having for the last six
years felt the necessity of providing a husband for Bessy,
had looked about for a young man who should have good
gifts and might probably make her happy. A couple of
thousand pounds added had at first suggested itself to Mrs.
Miles. Then love had ensnared her, and Bessy had become
dear to every one, and money was plenty. The thing should
be made so beautiful to all concerned that there should be
no doubt of its acceptance. The young parson didn't doubt.
Why should he? The living had been a wonderful stroke of
luck for him! The portion proposed would put him at once
among the easy-living gentlemen of the county; and then
the girl herself! Bessy had loomed upon him as feminine
perfection from the first moment he had seen her. It was to
him as though the heavens were raining their choicest
blessings on his head.

Nor had Mrs. Miles any reason to find fault with Bessy.
Had Bessy jumped into the man's arms directly he had
been offered to her as a lover, Mrs. Miles would herself
have been shocked. She knew enough of Bessy to be sure
that there would be no such jumping. Bessy had at first
been startled, and, throwing herself into her old friend's
arms, had pleaded her youth. Mrs. Miles had accepted the
embrace, had acknowledged the plea, and had expressed
herself quite satisfied, simply saying that Mr. Morrison
would be allowed to come about the house, and use his
own efforts to make himself agreeable. The young parson

had come about the house, and had shown himself to be good-humoured and pleasant. Bessy never said a word against him; did in truth try to persuade herself that it would be nice to have him as a lover; but she failed. "I think he is very good," she said one day, when she was pressed by Mrs. Miles.

"And he is a gentleman."

"Oh, yes," said Bessy.

"And good-looking."

"I don't know that that matters."

"No, my dear, no; only he is handsome. And then he is very fond of you." But Bessy would not commit herself, and certainly had never given any encouragement to the gentleman himself.

This had taken place just before Philip's return. At that time his stay at Launay was to be short; and during his sojourn his hands were to be very full. There would not be much danger during that fortnight, as Bessy was not prone to put herself forward in any man's way. She met him as his little pet of former days, and treated him quite as though he were a superior being. She ran about for him as he arranged his botanical treasures, and took in all that he said about the races. Mrs. Miles, as she watched them, still trusted that there might be no danger. But she went on with her safeguards. "I hope you like Mr. Morrison," she said to her son.

"Very much indeed, mother; but why do you ask?"

"It is a secret; but I'll tell you. I think he will become the husband of our dear Bessy."

"Marry Bessy!"

"Why not?" Then there was a pause. "You know how dearly I love Bessy. I hope you will not think me wrong when I tell you that I propose to give what will be for her a large fortune, considering all things."

"You should treat her just as though she were a daughter and a sister," said Philip.

"Not quite that! But you will not begrudge her six thousand pounds?"

"It is not half enough."

"Well, well. Six thousand pounds is a large sum of money to give away. However, I am sure we shall not differ about Bessy. Don't you think Mr. Morrison would make her a good husband?" Philip looked very serious, knitted his brows, and left the room, saying that he would think about it.

To make him think that the marriage was all but arranged would be a great protection. There was a protection to his mother also in hearing him speak of Bessy as being almost a sister. But there was still a further protection. Down away in Cornwall there was another Launay heiress coming up, some third or fourth cousin, and it had long since been settled among certain elders that the Launay properties should be combined. To this Philip had given no absolute assent; had even run away to Japan just when it had been intended that he should go to Cornwall. The Launay heiress had then only been seventeen, and it had been felt to be almost as well that there should be delay, so that the time was not passed by the young man in dangerous neighbourhoods. The South Sea Islands and Patagonia had been safe. And now when the idea of combining the properties was again mooted, he at first said nothing against it. Surely such precautions as these would suffice, especially as Bessy's retiring nature would not allow her to fall in love with any man within the short compass of a fortnight.

Not a word more was said between Mrs. Miles and her son as to the prospects of Mr. Morrison; not a word more then. She was intelligent enough to perceive that the match was not agreeable to him; but she attributed this feeling on his part to an idea that Bessy ought to be treated in all respects as though she were a daughter of the house of Launay. The idea was absurd, but safe. The match, if it could be managed, would of course go on, but should not be mentioned to him again till it could be named as a thing absolutely arranged. But there was no present danger. Mrs. Miles felt sure that there was no present danger. Mrs. Miles had seen Bessy grow out of meagre thinness and early want of ruddy health, into gradual proportions of perfect feminine loveliness; but, having seen the gradual growth, she did not know how lovely the girl was. A woman hardly ever does know how omnipotent may be the attraction which some feminine natures, and some feminine forms, diffuse unconsciously on the young men around them.

But Philip knew, or rather felt. As he walked about the park he declared to himself that Alexander Morrison was an insufferably impudent clerical prig; for which assertion there was, in truth, no ground whatsoever. Then he accused his mother of a sordid love of money and property, and swore to himself that he would never stir a step towards Cornwall. If they chose to have that red-haired Launay girl up from the far west, he would go away to London, or perhaps back to Japan. But what shocked him most was that such a girl as Bessy, a girl whom he treated always just like his own sister, should give herself to such a man as that young parson at the very first asking! He struck the trees among which he was walking with his stick as he thought of the meanness of feminine nature. And then such a greasy, ugly brute! But Mr. Morrison was not at all greasy, and would have been acknowledged by the world at large to be much better looking than Philip Launay.

Then came the day of his departure. He was going up to London in March to see his book through the press, make himself intimate at his club, and introduce himself generally to the ways of that life which was to be his hereafter. It had been understood that he was to pass the season in London, and that then the combined-property question should come on in earnest. Such was his mother's understanding; but by this time, by the day of his departure, he was quite determined that the combined-property question should never receive any consideration at his hands.

Early on that day he met Bessy somewhere about the house. She was very sweet to him on this occasion, partly because she loved him dearly,—as her adopted brother; partly because he was going; partly because it was her nature to be sweet! "There is one question I want to ask you," he said suddenly, turning round upon her with a frown. He had not meant to frown, but it was his nature to do so when his heart frowned within him.

"What is it, Philip?" She turned pale as she spoke, but looked him full in the face.

"Are you engaged to that parson?" She went on looking

at him, but did not answer a word. "Are you going to marry him? I have a right to ask." Then she shook her head. "You certainly are not?" Now as he spoke his voice was changed, and the frown had vanished. Again she shook her head. Then he got hold of her hand, and she left her hand with him, not thinking of him as other than a brother. "I am so glad. I detest that man."

"Oh, Philip; he is very good!"

"I do not care two-pence for his goodness. You are quite sure?" Now she nodded her head. "It would have been most awful, and would have made me miserable; miserable. Of course, my mother is the best woman in the world; but why can't she let people alone to find husbands and wives for themselves?" There was a slight frown, and then with a visible effort he completed his speech. "Bessy, you have grown to be the loveliest woman that ever I looked upon."

She withdrew her hand very suddenly. "Philip, you should not say such a thing as that."

"Why not, if I think it?"

"People should never say anything to anybody about themselves."

"Shouldn't they?"

"You know what I mean. It is not nice. It's the sort of stuff which people who ain't ladies and gentlemen put into books."

"I should have thought I might say anything."

"So you may; and of course you are different. But there are things that are so disagreeable!"

"And I am one of them?"

"No, Philip, you are the truest and best of brothers."

"At any rate you won't." Then he paused.

"No, I won't."

"That's a promise to your best and dearest brother?" She nodded her head again, and he was satisfied.

He went away, and when he returned to Launay at the end of four months he found that things were not going on pleasantly at the Park. Mr. Morrison had been refused, with a positive assurance from the young lady that she would never change her mind, and Mrs. Miles had become more stern than ever in the performance of her duty to her family.

Chapter III

How Bessy Pryor Came to Love the Heir of Launay

MATTERS became very unpleasant at the Park soon after Philip went away. There had been something in his manner as he left, and a silence in regard to him on Bessy's part, which created, not at first surprise, but uneasiness in the mind of Mrs. Miles. Bessy hardly mentioned his name, and Mrs. Miles knew enough of the world to feel that such restraint must have a cause. It would have been natural for a girl so circumstanced to have been full of Philip and his botany. Feeling this she instigated the parson to renewed attempts; but the parson had to tell her that there was no chance for him. "What has she said?" asked Mrs. Miles.

"That it can never be."

"But it shall be," said Mrs. Miles, stirred on this occasion to an assertion of the obstinacy which was in her nature. Then there was a most unpleasant scene between the old lady and her dependent. "What is it that you expect?" she asked.

"Expect, aunt!" Bessy had been instructed to call Mrs. Miles her aunt.

"What do you think is to be done for you?"

"Done for me! You have done everything. May I not stay with you?" Then Mrs. Miles gave utterance to a very long lecture, in which many things were explained to Bessy. Bessy's position was said to be one very peculiar in its nature. Were Mrs. Miles to die there would be no home for her. She could not hope to find a home in Philip's house as a real sister might have done. Everybody loved her because she had been good and gracious, but it was her duty to marry—especially her duty—so that there might be no future difficulty. Mr. Morrison was exactly the man that such a girl as Bessy ought to want as a husband. Bessy through her tears declared that she didn't want any husband, and that she certainly did not want Mr. Morrison.

"Has Philip said anything?" asked the imprudent old woman. Then Bessy was silent. "What has Philip said to you?"

"I told him, when he asked, that I should never marry Mr. Morrison." Then it was—in that very moment—that Mrs. Miles in truth suspected the blow that was to fall upon her; and in that same moment she resolved that, let the pain be what it might to any or all of them, she would do her duty by her family.

"Yes," she said to herself, as she sat alone in the unadorned, unattractive sanctity of her own bedroom, "I will do my duty at any rate now." With deep remorse she acknowledged to herself that she had been remiss. For a moment her anger was very bitter. She had warmed a reptile in her bosom. The very words came to her thoughts, though they were not pronounced. But the words were at once rejected. The girl had been no reptile. The girl had been true. The girl had been as sweet a girl as had ever brightened the hearth of an old woman. She acknowledged so much to herself even in this moment of her agony. But not the less would she do her duty by the family of the Launays. Let the girl do what she might, she must be sent away—got rid of—sacrificed in any way rather than that Philip should be allowed to make himself a fool. When for a couple of days she had turned it all in her mind she did not believe that there was as yet any understanding between the girl and Philip. But still she was sure that the danger existed. Not only had the girl refused her destined husband—just such a man as such a girl as Bessy ought to have loved—but she had communicated her purpose in that respect to Philip. There had been more of confidence between them than between her and the girl. How could they two have talked on such a subject unless there had been between them something of stricter, closer friendship even than that of brother and sister? There had been something of a conspiracy between them against her—her who at Launay was held to be omnipotent, against her who had in her hands all the income, all the power, all the ownership—the mother of one of them, and the protectress and only friend of the other! She would do her duty, let Bessy be ever so sweet. The girl must be made to marry Mr. Morrison—or must be made to go.

But whither should she go, and if that "whither" should be found, how should Philip be prevented from following her? Mrs. Miles, in her agony, conceived an idea that it would be easier to deal with the girl herself than with Philip. A woman, if she thinks it to be a duty, will more readily sacrifice herself in the performance of it than will a man. So at least thought Mrs. Miles, judging from her own feelings; and Bessy was very good, very affectionate, very grateful, had always been obedient. If possible she should be driven into the arms of Mr. Morrison. Should she stand firm against such efforts as could be made in that direction, then an appeal should be made to herself. After all that had been done for her, would she ruin the family of the Launays for the mere whim of her own heart?

During the process of driving her into Mr. Morrison's arms—a process which from first to last was altogether hopeless—not a word had been said about Philip. But Bessy understood the reticence. She had been asked as to her promise to Philip, and never forgot that she had been asked. Nor did she ever forget those words which at the moment so displeased her—"You have grown to be the loveliest woman that I have ever looked upon." She remembered now that he had held her hand tightly while he had spoken them, and that an effort had been necessary as she withdrew it. She had been perfectly serious in decrying the personal compliment; but still, still, there had been a flavour of love in the words which now remained among her heartstrings. Of course he was not her brother—not even her cousin. There was not a touch of blood between them to warrant such a compliment as a joke. He, as a young man, had told her that he thought her, as a young woman, to be lovely above all others. She was quite sure of this—that no possible amount of driving should drive her into the arms of Mr. Morrison.

The old woman became more and more stern. "Dear aunt," Bessy said to her one day, with an air of firmness which had evidently been assumed purposely for the occasion, "indeed, indeed, I cannot love Mr. Morrison." Then Mrs. Miles had resolved that she must resort to the other alternative. Bessy must go. She did believe that when everything should be explained Bessy herself would raise no difficulty as to her own going. Bessy had no more right to live at Launay than had any other fatherless, motherless, penniless living creature. But how to explain it? What reason should be given? And whither should the girl be sent?

Then there came delay, caused by another great trouble. On a sudden Mrs. Miles was very ill. This began about the end of May, when Philip was still up in London inhaling the incense which came up from the success of his book. At first she was very eager that her son should not be recalled to Launay. "Why should a young man be brought into the house with a sick old woman?" Of course she was eager. What evils might not happen if they two were brought together during her illness? At the end of three weeks, however, she was worse—so much worse that the people around her were afraid; and it became manifest to all of them that the truth must be told to Philip in spite of her injunctions. Bessy's position became one of great difficulty, because words fell from Mrs. Miles which explained to her almost with accuracy the condition of her aunt's mind. "You should not be here," she said over and over again. Now, it had been the case, as a matter of course, that Bessy, during the old lady's illness, had never left her bedside day or night. Of course she had been the nurse, of course she had tended the invalid in everything. It had been so much a matter of course that the poor lady had been impotent to prevent it,

ANTHONY TROLLOPE

in her ineffectual efforts to put an end to Bessy's influence. The servants, even the doctors, obeyed Bessy in regard to the household matters. Mrs. Miles found herself quite unable to repel Bessy from her bedside. And then, with her mind always intent on the necessity of keeping the young people apart, and when it was all but settled that Philip should be summoned, she said again and again, "You should not be here, Bessy. You must not be here, Bessy."

But whither should she go? No place was even suggested to her. And were she herself to consult some other friend as to a place—the clergyman of their own parish for instance, who out of that house was her most intimate friend—she would have to tell the whole story, a story which could not be told by her lips. Philip had never said a word to her, except that one word: "You have grown to be the loveliest woman that ever I looked upon." The word was very frequent in her thoughts, but she could tell no one of that!

If he did think her lovely, if he did love her, why should not things run smoothly? She had found it to be quite out of the question that she should be driven into the arms of Mr. Morrison, but she soon came to own to herself that she might easily be enticed into those other arms. But then perhaps he had meant nothing—so probably had meant nothing! But if not, why should she be driven away from Launay? As her aunt became worse and worse, and when Philip came down from London, and with Philip a London physician, nothing was settled about poor Bessy, and nothing was done. When Philip and Bessy stood together at the sick woman's bedside she was nearly insensible, wandering in her mind, but still with that care heavy at her heart. "No, Philip; no, no, no," she said. "What is it, mother ?" asked Philip. Then Bessy escaped from the room and resolved that she would always be absent when Philip was by his mother's bedside.

There was a week in which the case was almost hopeless; and then a week during which the mistress of Launay crept slowly back to life. It could not but be that they two should see much of each other during such weeks. At every meal they sat together. Bessy was still constant at the bedside of her aunt, but now and again she was alone with Philip. At first she struggled to avoid him, but she struggled altogether in vain. He would not be avoided. And then of course he spoke. "Bessy, I am sure you know that I love you."

"I am sure I hope you do," she replied, purposely misinterpreting him.

Then he frowned at her. "I am sure, Bessy, you are above all subterfuges."

"What subterfuges? Why do you say that?"

"You are no sister of mine; no cousin even. You know what I mean when I say that I love you. Will you be my wife?"

Oh! if she might only have knelt at his feet and hidden her face among her hands, and have gladly answered him with a little "Yes," extracted from amidst her happy blushes! But, in every way, there was no time for such joys. "Philip, think how ill your mother is," she said.

"That cannot change it. I have to ask you whether you

can love me. I am bound to ask you whether you will love me." She would not answer him then; but during that second week in which Mrs. Miles was creeping back to life she swore that she did love him, and would love him, and would be true to him for ever and ever.

Chapter IV

How Bessy Pryor Owned That She Was Engaged

WHEN these pretty oaths had been sworn, and while Mrs. Miles was too ill to keep her eyes upon them or to separate them, of course the two lovers were much together. For whispering words of love, for swearing oaths, for sweet kisses and looking into each other's eyes, a few minutes now and again will give ample opportunities. The long hours of the day and night were passed by Bessy with her aunt; but there were short moments, heavenly moments, which sufficed to lift her off the earth into an Elysium of joy. His love for her was so perfect, so assured! "In a matter such as this," he said in his fondly serious air, "my mother can have no right to interfere with me."

"But with me she may," said Bessy, foreseeing in the midst of her Paradise the storm which would surely come.

"Why should she wish to do so? Why should she not allow me to make myself happy in the only way in which it is possible?" There was such an ecstasy of bliss coming from such words as these, such a perfection of the feeling of mutual love, that she could not but be exalted to the heavens, although she knew that the storm would surely come. If her love would make him happy, then, then, surely he should be happy. "Of course she has given up her idea about that parson," he said.

"I fear she has not, Philip."

"It seems to me too monstrous that any human being should go to work and settle whom two other human beings are to marry."

"There was never a possibility of that."

"She told me it was to be so."

"It never could have been," said Bessy with great emphasis. "Not even for her, much as I love her—not even for her to whom I owe everything—could I consent to marry a man I did not love. But—"

"But what?"

"I do not know how I shall answer her when she bids me give you up. Oh, my love, how shall I answer her?"

Then he told her at considerable length what was the answer which he thought should in such circumstances be made to his mother. Bessy was to declare that nothing could alter her intentions, that her own happiness and that of her lover depended on her firmness, and that they two did, in fact, intend to have their own way in this matter sooner or later. Bessy, as she heard the lesson, made no direct reply, but she knew too well that it could be of no service to her. All that it would be possible for her to say, when the resolute old woman should declare her purpose, would be that come what might she must always love Philip Launay; that she never, never, never could become the wife of any other man. So much she thought she would say. But as to asserting her right to her lover, that she was sure would be beyond her.

Everyone in the house except Mrs. Miles was aware that Philip and Bessy were lovers, and from the dependents of the house the tidings spread through the parish. There had been no special secrecy. A lover does not usually pronounce his vows in public. Little half-lighted corners and twilight hours are chosen, or banks beneath the trees supposed to be safe from vulgar eyes, or lonely wanderings. Philip had followed the usual way of the world in his love-making, but had sought his secret moments with no special secrecy. Before the servants he would whisper to Bessy with that look of thorough confidence in his eyes which servants completely understand; and thus while the poor old woman was still in her bed, while she was unaware both of the danger and of her own immediate impotence, the secret—as far as it was a secret—became known, to all Launay. Mr. Morrison heard it over at Budcombe, and, with his heart down in his boots, told himself that now certainly there could be no chance for him. At Launay Mr. Gregory was the rector, and it was with his daughters that Bessy had become intimate. Knowing much of the mind of the first lady of the parish, he took upon himself to say a word or two to Philip. "I am so glad to hear that your mother is much better this morning."

"Very much better."

"It has been a most serious illness."

"Terribly serious, Mr. Gregory."

Then there was a pause, and sundry other faltering allusions were made to the condition of things up at the house, from which Philip was aware that words of counsel or perhaps reproach were coming. "I hope you will excuse me, Philip, if I tell you something."

"I think I shall excuse anything from you."

"People are saying about the place that during your mother's illness you have engaged yourself to Bessy Pryor."

"That's very odd," said Philip.

"Odd!" repeated the parson.

"Very odd indeed, because what the people about the place say is always supposed to be untrue. But this report is true."

"It is true?"

"Quite true, and I am proud to be in a position to assure you that I have been accepted. I am really sorry for Mr. Morrison, you know."

"But what will your mother say?"

"I do not think that she or anyone can say that Bessy is not fit to be the wife of the finest gentleman in the land." This he said with an air of pride which showed plainly enough that he did not intend to be talked out of his purpose.

"I should not have spoken, but that your dear mother is so ill," rejoined the parson.

"I understand that. I must fight my own battle and Bessy's as best I may. But you may be quite sure, Mr. Gregory, that I mean to fight it."

Nor did Bessy deny the fact when her friend Mary Gregory interrogated her. The question of Bessy's marriage with Mr. Morrison had, somewhat cruelly in regard to her and more cruelly still in regard to the gentleman, become public property in the neighbourhood. Everybody had known that Mrs. Miles intended to marry Bessy to the parson of Budcombe, and everybody had thought that Bessy would, as a matter of course, accept her destiny. Everybody now knew that Bessy had rebelled; and, as Mrs. Miles's auto-cratic disposition was well understood, everybody was waiting to see what would come of it. The neighbourhood generally thought that Bessy was unreasonable and un-grateful. Mr. Morrison was a very nice man, and nothing could have been more appropriate. Now, when the truth came out, everybody was very much interested indeed. That Mrs. Miles should assent to a marriage between the heir and Bessy Pryor was quite out of the question. She was too well known to leave a doubt on the mind of anyone either in Launay or Budcombe on that matter. Men and women drew their breath and looked at each other. It was just when the parishes thought that she was going to die that the parishioners first heard that Bessy would not marry Mr. Morrison because of the young squire. And now, when it was known that Mrs. Miles was not going to die, it was known that the young squire was absolutely engaged to Bessy Pryor. "There'll be a deal o' vat in the voir," said the old head ploughman of Launay, talking over the matter with the wife of Mr. Gregory's gardener. There was going to be "a deal of fat in the fire."

Mrs. Miles was not like other mothers. Everything in respect to present income was in her hands. And Bessy was not like other girls. She had absolutely no "locus standi" in the world, except what came to her from the bounty of the old lady. By favour of the Lady of Launay she held her head among the girls of that part of the country as high as any girl there. She was only Bessy Pryor; but, from love and kindness, she was the recognised daughter of the house of Launay. Everybody knew it all. Everybody was aware that she had done much towards reaching her present position by her own special sweetness. But should Mrs. Miles once frown, Bessy would be nobody. "Oh, Bessy, how is this all to be?" asked Mary Gregory.

"As God pleases," said Bessy, very solemnly.

"What does Mrs. Miles say?"

"I don't want anybody to ask me about it," said Bessy. "Of course I love him. What is the good of denying it? But I cannot talk about it." Then Mary Gregory looked as though some terrible secret had been revealed to her— some secret of which the burden might probably be too much for her to bear.

The first storm arose from an interview which took place between the mother and son as soon as the mother found herself able to speak on a subject which was near her heart. She sent for him and once again besought him to take steps towards that combining of the properties which was so essential to the Launay interests generally. Then he declared his purpose very plainly. He did not intend to combine the properties. He did not care for the red-haired Launay cousin. It was his intention to marry—Bessy Pryor; yes— he had proposed to her and she had accepted him. The poor sick mother was at first almost overwhelmed with despair. "What can I do but tell you the truth when you ask me?" he said.

"Do!" she screamed. "What could you do? You could have remembered your honour! You could have remembered your blood! You could have remembered your duty!" Then she bade him leave her, and after an hour passed in thought she sent for Bessy. "I have had my son with me," she said, sitting bolt upright in her bed, looking awful in her wanness, speaking with low, studied, harsh voice, with her two hands before her on the counterpane. "I have had my son with me and he has told me." Bessy felt that she was trembling. She was hardly able to support herself. She had not a word to say. The sick old woman was terrible in her severity. "Is it true?"

"Yes, it is true," whispered Bessy.

"And this is to be my return?"

"Oh, my dearest, my darling, oh, my aunt, dear, dearest, dearest aunt! Do not speak like that! Do not look at me like that! You know I love you. Don't you know I love you?" Then Bessy prostrated herself on the bed, and getting hold of the old woman's hand covered it with kisses. Yes, her aunt did know that the girl loved her, and she knew that she loved the girl perhaps better than any other human being in the world. The eldest son had become estranged from her. Even Philip had not been half so much to her as this girl. Bessy had wound herself round her very heart-strings. It made her happy even to sit and look at Bessy. She had denied herself all pretty things; but this prettiest of all things had grown up beneath her eyes. She did not draw away her hand; but, while her hand was being kissed, she made up her mind that she would do her duty.

"Of what service will be your love," she said, "if this is to be my return?" Bessy could only lie and sob and hide her face. "Say that you will give it up." Not to say that, not to give him up, was the only resolution at which Bessy had arrived. "If you will not say so, you must leave me, and I shall send you word what you are to do. If you are my enemy you shall not remain here."

"Pray—pray do not call me an enemy."

"You had better go." The woman's voice as she said this was dreadful in its harshness. Then Bessy, slowly creeping down from the bed, slowly slunk out of the room.

Chapter V

*How Bessy Pryor Ceased to Be a
Young Lady of Importance*

WHEN the old woman was alone she at once went to work in her own mind resolving what should be her course of proceeding. To yield in the matter, and to confirm the happiness of the young people, never occurred to her. Again and again she repeated to herself that she would do her duty; and again and again she repeated to herself that in allowing Philip and Bessy to come together she had neglected her duty. That her duty required her to separate them, in spite of their love, in spite of their engagement, though all the happiness of their lives might depend upon it, she did not in the least doubt. Duty is duty. And it was her duty to aggrandise the house of Launay, so that the old autocracy of the land might, so far as in her lay, be preserved. That it would be a good and pious thing to do,—to keep them apart, to force Philip to marry the girl in Cornwall, to drive Bessy into Mr. Morrison's arms, was to her so certain that it required no further thought. She had never indulged herself. Her life had been so led as to maintain the power of her own order, and relieve the wants of those below her. She had done nothing for her own pleasure. How should it occur to her that it would be well for her to change the whole course of her life in order that she might administer to the joys of a young man and a young woman?

It did not occur to her to do so. Lying thus all alone, white, sick, and feeble, but very strong of heart, she made her resolutions. As Bessy could not well be sent out of the house till a home should be provided for her elsewhere, Philip should be made to go. As that was to be the first step, she again sent for Philip that day. "No, mother; not while you are so ill." This he said in answer to her first command that he should leave Launay at once. It had not occurred to him that the house in which he had been born and bred, the house of his ancestors, the house which he had always supposed was at some future day to be his own, was not free to him. But, feeble as she was, she soon made him understand her purpose. He must go,—because she ordered him, because the house was hers and not his, because he was no longer welcome there as a guest unless he would promise to abandon Bessy. "This is tyranny, mother," he said.

"I do not mean to argue the question," said Mrs. Miles, leaning back among the pillows, gaunt, with hollow cheeks, yellow with her long sickness, seeming to be all eyes as she looked at him. "I tell you that you must go."

"Mother!"

Then, at considerable length, she explained her intended arrangements. He must go, and live upon the very modest income which she proposed. At any rate he must go, and go at once. The house was hers, and she would not have him there. She would have no one in the house who disputed her will. She had been an over-indulgent mother to him, and this had been the return made to her! She had condescended to explain to him her intention in regard to Bessy, and he had immediately resolved to thwart her. When she was dead and gone it might perhaps be in his power to ruin the family if he chose. As to that she would take further thought. But she, as long as she lived, would do her duty. "I suppose I may understand," she said, "that you will leave Launay early after breakfast to-morrow."

"Do you mean to turn me out of the house?"

"I do," she said, looking full at him, all eyes, with her grey hair coming dishevelled from under the large frill of her nightcap, with cheeks gaunt and yellow. Her extended hands were very thin. She had been very near death, and seemed, as he gazed at her, to be very near it now. If he went it might be her fate never to see him again.

"I cannot leave you like this," he said.

"Then obey me."

"Why should we not be married, mother?"

"I will not argue. You know as well as I do. Will you obey me?"

"Not in this, mother. I could not do so without perjuring myself."

"Then go you out of this house at once." She was sitting now bolt upright on her bed, supporting herself on her hands behind her. The whole thing was so dreadful that he could not endure to prolong the interview, and he left the room.

Then there came a message from the old housekeeper to Bessy, forbidding her to leave her own room. It was thus that Bessy first understood that her great sin was to be made public to all the household. Mrs. Knowl, who was the head of the domestics, had been told, and now felt that a sort of authority over Bessy had been confided to her. "No, Miss Bessy; you are not to go into her room at all. She says that she will not see you till you promise to be said by her."

"But why, Mrs. Knowl?"

"Well, miss; I suppose it's along of Mr. Philip. But you know that better than me. Mr. Philip is to go to-morrow morning and never come back any more."

"Never come back to Launay?"

"Not while things is as they is, miss. But you are to stay here and not go out at all. That's what Madam says." The servants about the place all called Mrs. Miles Madam.

There was a potency about Mrs. Miles which enabled her to have her will carried out, although she was lying ill in bed,—to have her will carried out as far as the immediate severance of the lovers was concerned. When the command had been brought by the mouth of a servant, Bessy determined that she would not see Philip again before he went. She understood that she was bound by her position, bound by gratitude, bound by a sense of propriety, to so much obedience as that. No earthly authority could be sufficient to make her abandon her troth. In that she could not allow even her aunt to sway her,—her aunt though she were sick and suffering, even though she were dying! Both her love and her vow were sacred to her. But obedience at the moment she did owe, and she kept her room. Philip came to the door, but she sat mute and would not speak to him. Mrs. Knowl, when she brought her some food, asked her whether she intended to obey the order. "Your aunt wants a promise from you, Miss Bessy?"

"I am sure my aunt knows that I shall obey her," said Bessy.

On the following morning Philip left the house. He sent a message to his mother, asking whether she would see him; but she refused. "I think you had better not disturb her, Mr. Philip," said Mrs. Knowl. Then he went, and as the waggonette took him away from the door, Bessy sat and listened to the sound of the wheels on the gravel.

All that day and all the next passed on and she was not allowed to see her aunt. Mrs. Knowl repeated that she could not take upon herself to say that Madam was better. No doubt the worry of the last day or two had been a great trouble to her. Mrs. Knowl grew much in self-importance at the time, and felt that she was overtopping Miss Bessy in the affairs of Launay.

It was no less true than singular that all the sympathies of the place should be on the side of the old woman. Her illness probably had something to do with it. And then she had been so autocratic, all Launay and Budcombe had been so accustomed to bow down to her, that rebellion on the part of anyone seemed to be shocking. And who was Bessy Pryor that she should dare to think of marrying the heir? Who, even, was the supposed heir that he should dare to think of marrying anyone in opposition to the actual owner of the acres? Heir though he was called, he was not necessarily the heir. She might do as she pleased with all Launay and all Budcombe, and there were those who thought that if Philip was still obstinate she would leave everything to her elder son. She did not love her elder son. In these days she never saw him. He was a gay man of the world, who had never been dutiful to her. But he might take the name of Launay, and the family would be perpetuated as well that way as the other. Philip was very foolish. And as for Bessy; Bessy was worse than foolish. That was the verdict of the place generally.

I think Launay liked it. The troubles of our neighbours are generally endurable, and any subject for conversation is a blessing. Launay liked the excitement; but, nevertheless, felt itself to be compressed into whispers and a solemn demeanour. The Gregory girls were solemn, conscious of the iniquity of their friend, and deeply sensitive of the danger to which poor Philip was exposed. When a rumour came to the vicarage that a fly had been up at the great house, it was immediately conceived that Mr. Jones, the lawyer from Taunton, had been sent for, with a view to an alteration of the will. This suddenness, this anger, this disruption of all things was dreadful! But when it was discovered that the fly contained no one but the doctor there was disappointment.

On the third day there came a message from Mrs. Miles to the rector. Would Mr. Gregory step up and see Mrs. Miles? Then it was thought at the rectory that the dear old lady was again worse, and that she had sent for her clergyman that she might receive the last comforts of religion. But this again was wrong. "Mr. Gregory," she said very suddenly, "I want to consult you as to a future home for Bessy Pryor."

"Must she go from this?"

"Yes; she must go from this. You have heard, perhaps, about her and my son." Mr. Gregory acknowledged that he had heard. "Of course she must go. I cannot have Philip banished from the house which is to be his own. In this matter he probably has been the most to blame."

"They have both, perhaps, been foolish."

"It is wickedness rather than folly. But he has been the wickeder. It should have been a duty to him, a great duty, and he should have been the stronger. But he is my son, and I cannot banish him."

"Oh, no!"

"But they must not be brought together. I love Bessy Pryor dearly, Mr. Gregory; oh, so dearly! Since she came to me, now so many years ago, she has been like a gleam of sunlight in the house. She has always been gentle with me. The very touch of her hand is sweet to me. But I must not on that account sacrifice the honour of the family. I have a duty to do; and I must do it, though I tear my heart in pieces. Where can I send her?"

"Permanently?"

"Well, yes; permanently. If Philip were married, of course she might come back. But I will still trust that she herself may be married first. I do not mean to cast her off;—only she must go. Anything that may be wanting in money shall be paid for her. She shall be provided for comfortably. You know what I had hoped about Mr. Morrison. Perhaps he may even yet be able to persuade her; but it must be away from here. Where can I send her?"

This was a question not very easy to answer, and Mr. Gregory said that he must take time to think of it. Mrs. Miles, when she asked the question, was aware that Mr. Gregory had a maiden sister, living at Avranches in Normandy, who was not in opulent circumstances.

Chapter VI

How Bessy Pryor Was to Be Banished

WHEN a man is asked by his friend if he knows of a horse to be sold he does not like immediately to suggest a transfer of the animal which he has in his own stable, though he may at the moment be in want of money and anxious to sell his steed. So it was with Mr. Gregory. His sister would be delighted to take as a boarder a young lady for whom liberal payment would be made; but at the first moment he had hesitated to make an offer by which his own sister would be benefited. On the next morning, however, he wrote as follows:—

"Dear Mrs. Miles,—My sister Amelia is living at Avranches, where she has a pleasant little house on the outskirts of the town, with a garden. An old friend was living with her, but she died last year, and my sister is now alone. If you think that Bessy would like to sojourn for awhile in Normandy, I will write to Amelia and make the proposition. Bessy will find my sister good-tempered and kindhearted.—Faithfully yours, Joshua Gregory."

Mrs. Miles did not care much for the good temper and the kind heart. Had she asked herself whether she wished Bessy to be happy she would no doubt have answered herself in the affirmative. She would probably have done so in regard to any human being or animal in the world. Of course, she wanted them all to be happy. But happiness was to her thinking of much less importance than duty; and at the present moment her duty and Bessy's duty and Philip's duty were so momentous that no idea of happiness ought to be considered in the matter at all. Had Mr. Gregory written to say that his sister was a woman of severe morals, of stern aspect, prone to repress all youthful ebullitions, and supposed to be disagreeable because of her temper, all that would have been no obstacle. In the present condition of things suffering would be better than happiness; more in accord with the feelings and position of the person concerned. It was quite intelligible to Mrs. Miles that Bessy should really love Philip almost to the breaking of her heart, quite intelligible that Philip should have set his mind upon the untoward marriage with all the obstinacy of a proud man. When young men and young women neglect their duty, hearts have to be broken. But it is not a soft and silken operation, which can be made pleasant by good temper and social kindness. It was necessary, for certain quite adequate reasons, that Bessy should be put on the wheel, and be racked and tormented. To talk to her of the good temper of the old woman who would have to turn the wheel would be to lie to her. Mrs. Miles did not want her to think that things could be made pleasant for her. Soon after the receipt of Mr. Gregory's letter she sent for Bessy, who was then brought into the room under the guard, as it were, of Mrs. Knowl. Mrs. Knowl accompanied her along the corridor, which was surely unnecessary, as Bessy's door had not been locked upon her. Her imprisonment had only come from obedience. But Mrs. Knowl felt that a great trust had been confided to her, and was anxious to omit none of her duties. She opened the door so that the invalid on the bed could see that this duty had been done, and then Bessy crept into the room. She crept in, but very quickly, and in a moment had her arms round the old woman's back and her lips pressed to the old woman's forehead. "Why may not I come and be with you?" she said.

"Because you are disobedient."

"No, no; I do all that you tell me. I have not stirred from my room, though it was hard to think you were ill so near me, and that I could do nothing. I did not try to say a word to him, or even to look at him; and now that he has gone, why should I not be with you?"

"It cannot be."

"But why not, aunt? Even though you would not speak to me I could be with you. Who is there to read to you?"

"There is no one. Of course it is dreary. But there are worse things than dreariness."

"Why should not I come back, now that he has gone?" She still had her arm round the old woman's back, and had now succeeded in dragging herself on to the bed and in crouching down by her aunt's side. It was her perseverance in this fashion that had so often forced Mrs. Miles out of her own ordained method of life, and compelled her to leave for a moment the strictness which was congenial to her. It was this that had made her declare to Mr. Gregory, in the midst of her severity, that Bessy had been like a gleam of sunshine in the house. Even now she knew not how to escape from the softness of an embrace which was in truth so grateful to her. It was a consciousness of this,—of the potency of Bessy's charm even over herself,—which had made her hasten to send her away from her. Bessy would read to her all the day, would hold her hand when she was half dozing, would assist in every movement with all the patience and much more than the tenderness of a waiting-maid. There was no voice so sweet, no hand so cool, no memory so mindful, no step so soft as Bessy's. And now Bessy was there, lying on her bed, caressing her, more closely bound to her than had ever been any other being in the world, and yet Bessy was an enemy from whom it was imperatively necessary that she should be divided.

"Get down, Bessy," she said; "go off from me."

"No, no, no," said Bessy, still clinging to her and kissing her.

"I have that to say to you which must be said calmly."

"I am calm,—quite calm. I will do whatever you tell me; only pray, pray, do not send me away from you."

"You say that you will obey me."

"I will; I have. I always have obeyed you."

"Will you give up your love for Philip?"

"Could I give up my love for you, if anybody told me? How can I do it? Love comes of itself. I did not try to love him. Oh, if you could know how I tried not to love him! If somebody came and said I was not to love you, would it be possible?"

"I am speaking of another love."

"Yes; I know. One is a kind of love that is always welcome. The other comes first as a shock, and one struggles to avoid it. But when it has come, how can it be helped? I do love him, better than all the world." As she said this she raised herself upon the bed, so as to look round upon her aunt's face; but still she kept her arm upon the old woman's shoulder. "Is it not natural? How could I have helped it?"

"You must have known that it was wrong."

"No!"

"You did not know that it would displease me?"

"I knew that it was unfortunate,—not wrong. What did I do that was wrong? When he asked me, could I tell him anything but the truth?"

"You should have told him nothing." At this reply Bessy shook her head. "It cannot be that you should think that in such a matter there should be no restraint. Did you expect that I should give my consent to such a marriage? I want to hear from yourself what you thought of my feelings."

"I knew you would be angry."

"Well?"

"I knew you must think me unfit to be Philip's wife."

"Well?"

"I knew that you wanted something else for him, and something else also for me."

"And did such knowledge go for nothing?"

"It made me feel that my love was unfortunate,—but not that it was wrong. I could not help it. He had come to me, and I loved him. The other man came, and I could not love him. Why should I be shut up for this in my own room? Why should I be sent away from you, to be miserable because I know that you want things done? He is not here. If he were here and you bade me not to go near him, I would not go. Though he were in the next room I would not see him. I would obey you altogether, but I must love

44

him. And as I love him I cannot love another. You would not wish me to marry a man when my heart has been given to another."

The old woman had not at all intended that there should be such arguments as these. It had been her purpose simply to communicate her plan, to tell Bessy that she would have to live probably for a few years at Avranches, and then to send her back to her prison. But Bessy had again got the best of her, and then had come caressing, talking, and excuses. Bessy had been nearly an hour in her room before Mrs. Miles had disclosed her purpose, and had hovered round her aunt, doing as had been her wont when she was recognised as having all the powers of head nurse in her hands. Then at last, in a manner very different from that which had been planned, Mrs. Miles proposed the Normandy scheme. She had been, involuntarily, so much softened that she condescended even to repeat what Mr. Gregory had said as to the good temper and general kindness of his maiden sister. "But why should I go?" asked Bessy, almost sobbing.

"I wonder that you should ask."

"He is not here."

"But he may come."

"If he came ever so I would not see him if you bade me not. I think you hardly understand me, aunt. I will obey you in everything. I am sure you will not now ask me to marry Mr. Morrison."

She could not say that Philip would be more likely to become amenable and marry the Cornish heiress if Bessy were away at Avranches than if she still remained shut up at

Launay. But that was her feeling. Philip, she knew, would be less obedient than Bessy. But then, too, Philip might be less obstinate of purpose. "You cannot live here, Bessy, unless you will say that you will never become the wife of my son."

"Never?"

"Never!"

"I cannot say that." There was a long pause before she found the courage to pronounce these words, but she did pronounce them at last.

"Then you must go."

"I may stay and nurse you till you are well. Let me do that. I will go whenever you may bid me."

"No. There shall be no terms between us. We must be friends, Bessy, or we must be enemies. We cannot be friends as long as you hold yourself to be engaged to Philip Launay. While that is so I will not take a cup of water from your hands. No, no," for the girl was again trying to embrace her. "I will not have your love, nor shall you have mine."

"My heart would break were I to say it."

"Then let it break! Is my heart not broken? What is it though our hearts do break,—what is it though we die,—if we do our duty? You owe this for what I have done for you."

"I owe you everything."

"Then say that you will give him up."

"I owe you everything, except this. I will not speak to him, I will not write to him, I will not even look at him, but I will not give him up. When one loves, one cannot give it up." Then she was ordered to go back to her room, and back to her room she went.

46

Chapter VII

How Bessy Pryor Was Banished to Normandy

THERE was nothing for it but to go, after the interview described in the last chapter. Mrs. Miles sent a message to the obstinate girl, informing her that she need not any longer consider herself as a prisoner, but that she had better prepare her clothes so as to be ready to start within a week. The necessary correspondence had taken place between Launay and Avranches, and within ten days from the time at which Mr. Gregory had made the proposition,—in less than a fortnight from the departure of her lover,—Bessy came down from her room all equipped, and took her place in the same waggonette which so short a time before had taken her lover away from her. During the week she had had liberty to go where she pleased, except into her aunt's room. But she had, in truth, been almost as much a prisoner as before. She did for a few minutes each day go out into the garden, but she would not go beyond the garden into the park, nor did she accept an invitation from the Gregory girls to spend an evening at the rectory. It would be so necessary, one of them wrote, that everything should be told to her as to the disposition and ways of life of Aunt Amelia! But Bessy would not see the Gregory girls. She was being sent away from home because of the wickedness of her love, and all Launay knew it. In such a condition of things she could not go out to eat sally-lunn and pound-cake, and to be told of the delights of a small Norman town. She would not even see the Gregory girls when they came up to the house, but wrote an affectionate note to the elder of them explaining that her misery was too great to allow her to see any friend.

She was in truth very miserable. It was not only because of her love, from which she had from the first been aware that misery must come,—undoubted misery, if not misery that would last through her whole life. But now there was added to this the sorrow of absolute banishment from her aunt. Mrs. Miles would not see her again before she started. Bessy was well aware of all that she owed to the mistress of Launay; and, being intelligent in the reading of character, was aware also that through many years she had succeeded in obtaining from the old woman more than the intended performance of an undertaken duty. She had forced the old woman to love her, and was aware that by means of that love the old woman's life had been brightened. She had not only received, but had conferred kindness,—and it is by conferring kindness that love is created. It was an agony to her that she should be compelled to leave this dearest friend, who was still sick and infirm, without seeing her. But Mrs. Miles was inexorable. These four words written on a scrap of paper were brought to her on that morning:—"Pray, pray, see me!" She was still inexorable. There had been long pencil-written notes between them on the previous day. If Bessy would pledge herself to give up her lover all might yet be changed. The old woman at Avranches should be compensated for her disappointment. Bessy should be restored to all her privileges at Launay. "You shall be my own, own child," said Mrs. Miles. She condescended even to promise that not a word more should be said about Mr. Morrison. But Bessy also could be inexorable. "I cannot say that I will give him up," she wrote. Thus it came to pass that she had to get into the waggonette without seeing her old friend. Mrs. Knowl went with her, having received instructions to wait upon Miss Bessy all the way to Avranches. Mrs. Knowl felt that she was sent as a guard against the lover. Mrs. Miles had known Bessy too well to have fear of that kind, and had sent Mrs. Knowl as general guardian against the wild beasts which are supposed to be roaming about the world in quest of unprotected young females.

In the distribution of her anger Mrs. Miles had for the moment been very severe towards Philip as to pecuniary matters. He had chosen to be rebellious, and therefore he was not only turned out of the house, but told that he must live on an uncomfortably small income. But to Bessy Mrs. Miles was liberal. She had astounded Miss Gregory by the nobility of the terms she had proposed, and on the evening before the journey had sent ten five-pound notes in a blank envelope to Bessy. Then in a subsequent note she had said that a similar sum would be paid to her every half-year. In none of these notes was there any expression of endearment. To none of them was there even a signature. But they all conveyed evidence of the amount of thought which Mrs. Miles was giving to Bessy and her affairs.

Bessy's journey was very comfortless. She had learned to hate Mrs. Knowl, who assumed all the airs of a duenna.

She would not leave Bessy out of sight for a moment, as though Philip might have been hidden behind every curtain or under every table. Once or twice the duenna made a little attempt at persuasion herself: "It ain't no good, miss, and it had better be give up." Then Bessy looked at her, and desired that she might be left alone. This had been at the hotel at Dover. Then again Mrs. Knowl spoke as the carriage was approaching Avranches: "If you wish to come back, Miss Bessy, the way is open." "Never mind my wishes, Mrs. Knowl," said Bessy. When, on her return to Launay, Mrs. Knowl once attempted to intimate to her mistress that Miss Bessy was very obstinate, she was silenced so sternly, so shortly, that the housekeeper began to doubt whether she might not have made a mistake and whether Bessy would not at last prevail. It was evident that Mrs. Miles would not hear a word against Bessy.

On her arrival at Avranches Miss Gregory was very kind to her. She found that she was received not at all as a naughty girl who had been sent away from home in order that she might be subjected to severe treatment. Miss Gregory fulfilled all the promises which her brother had made on her behalf, and was thoroughly kind and good-tempered. For nearly a month not a word was said about Philip or the love affairs. It seemed to be understood that Bessy had come to Avranches quite at her own desire. She was introduced to the genteel society with which that place abounds, and was conscious that a much freer life was vouchsafed to her than she had ever known before. At Launay she had of course been subject to Mrs. Miles. Now she was subject to no one. Miss Gregory exercised no authority over her,—was indeed rather subject to Bessy, as being recipient of the money paid for Bessy's board and lodging.

But by the end of the month there had grown up so much of friendship between the elder and the younger lady, that something came to be said about Philip. It was impossible that Bessy should be silent as to her past life. By degrees she told all that Mrs. Miles had done for her; how she herself had been a penniless orphan; how Mrs. Miles had taken her in from simple charity; how love had grown up between them two,—the warmest, truest love; and then how that other love had grown! The telling of secrets begets the telling of secrets. Miss Gregory, though she was now old, with the marks of little feeble crow's-feet round her gentle eyes, though she wore a false front and was much withered, had also had her love affair. She took delight in pouring forth her little tale; how she had loved an officer and had been beloved; how there had been no money; how the officer's parents had besought her to set the officer free, so that he might marry money; how she had set the officer free, and how, in consequence, the officer had married money and was now a major-general, with a large family, a comfortable house, and the gout. "And I have always thought it was right," said the excellent spinster. "What could I have done for him?"

"It couldn't be right if he loved you best," said Bessy.

"Why not, my dear? He has made an excellent husband. Perhaps he didn't love me best when he stood at the altar."

"I think love should be more holy."

"Mine has been very holy,—to me, myself. For a time I wept; but now I think I am happier than if I had never seen him. It adds something to one's life to have been loved once."

Bessy, who was of a stronger temperament, told herself that happiness such as that would not suffice for her. She wanted not only to be happy herself, but also to make him so. In the simplicity of her heart she wondered whether Philip would be different from that easy-changing major-general; but in the strength of her heart she was sure he would be very different. She would certainly not release him at the request of any parent;—but he should be free as air at the slightest hint of a request from himself. She did not believe for a moment that such a request would come; but, if it did,—if it did,—then there should be no difficulty. Then would she submit to banishment,—at Avranches or elsewhere as it might be decided for her,—till it might please the Lord to release her from her troubles.

At the end of six weeks Miss Gregory knew the whole secret of Philip and Bessy's love, and knew also that Bessy was quite resolved to persevere. There were many discussions about love, in which Bessy always clung to the opinion that when it was once offered and taken, given and received, it ought to be held as more sacred than any other bond. She owed much to Mrs. Miles;—she acknowledged that;—but she thought that she owed more to Philip. Miss Gregory would never quite agree with her;—was strong in her own opinion that women are born to yield and suffer and live mutilated lives, like herself; but not the less did they become fast friends. At the end of six weeks it was determined between them that Bessy should write to Mrs. Miles. Mrs. Miles had signified her wish not to be written to, and had not herself written. Messages as to the improving state of her health had come from the Gregory girls, but no letter had as yet passed. Then Bessy wrote as follows, in direct disobedience to her aunt's orders:

"Dearest Aunt,—I cannot help writing a line because I am so anxious about you. Mary Gregory says you have been up and out on the lawn in the sunshine, but it would make me so happy if I could see the words in your own dear handwriting. Do send me one little word. And though I know what you told me, still I think you will be glad to hear that your poor affectionate loving Bessy is well. I will not say that I am quite happy. I cannot be quite happy away from Launay and you. But Miss Gregory has been very, very kind to me, and there are nice people here. We live almost as quietly as at Launay, but sometimes we see the people. I am reading German and making lace, and I try not to be idle.

"Good-bye, dear, dearest aunt. Try to think kindly of me. I pray for you every morning and night. If you will send me a little note from yourself it will fill me with joy.— Your most affectionate and devoted niece,

"Bessy Pryor."

This was brought up to Mrs. Miles when she was still in bed, for as yet she had not returned to the early hours of her healthy life. When she had read it she at first held it apart from her. Then she put it close to her bosom, and wept bitterly as she thought how void of sunshine the house had been since that gleam had been turned away from it.

Chapter VIII

How Bessy Pryor Received Two Letters From Launay

THE same post brought Bessy two letters from England about the middle of August, both of which the reader shall see;—but first shall be given that which Bessy read the last. It was from Mrs. Miles, and had been sent when she was beginning to think that her aunt was still resolved not to write to her. The letter was as follows, and was written on square paper, which in these days is only used even by the old-fashioned when the letter to be sent is supposed to be one of great importance.

"My dear Bessy,—Though I had told you not to write to me, still I am glad to hear that you are well, and that your new home has been made as comfortable for you as circumstances will permit. Launay has not been comfortable since you went. I miss you very much. You have become so dear to me that my life is sad without you. My days have never been bright, but now they are less so than ever. I should scruple to admit so much as this to you, were it not that I intend it as a prelude to that which will follow.

"We have been sent into this world, my child, that we may do our duties, independent of that fleeting feeling which we call happiness. In the smaller affairs of life I am sure you would never seek a pleasure at the cost of your conscience. If not in the smaller things, then certainly should you not do so in the greater. To deny yourself, to remember the welfare of others, when temptation is urging you to do wrong, then do that which you know to be right,—that is your duty as a Christian, and especially your duty as a woman. To sacrifice herself is the special heroism which a woman can achieve. Men who are called upon to work may gratify their passions and still be heroes. A woman can soar only by suffering.

"You will understand why I tell you this. I and my son have been born into a special degree of life which I think it to be my duty and his to maintain. It is not that I or that he may enjoy any special delights that I hold fast to this opinion, but that I may do my part towards maintaining that order of things which has made my country more blessed than others. It would take me long to explain all this, but I know you will believe me when I say that an imperative sense of duty is my guide. You have not been born into that degree. That this does not affect my own personal feeling to you, you must know. You have had many signs how dear you are to me. At this moment my days are heavy to bear because I have not my Bessy with me,—my Bessy who has been so good to me, so loving, such an infinite blessing that to see the hem of her garments, to hear the sound of her foot, has made things bright around me. Now, there is nothing to see, nothing to hear, that is not unsightly and harsh of sound. Oh, Bessy, if you could come back to me!

"But I have to do that duty of which I have spoken, and I shall do it. Though I were never to see you again I shall do it. I am used to suffering, and sometimes think it wrong even to wish that you were back with me. But I write to you thus that you may understand everything. If you will say that you will give him up, you shall return to me and be my own, own beloved child. I tell you that you are not of the same degree. I am bound to tell you so. But you shall be so near my heart that nothing shall separate us.

"You two cannot marry while I am living. I do not think it possible that you should be longing to be made happy by my death. And you should remember that he cannot be the first to break away from this foolish engagement without dishonour. As he is the wealthy one, and the higher born, and as he is the man, he ought not to be the first to say the word.

"You may say it without falsehood and without disgrace. You may say it, and all the world will know that you have been actuated only by a sense of duty. It will be acknowledged that you have sacrificed yourself,—as it becomes a woman to do.

"One word from you will be enough to assure me. Since you came to me you have never been false. One word, and you shall come back to me and to Launay, my friend and my treasure! If it be that there must be suffering, we will suffer together. If tears are necessary there shall be joint tears. Though I am old still I can understand. I will acknowledge the sacrifice. But, Bessy, my Bessy, dearest Bessy, the sacrifice must be made.

"Of course he must live away from Launay for awhile. The fault will have been his, and what of inconvenience there may be he must undergo. He shall not come here till you yourself shall say that you can bear his presence without an added sorrow.

"I know you will not let this letter be in vain. I know you will think it over deeply, and that you will not keep me too long waiting for an answer. I need hardly tell you that I am

"Your most loving friend,

"M. Miles."

When Bessy was reading this, when the strong words with which her aunt had pleaded her cause were harrowing her heart, she had clasped in her hand this other letter from her lover. This too was written from Launay.

"My own dearest Bessy,—It is absolutely only now that I have found out where you are, and have done so simply because the people at the rectory could not keep the secret. Can anything be more absurd than supposing that my mother can have her way by whisking you away, and shutting you up in Normandy? It is too foolish! She has sent for me, and I have come like a dutiful son. I have, indeed, been rejoiced to see her looking again so much like herself. But I have not extended my duty to obeying her in a matter in which my own future happiness is altogether bound up; and in which, perhaps, the happiness of another person may be slightly concerned. I have told her that I would venture to say nothing of the happiness of the other person. The other person might be indifferent, though I did not believe it was so; but I was quite sure of my own. I have assured her that I know what I want myself, and that I do not mean to abandon my hope of achieving it. I know that she is writing to you. She can of course say what she pleases.

"The idea of separating two people who are as old as you and I, and who completely know our own minds,—you see that I do not really doubt as to yours,—is about as foolish as anything well can be. It is as though we were going back half a dozen centuries into the tyrannies of the middle ages. My object shall be to induce her to let you come home and be married properly from Launay. If she will not consent by the end of this month I shall go over to you, and we must contrive to be married at Avranches. When the thing has been once done all this rubbish will be swept away. I do not believe for a moment that my mother will punish us by any injustice as to money.

"Write and tell me that you agree with me, and be sure that I shall remain, as I am, always altogether your own,

"Truly and affectionately,

"Philip Miles."

When Bessy Pryor began to consider these two letters together, she felt that the task was almost too much for her. Her lover's letter had been the first read. She had known his handwriting, and of course had read his the first. And as she had read it everything seemed to be of rose colour. Of course she had been filled with joy. Something had been done by the warnings of Miss Gregory, something, but not much, to weaken her strong faith in her lover. The major-general had been worldly and untrue, and it had been possible that her Philip should be as had been the major-general. There had been moments of doubt in which her heart had fainted a little; but as she read her lover's words she acknowledged to herself how wrong she had been to faint at all. He declared it to be "a matter in which his own future happiness was altogether bound up." And then there had been his playful allusion to her happiness, which was not the less pleasant to her because he had pretended to think that the "other person might be indifferent." She pouted her lips at him, as though he were present while she was reading, with a joyous affectation of disdain. No, no; she could not consent to an immediate marriage at Avranches. There must be some delay. But she would write to him and explain all that. Then she read her aunt's letter.

It moved her very much. She had read it all twice before there came upon her a feeling of doubt, an acknowledgment to herself that she must reconsider the matter. But even when she was only reading it, before she had begun to consider, her former joy was repressed and almost quenched. So much of it was too true, terribly true. Of course her duty should be paramount. If she could persuade herself that duty required her to abandon Philip, she must abandon him, let the suffering to herself or to others be what it might. But then, what was it that duty required of her? "To sacrifice herself is the special heroism which a woman can achieve." Yes, she believed that. But then, how about sacrificing Philip, who, no doubt, was telling the truth when he said that his own happiness was altogether bound up in his love?

She was moved too by all that which Mrs. Miles said as to the grandeur of the Launay family. She had learned enough of the manners of Launay to be quite alive to the aristocratic idiosyncrasies of the old woman, She, Bessy Pryor, was nobody. It would have been well that Philip Launay should have founded his happiness on some girl of higher birth. But he had not done so. King Cophetua's marriage had been recognised by the world at large. Philip was no more than King Cophetua, nor was she less than the beggar-girl. Like to like in marriages was no doubt expedient,—but not indispensable. And though she was not Philip's equal, yet she was a lady. She would not disgrace him at his table, or among his friends. She was sure that she could be a comfort to him in his work.

But the parts of the old woman's letter which moved her most were those in which she gave full play to her own heart, and spoke, without reserve, of her own love for her dearest Bessy. "My days are heavy to bear because I have not my Bessy with me." It was impossible to read this and not to have some desire to yield. How good this lady had been to her! Was it not through her that she had known Philip? But for Mrs. Miles, what would her own life have been? She thought that had she been sure of Philip's happiness; could she have satisfied herself that he would bear the blow, she would have done as she was asked. She would have achieved her heroism, and shown the strength of her gratitude, and would have taken her delight in administering to the comforts of her old friend,—only that Philip had her promise. All that she could possibly owe to all the world beside must be less, so infinitely less, than what she owed to him.

She would have consulted Miss Gregory, but she knew so well what Miss Gregory would have advised. Miss Gregory would only have mentioned the major-general and her own experiences. Bessy determined, therefore, to lie awake and think of it, and to take no other counsellor beyond her own heart.

Chapter IX

How Bessy Pryor Answered the Two Letters,
and What Came of It

THE letters were read very often, and that from Mrs.
Miles I think the oftener. Philip's love was plainly expressed, and what more is expected from a lover's letter
than a strong, manly expression of love? It was quite satisfactory, declaring the one important fact that his happiness
was bound up in hers. But Mrs. Miles' was the stronger
letter, and by far the more suggestive. She had so mingled
hardness and softness, had enveloped her stern lesson of
feminine duty in so sweet a frame of personal love, that it
was hardly possible that such a girl as Bessy Pryor should
not be shaken by her arguments. There were moments during the night in which she had almost resolved to yield. "A
woman can soar only by suffering." She was not sure that
she wanted to soar, but she certainly did want to do her
duty, even though suffering should come of it. But there
was one word in her aunt's letter which militated against
the writer's purpose rather than assisted it. "Since you first
came to me, you have never been false." False! no; she
hoped she had not been false. Whatever might be the duty
of a man or a woman, that duty should be founded on
truth. Was it not her special duty at this moment to be true
to Philip? I do not know that she was altogether logical. I

do not know but that in so supporting herself in her love there may have been a bias of personal inclination. Bessy perhaps was a little prone to think that her delight and her duty went together. But that flattering assurance, that she had never yet been false, strengthened her resolution to be true, now, to Philip.

She took the whole of the next day to think, abstaining during the whole day from a word of confidential conversation with Miss Gregory. Then on the following morning she wrote her letters. That to Philip would be easily written. Words come readily when one has to give a hearty assent to an eager and welcome proposition. But to deny, to make denial to one loved and respected, to make denial of that which the loved one has a right to ask, must be difficult. Bessy, like a brave girl, went to the hard task first, and she rushed instantly at her subject, as a brave horseman rides at his fence without craning.

"Dearest Aunt,—I cannot do as you bid me. My word to him is so sacred to me that I do not dare to break it. I cannot say that I won't be his when I feel that I have already given myself to him.

"Dear, dearest aunt, my heart is very sad as I write this, because I feel that I am separating myself from you almost for ever. You know that I love you. You know that I am miserable because you have banished me from your side. All the sweet kind words of your love to me are like daggers to me, because I cannot show my gratitude by doing as you would have me. It seems so hard! I know it is probable that I may never see him again, and yet I am to be separated from you, and you will be my enemy. In all the world there are but two that I really love. Though I cannot and will not give him up, I desire to be back at Launay now only that I might be with you. My love for him would be contented with a simple permission that it should exist. My love for you cannot be satisfied unless I am allowed to be close to you once again. You say that a woman's duty consists in suffering. I am striving to do my duty, but I know how great is my suffering in doing it. However angry you may be with your Bessy, you will not think that she can appear even to be ungrateful without a pang.

"Though I will not give him up, you need not fear that I shall do anything. Should he come here I could not, I suppose, avoid seeing him, but I should ask him to go at once; and I should beg Miss Gregory to tell him that she could not make him welcome to her house. In all things I will do as though I were your daughter—though I know so well how far I am from any right to make use of so dear a name!

"But dear, dear aunt, no daughter could love you better, nor strive more faithfully to be obedient.

"I shall always be, even when you are most angry with me, your own, poor, loving, most affectionate

"Bessy."

The other letter need perhaps be not given in its entirety. Even in such a chronicle as this there seems to be something of treachery, something of a want of that forbearance to which young ladies are entitled, in making public the words of love which such a one may write to her lover. Bessy's letter was no doubt full of love, but it was full of prudence also. She begged him not to come to Avranches.

As to such a marriage as that of which he had spoken, it was, she assured him, quite impossible. She would never give him up, and so she had told Mrs. Miles. In that respect her duty to him was above her duty to her aunt. But she was so subject to her aunt that she would not in any other matter disobey her. For his sake—for Philip's sake—only for Philip's sake, she grieved that there should be more delay. Of course she was aware that it might possibly be a trouble in life too many for him to bear. In that case he might make himself free from it without a word of reproach from her. Of that he alone must be the judge. But, for the present, she could be no partner to any plans for the future. Her aunt had desired her to stay at Avranches, and at Avranches she must remain. There were words of love, no doubt; but the letter, taken altogether, was much sterner and less demonstrative of affection than that written to her aunt.

There very soon came a rejoinder from Mrs. Miles, but it was so curt and harsh as almost to crush Bessy by its laconic severity. "You are separated from me, and I am your enemy." That was all. Beneath that one line the old woman had signed her name, M. Miles, in large, plain angry letters. Bessy, who knew every turn of the woman's mind, understood exactly how it had been with her when she wrote those few words, and when, with care, she had traced that indignant signature. "Then everything shall be broken, and though there was but one gleam of sunshine left to me, that gleam shall be extinguished. No one shall say that I, as Lady of Launay, did not do my duty." It was thus the Lady of Launay had communed with herself when she penned that dreadful line. Bessy understood it all, and could almost see the woman as she wrote it.

Then in her desolation she told everything to Miss Gregory—showed the two former letters, showed that dreadful denunciation of lasting wrath, and described exactly what had been her own letter, both to Mrs. Miles and to her lover. Miss Gregory had but one recipe to offer in such a malady; that, namely, which she had taken herself in a somewhat similar sickness. The gentleman should be allowed to go forth into the world and seek a fitter wife, whereas Bessy should content herself, for the remainder of her life, with the pleasures of memory. Miss Gregory thought that it was much even to have been once loved by the major-general. When Bessy almost angrily declared that this would not be enough for her, Miss Gregory very meekly suggested that possibly affection might change in the lapse of years, and that some other suitor—perhaps Mr. Morrison—might in course of time suffice. But at the idea Bessy became indignant, and Miss Gregory was glad to confine herself to the remedy pure and simple which she acknowledged to have been good for herself.

Then there passed a month—a month without a line from Launay or from Philip. That Mrs. Miles should not write again was to be expected. She had declared her enmity, and there was an end of everything. During the month there had come a cheque to Miss Gregory from some man of business, and with the cheque there had been no intimation that the present arrangement was to be brought to a close. It appeared therefore that Mrs. Miles, in spite of her enmity, intended to provide for the mutinous girl a continuation of the comforts which she now enjoyed. Certainly nothing more than this could have been expected from her. But, in regard to Philip, though Bessy had assured herself, and had assured Miss Gregory also, that she did not at all desire a correspondence in the present condition of affairs, still she felt so total a cessation of all tidings to be hard to bear. Mary Gregory, when writing to her aunt, said nothing of Philip—merely remarked that Bessy Pryor would be glad to know that her aunt had nearly recovered her health, and was again able to go out among the poor. Then Bessy began to think—not that Philip was like the major-general, for to that idea she would not give way at all—but that higher and nobler motives had induced him to yield to his mother. If so she would never reproach him. If so she would forgive him in her heart of hearts. If so she would accept her destiny and entreat her old friend to allow her to return once more to Launay, and thenceforth to endure the evil thing which fate would have done to her in patient submission. If once the word should have come to her from Philip, then would she freely declare that everything should be over, then and for always, between her and her lover. After such suffering as that, while she was undergoing agony so severe, surely her friend would forgive her. That terrible word, "I am your enemy," would surely then be withdrawn.

But if it were to be so, if this was to be the end of her love, Philip, at least, would write. He would not leave her in doubt, after such a decision on his own part. That thought ought to have sustained her; but it was explained to her by Miss Gregory that the major-general had taken three months before he had been inspirited to send the fatal letter, and to declare his purpose of marrying money. There could be but little doubt, according to Miss Gregory, that Philip was undergoing the same process. It was, she thought, the natural end to such an affair. This was the kind of thing which young ladies without dowry, but with hearts to love, are doomed to suffer. There could be no doubt that Miss Gregory regarded the termination of the affair with a certain amount of sympathetic satisfaction. Could she have given Bessy all Launay, and her lover, she would have done so. But sadness and disappointment were congenial to her, and a heart broken, but still constant, was, to her thinking, a pretty feminine acquisition. She was to herself the heroine of her own romance, and she thought it good to be a heroine. But Bessy was indignant; not that Philip should be false, but that he should not dare to write and say so. "I think he ought to write," was on her lips, when the door was opened, and, lo, all of a sudden, Philip Miles was in the room.

Chapter X

How Bessy Pryor's Lover Argued His Case

WE must now go back to Launay. It will be remembered that Bessy received both her letters on the same day—those namely from Mrs. Miles and from Philip—and that they both came from Launay. Philip had been sent away from the place when the fact of his declared love was first made known to the old lady, as though into a banishment which was to be perpetual till he should have repented of his sin. Such certainly had been his mother's intention. He was to be sent one way, and the girl another, and everyone concerned was to be made to feel the terrible weight of her displeasure, till repentance and retractation should come.

He was to be starved into obedience by a minimised allowance, and she by the weariness of her life at Avranches. But the person most grievously punished by these arrangements was herself. She had declared to herself that she would endure anything, everything, in the performance of her duty. But the desolation of her life was so extreme that it was very hard to bear. She did not shrink and tell herself that it was unendurable, but after awhile she persuaded herself that now that Bessy was gone there could be no reason why Philip also should be exiled. Would not her influence be more potent over Philip if he were at Launay?

She therefore sent for him, and he came. Thus it was that the two letters were written from the same house.

Philip obeyed his mother's behest in coming as he had obeyed it in going; but he did not hesitate to show her that he felt himself to be aggrieved. Launay of course belonged to her. She could leave it and all the property to some hospital if she chose. He was well aware of that. But he had been brought up as the heir, and he could not believe that there should come such a ruin of heaven and earth as would be produced by any change in his mother's intentions as to the Launay property. Touching his marriage, he felt that he had a right to marry whom he pleased, as long as she was a lady, and that any dictation from his mother in such a matter was a tyranny not to be endured. He had talked it all over with the rector before he went. Of course it was possible that his mother should commit such an injustice as that at which the rector hinted. "There are," said Philip, "no bounds to possibilities." It was, however, he thought, all but impossible; and whether probable or improbable, no fear of such tyranny should drive him from his purpose. He was a little magniloquent, perhaps, in what he said, but he was very resolved.

It was, therefore, with some feeling of an injury inflicted upon him that he first greeted his mother on his return to the house. For a day or two not a word passed about Bessy. "Of course, I am delighted to be with you, and glad enough to have the shooting," he said, in answer to some word of hers. "I shouldn't have gone, as you know, unless you had driven me away." This was hard on the old woman; but she bore it, and, for some days, was simply affectionate and gentle to her son—more gentle than was her wont. Then she wrote to Bessy, and told her son that she was writing. "It is so impossible," she said, "that I cannot conceive that Bessy should not obey me when she comes to regard it at a distance."

"I see no impossibility; but Bessy can, of course, do as she pleases," replied Philip, almost jauntily. Then he determined that he also would write.

There were no further disputes on the matter till Bessy's answer came, and then Mrs. Miles was very angry indeed. She had done her best so to write her letter that Bessy should be conquered both by the weight of her arguments and by the warmth of her love. If reason would not prevail, surely gratitude would compel her to do as she was bidden. But the very first words of Bessy's letter contained a flat refusal. "I cannot do as you bid me." Who was this girl, that had been picked out of a gutter, that she should persist in the right of becoming the mistress of Launay? In a moment the old woman's love was turned into a feeling of condemnation, nearly akin to hatred. Then she sent off her short rejoinder, declaring herself to be Bessy's enemy.

On the following morning regret had come, and perhaps remorse. She was a woman of strong passion, subject to impulses which were, at the time, uncontrollable; but she was one who was always compelled by her conscience to quick repentance, and sometimes to an agonising feeling of wrong done by herself. To declare that Bessy was her enemy—Bessy, who for so many years had prevented all her wishes, who had never been weary of well-doing to her, who had been patient in all things, who had been her gleam of sunshine, of whom she had sometimes said to herself in her closet that the child was certainly nearer to perfection than any other human being that she had known! True, it was not fit that the girl should become mistress of Launay! A misfortune had happened which must be cured—if even by the severance of persons so dear to each other as she and her Bessy. But she knew that she had sinned in declaring one so good, and one so dear, to be her enemy.

But what should she do next? Days went on and she did nothing. She simply suffered. There was no pretext on which she could frame an affectionate letter to her child. She could not write and ask to be forgiven for the harshness of her letter. She could not simply revoke the sentence she had pronounced without any reference to Philip and his love. In great misery, with a strong feeling of self-degradation because she had allowed herself to be violent in her wrath, she went on, repentant but still obstinate, till Philip himself forced the subject upon her.

"Mother," he said one day, "is it not time that things should be settled?"

"What things, Philip?"

"You know my intention."

"What intention?"

"As to making Bessy my wife."

"That can never be."

"But it will be. It has to be. If as regards my own feelings I could bring myself to yield to you, how could I do so with honour in regard to her? But, for myself, nothing on earth would induce me to change my mind. It is a matter on which a man has to judge for himself, and I have not heard a word from you or from anyone to make me think that I have judged wrongly."

"Do birth and rank go for nothing?" He paused a moment, and then he answered her very seriously, standing up and looking down upon her as he did so. "For very much—with me. I do not think that I could have brought myself to choose a wife, whatever might have been a woman's charms, except among ladies. I found this one to be the chosen companion and dearest friend of the finest lady I know." At this the old woman, old as she was, first blushed, and then, finding herself to be sobbing, turned her face away from him. "I came across a girl of whose antecedents I could be quite sure, of whose bringing up I knew all the particulars, as to whom I could be certain that every hour of her life had been passed among the best possible associations. I heard testimony as to her worth and her temper which I could not but believe. As to her outward belongings, I had eyes of my own to judge. Could I be wrong in asking such a one to be my wife? Can I be regarded as unhappy in having succeeded with her? Could I be acquitted of dishonour if I were to desert her? Shall I be held to be contemptible if I am true to her?"

At every word he spoke he grew in her esteem. At this present crisis of her life she did not wish to think specially well of him, though he was her son, but she could not help herself. He became bigger before her than he had ever been before, and more of a man. It was, she felt, almost vain for a woman to lay her commands, either this way or that, upon a man who could speak to her as Philip had spoken.

But not the less was the power in her hands. She could

bid him go and marry—and be a beggar. She could tell him that all Launay should go to his brother, and she could instantly make a will to that effect. So strong was the desire for masterdom upon her that she longed to do it. In the very teeth of her honest wish to do what was right, there was another wish—a longing to do what she knew to be wrong. There was a struggle within, during which she strove to strengthen herself for evil. But it was vain. She knew of herself that were she to swear to-day to him that he was disinherited, were she to make a will before nightfall carrying out her threat, the pangs of conscience would be so heavy during the night that she would certainly change it all on the next morning. Of what use is a sword in your hand if you have not the heart to use it? Why seek to be turbulent with a pistol if your bosom be of such a nature that your finger cannot be forced to pull the trigger? Power was in her possession—but she could not use it. The power rather was in her hands. She could not punish her boy, even though he had deserved it. She had punished her girl, and from that moment she had been crushed by torments, because of the thing that she had done. Others besides Mrs. Miles have felt, with something of regret, that they have lacked the hardness necessary for cruelty and the courage necessary for its doing.

"How shall it be, mother?" asked Philip. As she knew not what to answer she rose slowly from her chair, and leaving the room went to the seclusion of her own chamber.

Days again passed before Philip renewed his question, and repeated it in the same words: "How shall it be, mother?" Wistfully she looked up at him, as though even yet something might be accorded by him to pity; as though the son might even yet be induced to accede to his mother's prayers. It was not that she thought so. No. She had thought much, and was aware that it could not be so. But as a dog will ask with its eyes when it knows that asking is in vain, so did she ask. "One word from you, mother, will make us all happy."

"No; not all of us."

"Will not my happiness make you happy?" Then he stooped over her and kissed her forehead. "Could you be happy if you knew that I were wretched?"

"I do not want to be happy. It should be enough that one does one's duty."

"And what is my duty? Can it be my duty to betray the girl I love in order that I may increase an estate which is already large enough?"

"It is for the family."

"What is a family but you, or I, or whoever for the moment may be its representative? Say that it shall be as I would have it, and then I will go to her and let her know that she may come back to your arms."

Not then, or on the next day, or on the next, did she yield; though she knew well during all these hours that it was her fate to yield. She had indeed yielded. She had confessed to herself that it must be so, and as she did so she felt once more the soft pressure of Bessy's arms as they would cling round her neck, and she could see once more the brightness of Bessy's eyes as the girl would hang over her bed early in the morning. "I do not want to be happy," she had said; but she did want, sorely want, to see her girl. "You may go and tell her," she said one night as she was preparing to go to her chamber. Then she turned quickly away, and was out of the room before he could answer her with a word.

Chapter XI

How Bessy Pryor Received Her Lover

MISS Gregory was certainly surprised when, on the entrance of the young man, Bessy jumped from her chair and rushed into his arms. She knew that Bessy had no brother, and her instinct rather than her experience told her that the greeting which she saw was more than fraternal,—more than cousinly. She did not doubt but that the young man was Philip Launay, and knowing what she knew she was not disposed to make spoken complaints. But when Bessy lifted her face to be kissed, Miss Gregory became red and very uneasy. It is probable that she herself had never progressed as far as this with the young man who afterwards became the major-general.

Bessy herself, had a minute been allowed to her for reflection, would have been less affectionate. She knew nothing of the cause which had brought Philip to Avranches. She only knew that her dear friend at Launay had declared her to be an enemy, and that she had determined that she could not, for years, become the wife of Philip Launay, without the consent of her who had used that cruel word. And at the moment of Philip's entering the room her heart had been sore with reproaches against him. "He ought at any rate to write." The words had been on her lips as the door had been opened, and the words had been spoken in the soreness of heart coming from a fear that she was to be abandoned.

Then he was there. In the moment that sufficed for the glance of his eye to meet hers she knew that she was not abandoned. With whatever tidings he had come that was not to be the burden of his news. No man desirous of being released from his vows ever looked like that. So up she jumped and flew to him, not quite knowing what she intended, but filled with delight when she found herself pressed to his bosom. Then she had to remember herself, and to escape from his arms. "Philip," she said, "this is Miss Gregory. Miss Gregory, I do not think you ever met Mr. Launay."

Then Miss Gregory had to endeavour to look as though nothing particular had taken place,—which was a trial. But Bessy bore her part, if not without a struggle, at least without showing it. "And now, Philip," she said, "how is my aunt?"

"A great deal stronger than when you left her."

"Quite well?"

"Yes; for her, I think I may say quite well."

"She goes out every day?"

"Every day,—after the old plan. The carriage toddles round to the door at three, and then toddles about the parish at the rate of four miles an hour, and toddles home exactly at five. The people at Launay, Miss Gregory, don't want clocks to tell them the hour in the afternoon."

"I do love punctuality," said Miss Gregory.

"I wish I were with her," said Bessy.

"I have come to take you," said Philip.

"Have you?" Then Bessy blushed,—for the first time. She blushed as a hundred various thoughts rushed across her mind. If he had been sent to take her back, sent by her aunt, instead of Mrs. Knowl, what a revulsion of circumstances must there not have been at Launay! How could it all have come to pass? Even to have been sent for at all, to be allowed to go back even in disgrace, would have been an inexpressible joy. Had Knowl come for her, with a grim look and an assurance that she was to be brought back because a prison at Launay was thought to be more secure than a prison at Avranches, the prospect of a return would have been hailed with joy. But now,—to be taken back by Philip to Launay! There was a whole heaven of delight in the thought of the very journey.

Miss Gregory endeavoured to look pleased, but in truth the prospect to her was not so pleasant as to Bessy. She was to be left alone again. She was to lose her pensioner. After so short a fruition of the double bliss of society and pay, she was to be deserted without a thought. But to be deserted without many thoughts had been her lot in life, and now she bore her misfortune like a heroine. "You will be glad to go back to your aunt, Bessy; will you not?"

"Glad!" The ecstasy was almost unkind, but poor Miss Gregory bore it, and maintained that pretty smile of gratified serenity as though everything were well with all of them.

But Bessy felt that she had as yet heard nothing of the real news, and that the real news could not be told in the presence of Miss Gregory. It had not even yet occurred to her that Mrs. Miles had actually given her sanction to the marriage. "This is a very pretty place," said Philip.

"What, Avranches?" said Miss Gregory, mindful of future possible pensioners. "Oh, delightful. It is the prettiest place in Normandy, and I think the most healthy town in all France."

"It seemed nice as I came up from the hotel. Suppose we go out for a walk, Bessy. We have to start back to-morrow."

"To-morrow!" ejaculated Bessy. She would have been ready to go in half an hour had he demanded it.

"If you can manage it. I promised my mother to be as quick as I could; and, when I arranged to come, I had ever so many engagements."

"If she must go to-morrow, she won't have much time for walking," said Miss Gregory, with almost a touch of anger in her voice. But Bessy was determined to have her walk. All her fate in life was to be disclosed to her within the next few minutes. She was already exultant, but she was beginning to think that there was a heaven, indeed, opening for her. So she ran away for her hat and gloves, leaving her lover and Miss Gregory together.

"It is very sudden," said the poor old lady with a gasp.

"My mother felt that, and bade me tell you that, of course, the full twelvemonth—"

"I was not thinking about that," said Miss Gregory. "I did not mean to allude to such a thing. Mrs. Miles has always been so kind to my brother, and anything I could have done I should have been so happy, without thinking of money. But—" Philip sat with the air of an attentive listener, so that Miss Gregory could get no answer to her question without absolutely asking it. "But there seems to be a change."

"Yes, there is a change, Miss Gregory."

"We were afraid that Mrs. Miles had been offended."

"It is the old story, Miss Gregory. Young people and old people very often will not think alike: but it is the young people who generally have their way."

She had not had her way. She remembered that at the moment. But then, perhaps, the major-general had had his. When a period of life has come too late for success, when all has been failure, the expanding triumphs of the glorious young grate upon the feelings even of those who are generous and self-denying. Miss Gregory was generous by nature and self-denying by practice, but Philip's paean and Bessy's wondrous prosperity were for a moment a little hard upon her. There had been a comfort to her in the conviction that Philip was no better than the major-general. "I suppose it is so," she said. "That is, if one of them has means."

"Exactly."

"But if they are both poor, I don't see how their being young can enable them to live upon nothing." She intended to imply that Philip probably would have been another major-general, but that he was heir to Launay.

Philip, who had never heard of the major-general, was a little puzzled; nevertheless, he acceded to the proposition, not caring, however, to say anything as to his own circumstances on so very short an acquaintance.

Then Bessy came down with her hat, and they started

for their walk. "Now tell me all about it," she said, in a fever of expectation, as soon as the front door was closed behind them.

"There is nothing more to tell," said he.

"Nothing more?"

"Unless you want me to say that I love you."

"Of course I do."

"Well, then,—I love you. There!"

"Philip, you are not half nice to me."

"Not after coming all the way from Launay to say that?"

"There must be so much to tell me? Why has my aunt sent for me?"

"Because she wants you."

"And why has she sent you?"

"Because I want you too."

"But does she want me?"

"Certainly she does."

"For you?" If he could say this, then everything would have been said. If he could say this truly, then everything would have been done necessary for the perfection of her happiness. "Oh, Philip, do tell me. It is so strange that she should send for me! Do you know what she said to me in her last letter? It was not a letter. It was only a word. She said that I was her enemy."

"All that is changed."

"She will be glad to have me again?"

"Very glad. I fancy that she has been miserable without you."

"I shall be as glad to be with her again, Philip. You do not know how I love her. Think of all she has done for me!"

"She has done something *now* that I hope will beat everything else."

"What has she done?"

"She has consented that you and I shall be man and wife. Isn't that more than all the rest?"

"But has she? Oh, Philip, has she really done that?"

Then at last he told his whole story. Yes; his mother had yielded. From the moment in which she had walked out of the room, having said that he might "go and tell her," she had never endeavoured to renew the fight. When he had spoken to her, endeavouring to draw from her some warmth of assent, she had generally been very silent. She had never brought herself absolutely to wish him joy. She had not as yet so crucified her own spirit in the matter as to be able to tell him that he had chosen his wife well; but she had shown him in a hundred ways that her anger was at an end, and that if any feeling was left opposed to his own happiness, it was simply one of sorrow. And there were signs which made him think that even that was not deep-seated. She would pat him, stroking his hair, and leaning on his shoulder, administering to his comforts with a nervous accuracy as to little things which was peculiar to her. And then she gave him an infinity of directions as to the way in which it would be proper that Bessy should travel, being anxious at first to send over a maid for her behoof,—not Mrs. Knowl, but a younger woman, who would have been at Bessy's command. Philip, however, objected to the maid. And when Mrs. Miles remarked that if it was Bessy's fate to become mistress of Launay, Bessy ought to have a maid to attend her, Philip said that that would be very well a month or two hence, when Bessy would have become,—not mistress of Launay, which was a place which he trusted might not be vacant for many a long day,—but first lieutenant to the mistress, by right of marriage. He refused altogether to take the maid with him, as he explained to Bessy with much laughter. And so they came to understand each other thoroughly, and Bessy knew that the great trouble of her life, which had been as a mountain in her way, had disappeared suddenly, as might some visionary mountain. And then, when they thoroughly understood each other, they started back to England and to Launay together.

Chapter XII

How Bessy Pryor Was Brought Back,
and What Then Became of Her

BESSY understood the condition of the old woman much better than did her son. "I am sad a little," she said, on her way home, "because of her disappointment."

"Sad, because she is to have you,—you yourself,— for her daughter-in-law?"

"Yes, indeed, Philip; because I know that she has not wanted me. She will be kind because I shall belong to you, and perhaps partly because she loves me; but she will always regret that that young lady down in Cornwall has not been allowed to add to the honour and greatness of the family. The Launays are everything to her, and what can I do for the Launays?" Of course he said many pretty things to her in answer to this, but he could not eradicate from her mind the feeling that, in regard to the old friend who had been so kind to her, she was returning evil for good.

But even Bessy did not quite understand the old woman. When she found that she had yielded, there was disappointment in the old woman's heart. Who can have indulged in a certain longing for a lifetime, in a special ambition, and seen that ambition and that longing crushed and trampled on, without such a feeling? And she had brought this failure on herself,—by her own weakness, as she told herself. Why had she given way to Bessy and to Bessy's blandishments? It was because she had not been strong to do her duty that this ruin had fallen upon her hopes. The power in her own hands had been sufficient. But for her Philip need never have seen Bessy Pryor. Might not Bessy Pryor have been sent somewhere out of the way when it became evident that she had charms of her own with which to be dangerous? And even after the first evil had been done her power had been sufficient. She need not have sent for Philip back. She need have written no letter to Bessy. She might have been calm and steady in her purpose, so that there should have been no violent ebullition of anger,—so violent as to induce repentance, and with repentance renewed softness and all the pangs of renewed repentance.

When Philip had left her on his mission to Normandy her heart was heavy with regret, and heavy also with anger. But it was with herself that she was angry. She had known her duty and she had not done it. She had known her duty, and had neglected it,—because Bessy had been soft to her, and dear, and pleasant. It was here that Bessy did not quite understand her friend. Bessy reproached herself because she had made to her friend a bad return to all the kindness she had received. The old woman would not allow herself to entertain any such a thought. Once she had spoken to herself of having warmed a serpent in her bosom; but instantly, with infinite self-scorn, she had declared to herself that Bessy was no serpent. For all that she had done for Bessy, Bessy had made ample return, the only possible return that could be full enough. Bessy had loved her. She too had loved Bessy, but that should have had no weight. Though they two had been linked together by their very heartstrings, it had been her duty to make a severance because their joint affection had been dangerous. She had allowed her own heart to over-ride her own sense of duty, and therefore she was angry,—not with Bessy, but with herself.

But the thing was done. To quarrel with Philip had been impossible to her. One feeling coming upon another, her own repentance, her own weakness, her acknowledgment of a certain man's strength on the part of her son, had brought her to such a condition that she had yielded. Then it was natural that she should endeavour to make the best of it. But even the doing of that was a trial to her. When she told herself that as far as the woman went, the mere woman, Philip could not have found a better wife had he searched the world all round, she found that she was being tempted from her proper path even in that. What right could she have to look for consolation there? For other reasons, which she still felt to be adequate, she had resolved that something else should be done. That something else had not been done, because she had failed in her duty. And now she was trying to salve the sore by the very poison which had created the wound. Bessy's sweet temper, and Bessy's soft voice, and Bessy's bright eye, and Bessy's devotion to the delight of others, were all so many temptations. Grovelling as she was in sackcloth and ashes because she had yielded to them, how could she console herself by a prospect of these future enjoyments either for herself or her son?

But there were various duties to which she could attend,

grievously afflicted as she was by her want of attention to that great duty. As Fate had determined that Bessy Pryor was to become mistress of Launay, it was proper that all Launay should know and recognise its future mistress. Bessy certainly should not be punished by any want of earnestness in this respect. No one should be punished but herself. The new mistress should be made as welcome as though she had been the red-haired girl from Cornwall. Knowl was a good deal put about because Mrs. Miles, remembering a few hard words which Knowl had allowed herself to use in the days of the imprisonment, became very stern. "It is settled that Miss Pryor is to become Mrs. Philip Launay, and you will obey her just as myself." Mrs. Knowl, who had saved a little money, began to consider whether it would not be as well to retire into private life.

When the day came on which the two travellers were to reach Launay Mrs. Miles was very much disturbed in her mind. In what way should she receive the girl? In her last communication,—her very last,—she had called Bessy her enemy; and now Bessy was being brought home to be made her daughter-in-law under her own roof. How sweet it would be to stand at the door and welcome her in the hall, among all the smiling servants, to make a tender fuss and hovering over her, as would be so natural with a mother-in-law who loved an adopted daughter as tenderly as Mrs. Miles loved Bessy! How pleasant to take her by the hand and lead her away into some inner sanctum where warm kisses as between mother and child would be given and taken; to hear her praises of Philip, and then to answer again with other praises; to tell her with words half serious and half drollery that she must now buckle on her armour and do her work, and take upon herself the task of managing the household! There was quite enough of softness in the old woman to make all this delightful. Her imagination revelled in thinking of it even at the moment in which she was telling herself that it was impossible. But it was impossible. Were she to force such a change upon herself Bessy would not believe in the sincerity of the change. She had told Bessy that she was her enemy!

At last the carriage which had gone to the station was here; not the waggonette on this occasion, but the real carriage itself, the carriage which was wont to toddle four miles an hour about the parish. "This is an honour meant for the prodigal daughter," said Philip, as he took his seat. "If you had never been naughty, we should only have had the waggonette, and we then should have been there in half the time." Mrs. Miles, when she heard the wheels on the gravel, was even yet uncertain where she would place herself. She was fluttered, moving about from the room into the hall and back, when the old butler spoke a careful word: "Go into the library, madam, and Mr. Philip will bring her to you there." Then she obeyed the butler,—as she had probably never done in her life before.

Bessy, as soon as her step was off the carriage, ran very quickly into the house. "Where is my aunt?" she said. The butler was there showing the way, and in a moment she had thrown her arms round the old woman. Bessy had a way of making her kisses obligatory, from which Mrs. Miles had never been able to escape. Then, when the old woman was seated, Bessy was at once upon her knees before her. "Say that you love me, aunt. Say that at once! Say that first of all!"

"You know I love you."

"I know I love you. Oh, I am so glad to have you again. It was so hard not to be with you when I thought that you were ill. I did not know how sick it would make me to be away from you." Neither then nor at any time afterwards was there a word spoken on the one side or the other as to that declaration of enmity.

There was nothing then said in way of explanation. There was nothing perhaps necessary. It was clear to Bessy that she was received at Launay as Philip's future wife,—not only by Mrs. Miles herself, but by the whole household,—and that all the honours of the place were to be awarded to her without stint. For herself that would have sufficed. To her any explanation of the circumstances which had led to a change so violent was quite unnecessary. But it was not so with Mrs. Miles herself. She could not but say some word in justification of herself,—in excuse rather than justification. She had Bessy into her bedroom that night, and said the word, holding between her two thin hands the hand of the girl she addressed. "You have known, Bessy, that I did not wish this." Bessy muttered that she did know it. "And I think you knew why."

"How could I help it, aunt?"

Upon this the old woman patted the hand. "I suppose he could not help it. And, if I had been a young man, I could not have helped it. I could not help it as I was, though I am an old woman. I think I am as foolish as he is."

"Perhaps he is foolish, but you are not."

"Well; I do not know. I have my misgivings about that, my dear. I had objects which I thought were sacred and holy, to which I had been wedded through many years. They have had to be thrust aside."

"Then you will hate me!"

"No, my child; I will love you with all my heart. You will be my son's wife now, and, as such, you will be dear to me, almost as he is dear. And you will still be my own Bessy, my gleam of sunlight, without whom the house is so gloomy that it is like a prison to me. For myself, do you think I could want any other young woman about the house than my own dear Bessy;—that any other wife for Philip could come as near my heart as you do?"

"But if I have stood in the way?"

"We will not think of it any more. You, at any rate, need not think of it," added the old woman, as she remembered all the circumstances. "You shall be made welcome with all the honours and all the privileges due to Philip's wife; and if there be a regret, it shall never trouble your path. It may be a comfort to you to hear me say that you, at least, in all things have done your duty." Then, at last, there were more tears, more embracings, and, before either of them went to their rest, a perfect ecstasy of love.

Little or nothing more is necessary for the telling of the story of the Lady of Launay. Before the autumn had quite gone, and the last tint had left the trees, Bessy Pryor became Bessy Launay, under the hand of Mr. Gregory, in the Launay parish church. Everyone in the neighbourhood around was there, except Mr. Morrison, who had taken this opportunity of having a holiday and visiting Switzerland.

But even he, when he returned, soon became reconciled to the arrangement, and again became a guest in the dining-room of the mansion. I hope I shall have no reader who will not think that Philip Launay did well in not following the example of the major-general.

THE COURTSHIP OF SUSAN BELL

J OHN MUNROE BELL had been a lawyer in Albany, State of New York, and as such had thriven well. He had thriven well as long as thrift and thriving on this earth had been allowed to him. But the Almighty had seen fit to shorten his span.

Early in life he had married a timid, anxious, pretty, good little wife, whose whole heart and mind had been given up to do his bidding and deserve his love. She had not only deserved it but had possessed it, and as long as John Munroe Bell had lived, Henrietta Bell—Hetta as he called her—had been a woman rich in blessings. After twelve years of such blessings he had left her, and had left with her two daughters, a second Hetta, and the heroine of our little story, Susan Bell.

A lawyer in Albany may thrive passing well for eight or ten years, and yet not leave behind him any very large sum of money if he dies at the end of that time. Some small modicum, some few thousand dollars, John Bell had amassed, so that his widow and daughters were not absolutely driven to look for work or bread.

In those happy days when cash had begun to flow in

plenteously to the young father of the family, he had taken it into his head to build for himself, or rather for his young female brood, a small neat house in the outskirts of Saratoga Springs. In doing so he was instigated as much by the excellence of the investment for his pocket as by the salubrity of the place for his girls. He furnished the house well, and then during some summer weeks his wife lived there, and sometimes he let it.

How the widow grieved when the lord of her heart and master of her mind was laid in the grave, I need not tell. She had already counted ten years of widowhood, and her children had grown to be young women beside her at the time of which I am now about to speak. Since that sad day on which they had left Albany they had lived together at the cottage at the Springs. In winter their life had been lonely enough; but as soon as the hot weather began to drive the fainting citizens out from New York, they had always received two or three boarders—old ladies generally, and occasionally an old gentleman—persons of very steady habits, with whose pockets the widow's moderate demands agreed better than the hotel charges. And so the Bells lived for ten years.

That Saratoga is a gay place in July, August, and September, the world knows well enough. To girls who go there with trunks full of muslin and crinoline, for whom a carriage and pair of horses is always waiting immediately after dinner, whose fathers' pockets are bursting with dollars, it is a very gay place. Dancing and flirtations come as a matter of course, and matrimony follows after with only too great rapidity. But the place was not very gay for Hetta or Susan Bell.

In the first place the widow was a timid woman, and among other fears feared greatly that she should be thought guilty of setting traps for husbands. Poor mothers! how often are they charged with this sin when their honest desires go no further than that their bairns may be "respectit like the lave." And then she feared flirtations; flirtations that should be that and nothing more, flirtations that are so destructive of the heart's sweetest essence. She feared love also, though she longed for that as well as feared it;—for her girls, I mean; all such feelings for herself were long laid under ground;—and then, like a timid creature as she was, she had other indefinite fears, and among them a great fear that those girls of hers would be left husbandless,—a phase of life which after her twelve years of bliss she regarded as anything but desirable. But the upshot was,—the upshot of so many fears and such small means,—that Hetta and Susan Bell had but a dull life of it.

Were it not that I am somewhat closely restricted in the number of my pages, I would describe at full the merits and beauties of Hetta and Susan Bell. As it is I can but say a few words. At our period of their lives Hetta was nearly one-and-twenty, and Susan was just nineteen. Hetta was a short, plump, demure young woman, with the softest smoothed hair, and the brownest brightest eyes. She was very useful in the house, good at corn cakes, and thought much, particularly in these latter months, of her religious duties. Her sister in the privacy of their own little room would sometimes twit her with the admiring patience with which she would listen to the lengthened eloquence of Mr. Phineas Beckard, the Baptist minister. Now Mr. Phineas Beckard was a bachelor.

Susan was not so good a girl in the kitchen or about the house as was her sister; but she was bright in the parlour, and if that motherly heart could have been made to give out its inmost secret—which however, it could not have been made to give out in any way painful to dear Hetta— perhaps it might have been found that Susan was loved with the closest love. She was taller than her sister, and lighter; her eyes were blue as were her mother's; her hair was brighter than Hetta's, but not always so singularly neat. She had a dimple on her chin, whereas Hetta had none; dimples on her cheeks too, when she smiled; and, oh, such a mouth! There; my allowance of pages permits no more.

One piercing cold winter's day there came knocking at the widow's door—a young man. Winter days, when the ice of January is refrozen by the wind of February, are very cold at Saratoga Springs. In these days there was not often much to disturb the serenity of Mrs. Bell's house; but on the day in question there came knocking at the door—a young man.

Mrs. Bell kept an old domestic, who had lived with them in those happy Albany days. Her name was Kate O'Brien, but though picturesque in name she was hardly so in person. She was a thick-set, noisy, good-natured old Irishwoman, who had joined her lot to that of Mrs. Bell when the latter first began housekeeping, and knowing when she was well off, had remained in the same place from that day forth. She had known Hetta as a baby, and, so to say, had seen Susan's birth.

"And what might you be wanting, sir?" said Kate O'Brien, apparently not quite pleased as she opened the door and let in all the cold air.

"I wish to see Mrs. Bell. Is not this Mrs. Bell's house?" said the young man, shaking the snow from out of the breast of his coat.

He did see Mrs. Bell, and we will now tell who he was, and why he had come, and how it came to pass that his carpet-bag was brought down to the widow's house and one of the front bedrooms was prepared for him, and that he drank tea that night in the widow's parlour.

His name was Aaron Dunn, and by profession he was an engineer. What peculiar misfortune in those days of frost and snow had befallen the line of rails which runs from Schenectady to Lake Champlain, I never quite understood. Banks and bridges had in some way come to grief, and on Aaron Dunn's shoulders was thrown the burden of seeing that they were duly repaired. Saratoga Springs was the centre of these mishaps, and therefore at Saratoga Springs it was necessary that he should take up his temporary abode.

Now there was at that time in New York City a Mr. Bell, great in railway matters—an uncle of the once thriving but now departed Albany lawyer. He was a rich man, but he liked his riches himself; or at any rate had not found himself called upon to share them with the widow and daughters of his nephew. But when it chanced to come to pass that he had a hand in despatching Aaron Dunn to Saratoga, he took the young man aside and recommended him to lodge with the widow. "There," said he, "show her my card." So much the rich uncle thought he might vouchsafe to do for the nephew's widow.

Mrs. Bell and both her daughters were in the parlour when Aaron Dunn was shown in, snow and all. He told his story in a rough, shaky voice, for his teeth chattered; and he gave the card, almost wishing that he had gone to the empty big hotel, for the widow's welcome was not at first quite warm.

The widow listened to him as he gave his message, and then she took the card and looked at it. Hetta, who was sitting on the side of the fireplace facing the door, went on demurely with her work. Susan gave one glance round— her back was to the stranger—and then another; and then she moved her chair a little nearer to the wall, so as to give the young man room to come to the fire, if he would. He did not come, but his eyes glanced upon Susan Bell; and he thought that the old man in New York was right, and that the big hotel would be cold and dull. It was a pretty face to look on that cold evening as she turned it up from the stocking she was mending.

"Perhaps you don't wish to take winter boarders, ma'am?" said Aaron Dunn.

"We never have done so yet, sir," said Mrs. Bell timidly. Could she let this young wolf in among her lamb-fold? He might be a wolf;—who could tell?

"Mr. Bell seemed to think it would suit," said Aaron.

Had he acquiesced in her timidity and not pressed the point, it would have been all up with him. But the widow did not like to go against the big uncle; and so she said,

"Perhaps it may, sir."

"I guess it will, finely," said Aaron. And then the widow, seeing that the matter was so far settled, put down her work and came round into the passage. Hetta followed her, for there would be housework to do. Aaron gave himself another shake, settled the weekly number of dollars—with very little difficulty on his part, for he had caught another glance at Susan's face; and then went after his bag. 'Twas thus that Aaron Dunn obtained an entrance into Mrs. Bell's house. "But what if he be a wolf?" she said to herself over and over again that night, though not exactly in those words. Ay, but there is another side to that question. What if he be a stalwart man, honest-minded, with clever eye, cunning hand, ready brain, broad back, and warm heart; in want of a wife mayhap; a man that can earn his own bread and another's;—half a dozen others' when the half dozen come? Would not that be a good sort of lodger? Such a question as that too did flit, just flit, across the widow's sleepless mind. But then she thought so much more of the wolf! Wolves, she had taught herself to think, were more common than stalwart, honest-minded, wife-desirous men.

"I wonder mother consented to take him," said Hetta, when they were in the little room together.

"And why shouldn't she?" said Susan. "It will be a help."

"Yes, it will be a little help," said Hetta. "But we have done very well hitherto without winter lodgers."

"But uncle Bell said she was to."

"What is uncle Bell to us?" said Hetta, who had a spirit of her own. And she began to surmise within herself whether Aaron Dunn would join the Baptist congregation, and whether Phineas Beckard would approve of this new move.

"He is a very well-behaved young man at any rate," said Susan, "and he draws beautifully. Did you see those things he was doing?"

"He draws very well, I dare say," said Hetta, who regarded this as but a poor warranty for good behaviour. Hetta also had some fear of wolves—not for herself perhaps; but for her sister.

Aaron Dunn's work—the commencement of his work—lay at some distance from the Springs, and he left every morning with a lot of workmen by an early train—almost before daylight. And every morning, cold and wintry as the mornings were, the widow got him his breakfast with her own hands. She took his dollars and would not leave him altogether to the awkward mercies of Kate O'Brien; nor would she trust her girls to attend upon the young man. Hetta she might have trusted; but then Susan would have asked why she was spared her share of such hardship.

In the evening, leaving his work when it was dark, Aaron always returned, and then the evening was passed together. But they were passed with the most demure propriety. These women would make the tea, cut the bread and butter, and then sew; while Aaron Dunn, when the cups were removed, would always go to his plans and drawings.

On Sundays they were more together; but even on this day there was cause of separation, for Aaron went to the Episcopalian church, rather to the disgust of Hetta. In the afternoon, however, they were together; and then Phineas Beckard came in to tea on Sundays, and he and Aaron got to talking on religion; and though they disagreed pretty much, and would not give an inch either one or the other, nevertheless the minister told the widow, and Hetta too probably, that the lad had good stuff in him, though he was so stiff-necked.

"But he should be more modest in talking on such matters with a minister," said Hetta.

The Rev. Phineas acknowledged that perhaps he should; but he was honest enough to repeat that the lad had stuff in him. "Perhaps after all he is not a wolf," said the widow to herself.

Things went on in this way for above a month. Aaron had declared to himself over and over again that that face was sweet to look upon, and had unconsciously promised to himself certain delights in talking and perhaps walking with the owner of it. But the walkings had not been achieved—nor even the talkings as yet. The truth was that Dunn was bashful with young women, though he could be so stiff-necked with the minister.

And then he felt angry with himself, inasmuch as he had advanced no further; and as he lay in his bed—which perhaps those pretty hands had helped to make—he resolved that he would be a thought bolder in his bearing. He had no idea of making love to Susan Bell; of course not. But why should he not amuse himself by talking to a pretty girl when she sat so near him, evening after evening?

"What a very quiet young man he is," said Susan to her sister.

"He has his bread to earn, and sticks to his work," said Hetta. "No doubt he has his amusement when he is in the city," added the elder sister, not wishing to leave too strong an impression of the young man's virtue.

They had all now their settled places in the parlour. Hetta sat on one side of the fire, close to the table, having that side to herself. There she sat always busy. She must have made every dress and bit of linen worn in the house, and hemmed every sheet and towel, so busy was she always. Sometimes, once in a week or so, Phineas Beckard would come in, and then place was made for him between Hetta's usual seat and the table. For when there he would read out loud. On the other side, close also to the table, sat the widow, busy, but not savagely busy as her elder daughter. Between Mrs. Bell and the wall, with her feet ever on the fender, Susan used to sit; not absolutely idle, but doing work of some slender pretty sort, and talking ever and anon to her mother. Opposite to them all, at the other side of the table, far away from the fire, would Aaron Dunn place himself with his plans and drawings before him.

"Are you a judge of bridges, ma'am?" said Aaron, the evening after he had made his resolution. 'Twas thus he began his courtship.

"Of bridges?" said Mrs. Bell—"Oh, dear no, sir"; but she put out her hand to take the little drawing which Aaron handed to her.

"Because that's one I've planned for our bit of a new branch from Moreau up to Lake George. I guess Miss Susan knows something about bridges."

"I guess I don't," said Susan—"only that they oughtn't to tumble down when the frost comes."

"Ha, ha, ha; no more they ought. I'll tell McEvoy that."

McEvoy had been a former engineer on the line. "Well, that won't burst with any frost, I guess."

"Oh my! how pretty!" said the widow, and then Susan of course jumped up to look over her mother's shoulder.

The artful dodger! he had drawn and coloured a beautiful little sketch of a bridge; not an engineer's plan with sections and measurements, vexatious to a woman's eye, but a graceful little bridge with a string of cars running under it. You could almost hear the bell going.

"Well; that is a pretty bridge," said Susan. "Isn't it, Hetta?"

"I don't know anything about bridges," said Hetta, to whose clever eyes the dodge was quite apparent. But in spite of her cleverness Mrs. Bell and Susan had soon moved their chairs round to the table, and were looking through the contents of Aaron's portfolio. "But yet he may be a wolf," thought the poor widow, just as she was kneeling down to say her prayers.

That evening certainly made a commencement. Though Hetta went on pertinaciously with the body of a new dress, the other two ladies did not put in another stitch that night. From his drawings Aaron got to his instruments, and before bedtime was teaching Susan how to draw parallel lines. Susan found that she had quite an aptitude for parallel lines, and altogether had a good time of it that evening. It is dull to go on week after week, and month after month, talking only to one's mother and sister. It is dull though one does not oneself recognise it to be so. A little change in such matters is so very pleasant. Susan had not the slightest idea of regarding Aaron as even a possible lover. But young ladies do like the conversation of young gentlemen. Oh, my exceedingly proper prim old lady, you who are so shocked at this as a general doctrine, has it never occurred to you that the Creator has so intended it?

Susan understanding little of the how and why, knew that she had had a good time, and was rather in spirits as she went to bed. But Hetta had been frightened by the dodge.

"Oh, Hetta, you should have looked at those drawings. He is so clever!" said Susan.

"I don't know that they would have done me much good," replied Hetta.

"Good! Well, they'd do me more good than a long sermon, I know," said Susan; "except on a Sunday, of course," she added apologetically. This was an ill-tempered attack both on Hetta and Hetta's admirer. But then why had Hetta been so snappish?

"I'm sure he's a wolf," thought Hetta as she went to bed.

"What a very clever young man he is!" thought Susan to herself as she pulled the warm clothes round about her shoulders and ears.

"Well that certainly was an improvement," thought Aaron as he went through the same operation, with a stronger feeling of self-approbation than he had enjoyed for some time past.

In the course of the next fortnight the family arrangements all altered themselves. Unless when Beckard was there Aaron would sit in the widow's place, the widow would take Susan's chair, and the two girls would be opposite. And then Dunn would read to them; not sermons, but passages from Shakespeare, and Byron, and Longfellow. "He reads much better than Mr. Beckard," Susan had said one night. "Of course you're a competent judge!" had been Hetta's retort. "I mean that I like it better," said Susan. "It's well that all people don't think alike," replied Hetta.

And then there was a deal of talking. The widow herself, as unconscious in this respect as her youngest daughter, certainly did find that a little variety was agreeable on those long winter nights; and talked herself with unaccustomed freedom. And Beckard came there oftener and talked very much. When he was there the two young men did all the talking, and they pounded each other immensely. But still there grew up a sort of friendship between them.

"Mr. Beckard seems quite to take to him," said Mrs. Bell to her eldest daughter.

"It is his great good nature, mother," replied Hetta.

It was at the end of the second month when Aaron took another step in advance—a perilous step. Sometimes on evenings he still went on with his drawing for an hour or so; but during three or four evenings he never asked any one to look at what he was doing. On one Friday he sat over his work till late, without any reading or talking at all; so late that at last Mrs. Bell said, "If you're going to sit much longer, Mr. Dunn, I'll get you to put out the candles." Thereby showing, had he known it or had she, that the mother's confidence in the young man was growing fast. Hetta knew all about it, and dreaded that the growth was too quick.

"I've finished now," said Aaron; and he looked carefully at the card-board on which he had been washing in his water-colours. "I've finished now." He then hesitated a moment; but ultimately he put the card into his portfolio and carried it up to his bedroom. Who does not perceive that it was intended as a present to Susan Bell?

The question which Aaron asked himself that night, and which he hardly knew how to answer, was this. Should he offer the drawing to Susan in the presence of her mother and sister, or on some occasion when they two might be alone together? No such occasion had ever yet occurred, but Aaron thought that it might probably be brought about. But then he wanted to make no fuss about it. His first intention had been to chuck the drawing lightly across the table when it was completed, and so make nothing of it. But he had finished it with more care than he had at first intended; and then he had hesitated when he had finished it. It was too late now for that plan of chucking it over the table.

On the Saturday evening when he came down from his room, Mr. Beckard was there, and there was no opportunity that night. On the Sunday, in conformity with a previous engagement, he went to hear Mr. Beckard preach, and walked to and from meeting with the family. This pleased Mrs. Bell, and they were all very gracious that afternoon. But Sunday was no day for the picture.

On Monday the thing had become of importance to him. Things always do when they are kept over. Before tea that evening when he came down Mrs. Bell and Susan only were in the room. He knew Hetta for his foe, and therefore determined to use this occasion.

"Miss Susan," he said, stammering somewhat, and

blushing too, poor fool! "I have done a little drawing which I want you to accept," and he put his portfolio down on the table.

"Oh! I don't know," said Susan, who had seen the blush.

Mrs. Bell had seen the blush also, and pursed her mouth up, and looked grave. Had there been no stammering and no blush, she might have thought nothing of it.

Aaron saw at once that his little gift was not to go down smoothly. He was, however, in for it now, so he picked it out from among the other papers in the case and brought it over to Susan. He endeavoured to hand it to her with an air of indifference, but I cannot say that he succeeded.

It was a very pretty, well-finished, water-coloured drawing, representing still the same bridge, but with more adjuncts. In Susan's eyes it was a work of high art. Of pictures probably she had seen but little, and her liking for the artist no doubt added to her admiration. But the more she admired it and wished for it, the stronger was her feeling that she ought not to take it.

Poor Susan! she stood for a minute looking at the drawing, but she said nothing; not even a word of praise. She felt that she was red in the face, and uncourteous to their lodger; but her mother was looking at her and she did not know how to behave herself.

Mrs. Bell put out her hand for the sketch, trying to bethink herself as she did so in what least uncivil way she could refuse the present. She took a moment to look at it collecting her thoughts, and as she did so her woman's wit came to her aid.

"Oh dear, Mr. Dunn, it is very pretty; quite a beautiful picture. I cannot let Susan rob you of that. You must keep that for some of your own particular friends."

"But I did it for her," said Aaron innocently.

Susan looked down at the ground, half pleased at the declaration. The drawing would look very pretty in a small gilt frame put over her dressing-table. But the matter now was altogether in her mother's hands.

"I am afraid it is too valuable, sir, for Susan to accept."

"It is not valuable at all," said Aaron, declining to take it back from the widow's hand.

"Oh, I am quite sure it is. It is worth ten dollars at least—or twenty," said poor Mrs. Bell, not in the very best taste. But she was perplexed, and did not know how to get out of the scrape. The article in question now lay upon the table-cloth, appropriated by no one, and at this moment Hetta came into the room.

"It is not worth ten cents," said Aaron, with something like a frown on his brow. "But as we had been talking about the bridge, I thought Miss Susan would accept it."

"Accept what?" said Hetta. And then her eye fell upon the drawing and she took it up.

"It is beautifully done," said Mrs. Bell, wishing much to soften the matter; perhaps the more so that Hetta the demure was now present. "I am telling Mr. Dunn that we can't take a present of anything so valuable."

"Oh dear no," said Hetta. "It wouldn't be right."

It was a cold frosty evening in March, and the fire was burning brightly on the hearth. Aaron Dunn took up the drawing quietly—very quietly—and rolling it up, as such drawings are rolled, put it between the blazing logs. It was the work of four evenings, and his chef-d'oeuvre in the way of art.

Susan, when she saw what he had done, burst out into tears. The widow could very readily have done so also, but she was able to refrain herself, and merely exclaimed—"Oh, Mr. Dunn!"

"If Mr. Dunn chooses to burn his own picture, he has certainly a right to do so," said Hetta.

Aaron immediately felt ashamed of what he had done; and he also could have cried, but for his manliness. He walked away to one of the parlour-windows, and looked out upon the frosty night. It was dark, but the stars were bright, and he thought that he should like to be walking fast by himself along the line of rails towards Balston. There he stood, perhaps for three minutes. He thought it would be proper to give Susan time to recover from her tears.

"Will you please to come to your tea, sir?" said the soft voice of Mrs. Bell.

He turned round to do so, and found that Susan was gone. It was not quite in her power to recover from her tears in three minutes. And then the drawing had been so beautiful! It had been done expressly for her too! And there had been something, she knew not what, in his eye as he had so declared. She had watched him intently over those four evenings' work, wondering why he did not show it, till her feminine curiosity had become rather strong. It was something very particular, she was sure, and she had learned that all that precious work had been for her. Now all that precious work was destroyed. How was it possible that she should not cry for more than three minutes?

The others took their meal in perfect silence, and when it was over the two women sat down to their work. Aaron had a book which he pretended to read, but instead of reading he was bethinking himself that he had behaved badly. What right had he to throw them all into such confusion by indulging in his passion? He was ashamed of what he had done, and fancied that Susan would hate him. Fancying that, he began to find at the same time that he by no means hated her.

At last Hetta got up and left the room. She knew that her sister was sitting alone in the cold, and Hetta was affectionate. Susan had not been in fault, and therefore Hetta went up to console her.

"Mrs. Bell," said Aaron, as soon as the door was closed, "I beg your pardon for what I did just now."

"Oh, sir, I'm so sorry that the picture is burnt," said poor Mrs. Bell.

"The picture does not matter a straw," said Aaron. "But I see that I have disturbed you all,—and I am afraid I have made Miss Susan unhappy."

"She was grieved because your picture was burnt," said Mrs. Bell, putting some emphasis on the "your," intending to show that her daughter had not regarded the drawing as her own. But the emphasis bore another meaning; and so the widow perceived as soon as she had spoken.

"Oh, I can do twenty more of the same if anybody wanted them," said Aaron. "If I do another like it, will you let her take it, Mrs. Bell?—just to show that you have for-given me, and that we are friends as we were before?"

Was he, or was he not a wolf? That was the question which Mrs. Bell scarcely knew how to answer. Hetta had given her voice, saying he was lupine. Mr. Beckard's opin-ion she had not liked to ask directly. Mr. Beckard she thought would probably propose to Hetta; but as yet he had not done so. And, as he was still a stranger in the fam-ily, she did not like in any way to compromise Susan's name. Indirectly she had asked the question, and, indi-rectly also, Mr. Beckard's answer had been favourable.

"But it mustn't mean anything, sir," was the widow's weak answer, when she had paused on the question for a moment.

"Oh no, of course not," said Aaron, joyously, and his face became radiant and happy. "And I do beg your pardon for burning it; and the young ladies' pardon too." And then he rapidly got out his card-board, and set himself to work about another bridge. The widow, meditating many things in her heart, commenced the hemming of a handkerchief.

In about an hour the two girls came back to the room and silently took their accustomed places. Aaron hardly looked up, but went on diligently with his drawing. This bridge should be a better bridge than that other. Its accep-tance was now assured. Of course it was to mean nothing. That was a matter of course. So he worked away diligently, and said nothing to anybody.

When they went off to bed the two girls went into the mother's room. "Oh, mother, I hope he is not very angry," said Susan.

"Angry!" said Hetta, "if anybody should be angry, it is mother. He ought to have known that Susan could not accept it. He should never have offered it."

"But he's doing another," said Mrs. Bell.

"Not for her," said Hetta.

"Yes he is," said Mrs. Bell, "and I have promised that she shall take it." Susan as she heard this sank gently into the chair behind her, and her eyes became full of tears. The intimation was almost too much for her.

"Oh, mother!" said Hetta.

"But I particularly said that it was to mean nothing."

"Oh, mother, that makes it worse."

Why should Hetta interfere in this way, thought Susan to herself. Had she interfered when Mr. Beckard gave Hetta a Testament bound in Morocco? Had not she smiled, and looked gratified, and kissed her sister, and declared that Phineas Beckard was a nice dear man, and by far the most elegant preacher at the Springs? Why should Hetta be so cruel?

"I don't see that, my dear," said the mother. Hetta would not explain before her sister, so they all went to bed.

On the Thursday evening the drawing was finished. Not a word had been said about it, at any rate in his presence, and he had gone on working in silence. "There," said he, late on the Thursday evening, "I don't know that it will be any better if I go on daubing for another hour. There, Miss Susan; there's another bridge. I hope that will neither burst with the frost, nor yet be destroyed by fire," and he gave it a light flip with his fingers and sent it skimming over the table.

Susan blushed and smiled, and took it up. "Oh, it is beautiful," she said. "Isn't it beautifully done, mother?" And then all the three got up to look at it, and all confessed that it was excellently done.

"And I am sure we are very much obliged to you," said Susan after a pause, remembering that she had not yet thanked him.

"Oh, it's nothing," said he, not quite liking the word "we." On the following day he returned from his work to Saratoga about noon. This he had never done before, and therefore no one expected that he would be seen in the house before the evening. On this occasion, however, he went straight thither, and as chance would have it, both the widow and her elder daughter were out. Susan was there alone in charge of the house.

He walked in and opened the parlour door. There she sat, with her feet on the fender, with her work unheeded on the table behind her, and the picture, Aaron's drawing, lying on her knees. She was gazing at it intently as he entered, thinking in her young heart that it possessed all the beauties which a picture could possess.

"Oh, Mr. Dunn," she said, getting up and holding the telltale sketch behind the skirt of her dress.

"Miss Susan, I have come here to tell your mother that I must start for New York this afternoon and be there for six weeks, or perhaps longer."

"Mother is out," said she; "I'm so sorry."

"Is she?" said Aaron.

"And Hetta too. Dear me. And you'll be wanting dinner. I'll go and see about it."

Aaron began to swear that he could not possibly eat any dinner. He had dined once, and was going to dine again;— anything to keep her from going.

"But you must have something, Mr. Dunn," and she walked towards the door.

But he put his back to it. "Miss Susan," said he, "I guess I've been here nearly two months."

"Yes, sir, I believe you have," she replied, shaking in her shoes, and not knowing which way to look.

"And I hope we have been good friends."

"Yes, sir," said Susan, almost beside herself as to what she was saying.

"I'm going away now, and it seems to be such a time before I'll be back."

"Will it, Sir?"

"Six weeks, Miss Susan!" and then he paused, looking into her eyes, to see what he could read there. She leant against the table, pulling to pieces a morsel of half-ravelled muslin which she held in her hand; but her eyes were turned to the ground, and he could hardly see them.

"Miss Susan," he continued, "I may as well speak out now as at another time." He too was looking towards the ground, and clearly did not know what to do with his hands. "The truth is just this. I—I love you dearly, with all my heart. I never saw any one I ever thought so beautiful, so nice, and so good;—and what's more, I never shall. I'm not very good at this sort of thing, I know; but I couldn't go away from Saratoga for six weeks and not tell you." And then he ceased. He did not ask for any love in return. His presumption had not got so far as that yet. He merely declared his passion, leaning against the door, and there he stood twiddling his thumbs.

Susan had not the slightest conception of the way in which she ought to receive such a declaration. She had never had a lover before; nor had she ever thought of Aaron absolutely as a lover, though something very like love for him had been crossing over her spirit. Now, at this moment, she felt that he was the beau-ideal of manhood, though his boots were covered with the railway mud, and though his pantaloons were tucked up in rolls round his ankles. He was a fine, well-grown, open-faced fellow, whose eye was bold and yet tender, whose brow was full and broad, and all his bearing manly. Love him! Of course she loved him. Why else had her heart melted with pleasure when her mother said that that second picture was to be accepted?

But what was she to say? Anything but the open truth; she well knew that. The open truth would not do at all. What would her mother say and Hetta if she were rashly to say that? Hetta, she knew, would be dead against such a lover, and of her mother's approbation she had hardly more hope. Why they should disapprove of Aaron as a lover she had never asked herself. There are many nice things that seem to be wrong only because they are so nice. Maybe that Susan regarded a lover as one of them. "Oh, Mr. Dunn, you shouldn't." That in fact was all that she could say.

"Should not I?" said he. "Well, perhaps not; but there's the truth, and no harm ever comes of that. Perhaps I'd better not ask you for an answer now, but I thought it better you should know it all. And remember this—I only care for one thing now in the world, and that is for your love." And then he paused, thinking possibly that in spite of what he had said he might perhaps get some sort of an answer, some inkling of the state of her heart's disposition towards him.

But Susan had at once resolved to take him at his word when he suggested that an immediate reply was not necessary. To say that she loved him was of course impossible, and to say that she did not was equally so. She determined therefore to close at once with the offer of silence.

When he ceased speaking there was a moment's pause, during which he strove hard to read what might be written on her down-turned face. But he was not good at such reading. "Well, I guess I'll go and get my things ready now," he said, and then turned round to open the door.

"Mother will be in before you are gone, I suppose," said Susan.

"I have only got twenty minutes," said he, looking at his watch. "But, Susan, tell her what I have said to you. Good-bye." And he put out his hand. He knew he should see her again, but this had been his plan to get her hand in his.

"Good-bye, Mr. Dunn," and she gave him her hand.

He held it tight for a moment, so that she could not draw it away,—could not if she would. "Will you tell your mother?" he asked.

"Yes," she answered, quite in a whisper. "I guess I'd better tell her." And then she gave a long sigh. He pressed her hand again and got it up to his lips.

"Mr. Dunn, don't," she said. But he did kiss it. "God bless you, my own dearest, dearest girl! I'll just open the door as I come down. Perhaps Mrs. Bell will be here." And then he rushed up stairs.

But Mrs. Bell did not come in. She and Hetta were at a weekly service at Mr. Beckard's meeting-house, and Mr. Beckard it seemed had much to say. Susan, when left alone, sat down and tried to think. But she could not think; she could only love. She could use her mind only in recounting to herself the perfections of that demigod whose heavy steps were so audible overhead, as he walked to and fro collecting his things and putting them into his bag.

And then, just when he had finished, she bethought herself that he must be hungry. She flew to the kitchen, but she was too late. Before she could even reach at the loaf of bread he descended the stairs, with a clattering noise, and heard her voice as she spoke quickly to Kate O'Brien.

"Miss Susan," he said, "don't get anything for me, for I'm off."

"Oh, Mr. Dunn, I am so sorry. You'll be so hungry on your journey," and she came out to him in the passage.

"I shall want nothing on the journey, dearest, if you'll say one kind word to me."

Again her eyes went to the ground. "What do you want me to say, Mr. Dunn?"

"Say, God bless you, Aaron."

"God bless you, Aaron," said she; and yet she was sure that she had not declared her love. He however thought otherwise, and went up to New York with a happy heart.

Things happened in the next fortnight rather quickly.

Susan at once resolved to tell her mother, but she resolved also not to tell Hetta. That afternoon she got her mother to herself in Mrs. Bell's own room, and then she made a clean breast of it.

"And what did you say to him, Susan?"

"I said nothing, mother."

"Nothing, dear!"

"No, mother; not a word. He told me he didn't want it." She forgot how she had used his Christian name in bidding God bless him.

"Oh dear!" said the widow.

"Was it very wrong?" asked Susan.

"But what do you think yourself, my child?" asked Mrs. Bell after a while. "What are your own feelings."

Mrs. Bell was sitting on a chair and Susan was standing opposite to her against the post of the bed. She made no answer, but moving from her place, she threw herself into her mother's arms, and hid her face on her mother's shoulder. It was easy enough to guess what were her feelings.

"But, my darling," said her mother, "you must not think that it is an engagement."

"No," said Susan, sorrowfully.

"Young men say those things to amuse themselves." Wolves, she would have said, had she spoken out her mind freely.

"Oh, mother, he is not like that."

The daughter contrived to extract a promise from the mother that Hetta should not be told just at present. Mrs. Bell calculated that she had six weeks before her; as yet Mr. Beckard had not spoken out, but there was reason to suppose that he would do so before those six weeks would be over, and then she would be able to seek counsel from him.

Mr. Beckard spoke out at the end of six days, and Hetta frankly accepted him. "I hope you'll love your brother-in-law," said she to Susan.

"Oh, I will indeed," said Susan; and in the softness of her heart at the moment she almost made up her mind to tell; but Hetta was full of her own affairs, and thus it passed off.

It was then arranged that Hetta should go and spend a week with Mr. Beckard's parents. Old Mr. Beckard was a farmer living near Utica, and now that the match was declared and approved, it was thought well that Hetta should know her future husband's family. So she went for a week, and Mr. Beckard went with her. "He will be back in plenty of time for me to speak to him before Aaron Dunn's six weeks are over," said Mrs. Bell to herself.

But things did not go exactly as she expected. On the very morning after the departure of the engaged couple, there came a letter from Aaron, saying that he would be at Saratoga that very evening. The railway people had ordered him down again for some days' special work; then he was to go elsewhere, and not to return to Saratoga till June. "But he hoped," so said the letter, "that Mrs. Bell would not turn him into the street even then, though the summer might have come, and her regular lodgers might be expected."

"Oh dear, oh dear!" said Mrs. Bell to herself, reflecting that she had no one of whom she could ask advice, and that she must decide that very day. Why had she let Mr. Beckard go without telling him? Then she told Susan, and Susan spent the day trembling. Perhaps, thought Mrs. Bell, he will say nothing about it. In such case, however, would it not be her duty to say something? Poor mother! She trembled nearly as much as Susan.

It was dark when the fatal knock came at the door. The tea-things were already laid, and the tea-cake was already baked; for it would at any rate be necessary to give Mr. Dunn his tea. Susan, when she heard the knock, rushed from her chair and took refuge upstairs. The widow gave a long sigh and settled her dress. Kate O'Brien with willing step opened the door, and bade her old friend welcome.

"How are the ladies?" asked Aaron, trying to gather something from the face and voice of the domestic.

"Miss Hetta and Mr. Beckard be gone off to Utica, just man-and-wife like! and so they are, more power to them."

"Oh indeed; I'm very glad," said Aaron—and so he was; very glad to have Hetta the demure out of the way. And then he made his way into the parlour, doubting much, and hoping much.

Mrs. Bell rose from her chair, and tried to look grave. Aaron glancing round the room saw that Susan was not there. He walked straight up to the widow, and offered her his hand, which she took. It might be that Susan had not thought fit to tell, and in such case it would not be right for him to compromise her; so he said never a word.

But the subject was too important to the mother to allow of her being silent when the young man stood before her. "Oh, Mr. Dunn," said she, "what is this you have been saying to Susan?"

"I have asked her to be my wife," said he, drawing himself up and looking her full in the face. Mrs. Bell's heart was almost as soft as her daughter's, and it was nearly gone; but at the moment she had nothing to say but, "Oh dear, oh dear!"

"May I not call you mother?" said he, taking both her hands in his.

"Oh dear—oh dear! But will you be good to her? Oh, Aaron Dunn, if you deceive my child!"

In another quarter of an hour, Susan was kneeling at her mother's knee, with her face on her mother's lap; the mother was wiping tears out of her eyes; and Aaron was standing by holding one of the widow's hands.

"You are my mother too, now," said he. What would Hetta and Mr. Beckard say, when they came back? But then he surely was not a wolf!

There were four or five days left for courtship before Hetta and Mr. Beckard would return; four or five days during which Susan might be happy, Aaron triumphant, and Mrs. Bell nervous. Days I have said, but after all it was only the evenings that were so left. Every morning Susan got up to give Aaron his breakfast, but Mrs. Bell got up also. Susan boldly declared her right to do so, and Mrs. Bell found no objection which she could urge.

But after that Aaron was always absent till seven or eight in the evening, when he would return to his tea. Then came the hour or two of lovers' intercourse.

But they were very tame, those hours. The widow still felt an undefined fear that she was wrong, and though her heart yearned to know that her daughter was happy in the sweet happiness of accepted love, yet she dreaded to be too confident. Not a word had been said about money matters; not a word of Aaron Dunn's relatives. So she did not leave them by themselves, but waited with what patience she could for the return of her wise counsellors.

And then Susan hardly knew how to behave herself with her accepted suitor. She felt that she was very happy; but perhaps she was most happy when she was thinking about him through the long day, assisting in fixing little things for his comfort, and waiting for his evening return. And as he sat there in the parlour, she could be happy then too, if she were but allowed to sit still and look at him,—not stare at him, but raise her eyes every now and again to his face for the shortest possible glance, as she had been used to do ever since he came there.

But he, unconscionable lover, wanted to hear her speak, was desirous of being talked to, and perhaps thought that he should by rights be allowed to sit by her, and hold her hand. No such privileges were accorded to him. If they had been alone together, walking side by side on the green turf, as lovers should walk, she would soon have found the use of her tongue,—have talked fast enough no doubt. Under such circumstances, when a girl's shyness has given way to real intimacy, there is in general no end to her power of chatting. But though there was much love between Aaron and Susan, there was as yet but little intimacy. And then, let a mother be ever so motherly—and no mother could have more of a mother's tenderness than Mrs. Bell—still her presence must be a restraint. Aaron was very fond of Mrs. Bell; but nevertheless he did sometimes wish that some domestic duty would take her out of the parlour for a few happy minutes. Susan went out very often, but Mrs. Bell seemed to be a fixture.

Once for a moment he did find his love alone, immediately as he came into the house. "My own Susan, you do love me? do say so to me once." And he contrived to slip his arm round her waist. "Yes," she whispered; but she slipped like an eel from his hands, and left him only preparing himself for a kiss. And then when she got to her room, half frightened, she clasped her hands together, and bethought herself that she did really love him with a strength and depth of love which filled her whole existence. Why could she not have told him something of all this?

And so the few days of his second sojourn at Saratoga passed away, not altogether satisfactorily. It was settled that he should return to New York on Saturday night, leaving Saratoga on that evening; and as the Beckards—Hetta was already regarded quite as a Beckard—were to be back to dinner on that day, Mrs. Bell would have an opportunity of telling her wondrous tale. It might be well that Mr. Beckard should see Aaron before his departure.

On that Saturday the Beckards did arrive just in time for dinner. It may be imagined that Susan's appetite was not very keen, nor her manner very collected. But all this passed by unobserved in the importance attached to the various Beckard arrangements which came under discussion. Ladies and gentlemen circumstanced as were Hetta and Mr. Beckard are perhaps a little too apt to think that their own affairs are paramount. But after dinner Susan vanished at once, and when Hetta prepared to follow her, desirous of further talk about matrimonial arrangements, her mother stopped her, and the disclosure was made.

"Proposed to her!" said Hetta, who perhaps thought that one marriage in a family was enough at a time.

"Yes, my love—and he did it, I must say, in a very honourable way, telling her not to make any answer till she had spoken to me;—now that was very nice; was it not, Phineas?" Mrs. Bell had become very anxious that Aaron should not be voted a wolf.

"And what has been said to him since?" asked the discreet Phineas.

"Why—nothing absolutely decisive." Oh, Mrs. Bell! "You see I know nothing as to his means."

"Nothing at all," said Hetta.

"He is a man that will always earn his bread," said Mr. Beckard; and Mrs. Bell blessed him in her heart for saying it.

"But has he been encouraged?" asked Hetta.

"Well; yes, he has," said the widow.

"Then Susan I suppose likes him?" asked Phineas.

"Well; yes, she does," said the widow. And the conference ended in a resolution that Phineas Beckard should have a conversation with Aaron Dunn, as to his worldly means and position; and that he, Phineas, should decide whether Aaron might, or might not be at once accepted as a lover, according to the tenor of that conversation. Poor Susan was not told anything of all this. "Better not," said Hetta the demure. "It will only flurry her the more." How would she have liked it, if without consulting her, they had left it to Aaron to decide whether or no she might marry Phineas?

They knew where on the works Aaron was to be found, and thither Mr. Beckard rode after dinner. We need not narrate at length the conference between the young men. Aaron at once declared that he had nothing but what he made as an engineer, and explained that he held no permanent situation on the line. He was well paid at that present moment, but at the end of summer he would have to look for employment.

"Then you can hardly marry quite at present," said the discreet minister.

"Perhaps not quite immediately."

"And long engagements are never wise," said the other.

"Three or four months," suggested Aaron. But Mr. Beckard shook his head.

The afternoon at Mrs. Bell's house was melancholy. The final decision of the three judges was as follows. There was to be no engagement; of course no correspondence. Aaron was to be told that it would be better that he should get lodgings elsewhere when he returned; but that he would be allowed to visit at Mrs. Bell's house,—and at Mrs. Beckard's, which was very considerate. If he should succeed in getting a permanent appointment, and if he and Susan still held the same mind, why then—&c. &c. Such was Susan's fate, as communicated to her by Mrs. Bell and Hetta. She sat still and wept when she heard it; but she did not complain. She had always felt that Hetta would be against her.

"Mayn't I see him, then?" she said through her tears.

Hetta thought she had better not. Mrs. Bell thought she might. Phineas decided that they might shake hands, but only in full conclave. There was to be no lovers' farewell.

Aaron was to leave the house at half-past five; but before he went Susan should be called down. Poor Susan! She sat down and bemoaned herself; uncomplaining, but very sad.

Susan was soft, feminine, and manageable. But Aaron Dunn was not very soft, was especially masculine, and in some matters not easily manageable. When Mr. Beckard in the widow's presence—Hetta had retired in obedience to her lover—informed him of the court's decision, there came over his face the look which he had worn when he burned the picture. "Mrs. Bell," he said, "had encouraged his engagement; and he did not understand why other people should now come and disturb it."

"Not an engagement, Aaron," said Mrs. Bell piteously.

"He was able and willing to work," he said, "and knew his profession. What young man of his age had done better than he had?" and he glanced round at them with perhaps more pride than was quite becoming.

Then Mr. Beckard spoke out, very wisely no doubt, but perhaps a little too much at length. Sons and daughters, as well as fathers and mothers, will know very well what he said; so I need not repeat his words. I cannot say that Aaron listened with much attention, but he understood perfectly what the upshot of it was. Many a man understands the purport of many a sermon without listening to one word in ten. Mr. Beckard meant to be kind in his manner; indeed was so, only that Aaron could not accept as kindness any interference on his part.

"I'll tell you what, Mrs. Bell," said he. "I look upon myself as engaged to her. And I look on her as engaged to me. I tell you so fairly; and I believe that's her mind as well as mine."

"But, Aaron, you won't try to see her—or to write to her,—not in secret; will you?"

"When I try to see her, I'll come and knock at this door; and if I write to her, I'll write to her full address by the post. I never did and never will do anything in secret."

"I know you're good and honest," said the widow with her handkerchief to her eyes.

"Then why do you separate us?" asked he, almost roughly. "I suppose I may see her at any rate before I go. My time's nearly up now, I guess."

And then Susan was called for, and she and Hetta came down together. Susan crept in behind her sister. Her eyes were red with weeping, and her appearance was altogether disconsolate. She had had a lover for a week, and now she was to be robbed of him.

"Good-bye, Susan," said Aaron, and he walked up to her without bashfulness or embarrassment. Had they all been compliant and gracious to him he would have been as bashful as his love; but now his temper was hot. "Good-bye, Susan," and she took his hand, and he held hers till he had finished. "And remember this, I look upon you as my promised wife, and I don't fear that you'll deceive me. At any rate I shan't deceive you."

"Good-bye, Aaron," she sobbed.

"Good-bye, and God bless you, my own darling!" And then without saying a word to any one else, he turned his back upon them and went his way.

There had been something very consolatory, very sweet, to the poor girl in her lover's last words. And yet they had almost made her tremble. He had been so bold, and stern, and confident. He had seemed so utterly to defy the impregnable discretion of Mr. Beckard, so to despise the demure propriety of Hetta. But of this she felt sure, when she came to question her heart, that she could never, never, never cease to love him better than all the world beside. She would wait—patiently if she could find patience—and then, if he deserted her, she would die.

In another month Hetta became Mrs. Beckard. Susan brisked up a little for the occasion, and looked very pretty as bridesmaid. She was serviceable too in arranging household matters, hemming linen and sewing table-cloths; though of course in these matters she did not do a tenth of what Hetta did.

Then the summer came, the Saratoga summer of July, August, and September, during which the widow's house was full; and Susan's hands saved the pain of her heart, for she was forced into occupation. Now that Hetta was gone to her own duties, it was necessary that Susan's part in the household should be more prominent.

Aaron did not come back to his work at Saratoga. Why he did not they could not then learn. During the whole long summer they heard not a word of him nor from him; and then when the cold winter months came and their boarders had left them, Mrs. Beckard congratulated her sister in that she had given no further encouragement to a lover who cared so little for her. This was very hard to bear. But Susan did bear it.

That winter was very sad. They learned nothing of Aaron Dunn till about January; and then they heard that he was doing very well. He was engaged on the Erie trunk line, was paid highly, and was much esteemed. And yet he neither came nor sent! "He has an excellent situation," their informant told them. "And a permanent one?" asked the widow. "Oh, yes, no doubt," said the gentleman, "for I happen to know that they count greatly on him." And yet he sent no word of love.

After that the winter became very sad indeed. Mrs. Bell thought it to be her duty now to teach her daughter that in all probability she would see Aaron Dunn no more. It was open to him to leave her without being absolutely a wolf. He had been driven from the house when he was poor, and they had no right to expect that he would return, now that he had made some rise in the world. "Men do amuse themselves in that way," the widow tried to teach her.

"He is not like that, mother," she said again.

"But they do not think so much of these things as we do," urged the mother.

"Don't they?" said Susan, oh, so sorrowfully; and so through the whole long winter months she became paler and paler, and thinner and thinner.

And then Hetta tried to console her with religion, and that perhaps did not make things any better. Religious consolation is the best cure for all griefs; but it must not be looked for specially with regard to any individual sorrow. A religious man, should he become bankrupt through the misfortunes of the world, will find true consolation in his religion even for that sorrow. But a bankrupt, who has not thought much of such things, will hardly find solace by taking up religion for that special occasion.

And Hetta perhaps was hardly prudent in her attempts.

She thought that it was wicked in Susan to grow thin and pale for love of Aaron Dunn, and she hardly hid her thoughts. Susan was not sure but that it might be wicked, but this doubt in no way tended to make her plump or rosy. So that in those days she found no comfort in her sister.

But her mother's pity and soft love did ease her sufferings, though it could not make them cease. Her mother did not tell her that she was wicked, or bid her read long sermons, or force her to go oftener to the meeting-house.

"He will never come again, I think," she said one day, as with a shawl wrapped around her shoulders, she leant with her head upon her mother's bosom.

"My own darling," said the mother, pressing her child closely to her side.

"You think he never will, eh, mother?" What could Mrs. Bell say? In her heart of hearts she did not think he ever would come again.

"No, my child. I do not think he will." And then the hot tears ran down, and the sobs came thick and frequent.

"My darling, my darling!" exclaimed the mother; and they wept together.

"Was I wicked to love him at the first?" she asked that night.

"No, my child; you were not wicked at all. At least I think not."

"Then why—" Why was he sent away? It was on her tongue to ask that question; but she paused and spared her mother. This was as they were going to bed. The next morning Susan did not get up. She was not ill, she said; but weak and weary. Would her mother let her lie that day? And then Mrs. Bell went down alone to her room, and sorrowed with all her heart for the sorrow of her child. Why, oh why, had she driven away from her door-sill the love of an honest man?

On the next morning Susan again did not get up;—nor did she hear, or if she heard she did not recognise, the step of the postman who brought a letter to the door. Early, before the widow's breakfast, the postman came, and the letter which he brought was as follows:

> "MY DEAR MRS. BELL,
> "I have now got a permanent situation on the Erie line, and the salary is enough for myself and a wife. At least I think so, and I hope you will too. I shall be down at Saratoga to-morrow evening, and I hope neither Susan nor you will refuse to receive me.
> > "Yours affectionately,
> > "AARON DUNN."

That was all. It was very short, and did not contain one word of love; but it made the widow's heart leap for joy. She was rather afraid that Aaron was angry, he wrote so curtly and with such a brusque business-like attention to mere facts; but surely he could have but one object in coming there. And then he alluded specially to a wife. So the widow's heart leapt with joy.

But how was she to tell Susan? She ran upstairs almost breathless with haste, to the bedroom door; but then she stopped; too much joy she had heard was as dangerous as too much sorrow; she must think it over for a while, and so she crept back again.

But after breakfast—that is, when she had sat for a while over her teacup—she returned to the room, and this time she entered it. The letter was in her hand, but held so as to be hidden;—in her left hand as she sat down with her right arm towards the invalid.

"Susan dear," she said, and smiled at her child, "you'll be able to get up this morning? eh, dear?"

"Yes, mother," said Susan, thinking that her mother objected to this idleness of her lying in bed. And so she began to bestir herself.

"I don't mean this very moment, love. Indeed, I want to sit with you for a little while," and she put her right arm affectionately round her daughter's waist.

"Dearest mother," said Susan.

"Ah! there's one dearer than me, I guess," and Mrs. Bell smiled sweetly, as she made the maternal charge against her daughter.

Susan raised herself quickly in the bed, and looked straight into her mother's face. "Mother, mother," she said, "what is it? You've something to tell. Oh, mother!" And stretching herself over, she struck her hand against the corner of Aaron's letter. "Mother, you've a letter. Is he coming, mother?" and with eager eyes and open lips, she sat up, holding tight to her mother's arm.

"Yes, love. I have got a letter."

"Is he—is he coming?"

How the mother answered, I can hardly tell; but she did answer, and they were soon lying in each other's arms, warm with each other's tears. It was almost hard to say which was the happier.

Aaron was to be there that evening—that very evening. "Oh, mother, let me get up," said Susan.

But Mrs. Bell said no, not yet; her darling was pale and thin, and she almost wished that Aaron was not coming for another week. What if he should come and look at her, and finding her beauty gone, vanish again and seek a wife elsewhere!

So Susan lay in bed, thinking of her happiness, dozing now and again, and fearing as she waked that it was a dream, looking constantly at that drawing of his, which she kept outside upon the bed, nursing her love and thinking of it, and endeavouring, vainly endeavouring, to arrange what she would say to him.

"Mother," she said, when Mrs. Bell once went up to her, "you won't tell Hetta and Phineas, will you? Not to-day, I mean?" Mrs. Bell agreed that it would be better not to tell them. Perhaps she thought that she had already depended too much on Hetta and Phineas in the matter.

Susan's finery in the way of dress had never been extensive, and now lately, in these last sad winter days, she had thought but little of the fashion of her clothes. But when she began to dress herself for the evening, she did ask her mother with some anxiety what she had better wear. "If he loves you he will hardly see what you have on," said the mother. But not the less was she careful to smooth her daughter's hair, and make the most that might be made of those faded roses.

How Susan's heart beat,—how both their hearts beat as

the hands of the clock came round to seven! And then, sharp at seven, came the knock; that same short bold ringing knock which Susan had so soon learned to know as belonging to Aaron Dunn. "Oh mother, I had better go upstairs," she cried, starting from her chair.

"No dear; you would only be more nervous."

"I will, mother."

"No, no, dear; you have not time"; and then Aaron Dunn was in the room.

She had thought much what she would say to him, but had not yet quite made up her mind. It mattered however but very little. On whatever she might have resolved, her resolution would have vanished to the wind. Aaron Dunn came into the room, and in one second she found herself in the centre of a whirlwind, and his arms were the storms that enveloped her on every side.

"My own, own darling girl," he said over and over again, as he pressed her to his heart, quite regardless of Mrs. Bell, who stood by, sobbing with joy. "My own Susan."

"Aaron, dear Aaron," she whispered. But she had already recognised the fact that for the present meeting a passive part would become her well, and save her a deal of trouble. She had her lover there quite safe, safe beyond any thing that Mr. or Mrs. Beckard might have to say to the contrary. She was quite happy; only that there were symptoms now and again that the whirlwind was about to engulf her yet once more.

"Dear Aaron, I am so glad you are come," said the innocent-minded widow, as she went upstairs with him, to show him his room; and then he embraced her also. "Dear, dear mother," he said.

On the next day there was, as a matter of course, a family conclave. Hetta and Phineas came down, and discussed the whole subject of the coming marriage with Mrs. Bell. Hetta at first was not quite certain;—ought they not to inquire whether the situation was permanent?

"I won't inquire at all," said Mrs. Bell, with an energy that startled both the daughter and son-in-law. "I would not part them now; no, not if—" and the widow shuddered as she thought of her daughter's sunken eyes, and pale cheeks.

"He is a good lad," said Phineas, "and I trust she will make him a sober steady wife"; and so the matter was settled.

During this time, Susan and Aaron were walking along the Balston road; and they also had settled the matter— quite as satisfactorily.

Such was the courtship of Susan Dunn.

THE PARSON'S DAUGHTER
OF OXNEY COLNE

THE prettiest scenery in all England—and if I am contradicted in that assertion, I will say in all Europe—is in Devonshire, on the southern and south-eastern skirts of Dartmoor, where the rivers Dart, and Avon, and Teign form themselves, and where the broken moor is half cultivated, and the wild-looking upland fields are half moor. In making this assertion I am often met with much doubt, but it is by persons who do not really know the locality. Men and women talk to me on the matter, who have travelled down the line of railway from Exeter to Plymouth, who have spent a fortnight at Torquay, and perhaps made an excursion from Tavistock to the convict prison on Dartmoor. But who knows the glories of Chagford? Who has walked through the parish of Manaton? Who is conversant with Lustleigh Cleeves and Withycombe in the moor? Who has explored Holne Chase? Gentle reader, believe me that you will be rash in contradicting me, unless you have done these things.

There or thereabouts—I will not say by the waters of which little river it is washed—is the parish of Oxney Colne. And for those who wish to see all the beauties of this lovely country, a sojourn in Oxney Colne would be most desirable, seeing that the sojourner would then be brought nearer to all that he would wish to visit, than at any other spot in the country. But there is an objection to any such arrangement. There are only two decent houses in the whole parish, and these are—or were when I knew the locality—small and fully occupied by their possessors. The larger and better is the parsonage, in which lived the parson and his daughter; and the smaller is a freehold residence of a certain Miss Le Smyrger, who owned a farm of a hundred acres, which was rented by one Farmer Cloysey, and who also possessed some thirty acres round her own house, which she managed herself; regarding herself to be quite as great in cream as Mr. Cloysey, and altogether superior to him in the article of cider. "But yeu has to pay no rent, Miss," Farmer Cloysey would say, when Miss Le Smyrger expressed this opinion of her art in a manner too defiant. "Yeu pays no rent, or yeu couldn't do it." Miss Le Smyrger was an old maid, with a pedigree and blood of her own, a hundred and thirty acres of fee-simple land on the borders of Dartmoor, fifty years of age, a constitution of iron, and an opinion of her own on every subject under the sun.

And now for the parson and his daughter. The parson's name was Woolsworthy—or Woolathy, as it was pronounced by all those who lived around him—the Rev. Saul Woolsworthy; and his daughter was Patience Woolsworthy, or Miss Patty, as she was known to the Devonshire world of those parts. That name of Patience had not been well chosen for her, for she was a hot-tempered damsel, warm in her convictions, and inclined to express them freely. She had but two closely intimate friends in the world, and by both of them this freedom of expression had now been fully permitted to her since she was a child. Miss Le Smyrger and her father were well accustomed to her ways, and on the whole well satisfied with them. The former was equally free and equally warm-tempered as herself, and as Mr. Woolsworthy was allowed by his daughter to be quite paramount on his own subject—for he had a subject—he did not object to his daughter being paramount on all others. A pretty girl was Patience Woolsworthy at the time of which I am writing, and one who possessed much that was worthy of remark and admiration, had she lived where beauty meets with admiration, or where force of character is remarked. But at Oxney Colne, on the borders of Dartmoor, there were few to appreciate her, and it seemed as though she herself had but little idea of carrying her talent further afield, so that it might not remain for ever wrapped in a blanket.

She was a pretty girl, tall and slender, with dark eyes and black hair. Her eyes were perhaps too round for regular beauty, and her hair was perhaps too crisp; her mouth was large and expressive; her nose was finely formed, though a critic in female form might have declared it to be somewhat broad. But her countenance altogether was wonderfully attractive—if only it might be seen without that resolution for dominion which occasionally marred it, though sometimes it even added to her attractions.

It must be confessed on behalf of Patience Woolsworthy, that the circumstances of her life had peremptorily called upon her to exercise dominion. She had lost her mother when she was sixteen, and had had neither brother nor sister. She had no neighbours near her fit either from education or rank to interfere in the conduct of her life, excepting always Miss Le Smyrger. Miss Le Smyrger would have done anything for her, including the whole management of her morals and of the parsonage household, had Patience been content with such an arrangement. But much as Patience had ever loved Miss Le Smyrger, she was not content with this, and therefore she had been called on to put forth a strong hand of her own. She had put forth this strong hand early, and hence had come the character which I am attempting to describe. But I must say on behalf of this girl, that it was not only over others that she thus exercised dominion. In acquiring that power she had also acquired the much greater power of exercising rule over herself.

But why should her father have been ignored in these family arrangements? Perhaps it may almost suffice to say, that of all living men her father was the man best conversant with the antiquities of the county in which he lived. He was the Jonathan Oldbuck of Devonshire, and especially of Dartmoor, without that decision of character which enabled Oldbuck to keep his womenkind in some kind of subjection, and probably enabled him also to see that his weekly bills did not pass their proper limits. Our Mr. Oldbuck, of Oxney Colne, was sadly deficient in these. As a parish pastor with but a small cure, he did his duty with sufficient energy to keep him, at any rate, from reproach. He was kind and charitable to the poor, punctual in his services, forbearing with the farmers around him, mild with his brother clergymen, and indifferent to aught that bishop or archdeacon might think or say of him. I do not name this latter attribute as a virtue, but as a fact. But all these points were as nothing in the known character of Mr. Woolsworthy, of Oxney Colne. He was the antiquarian of Dartmoor. That was his line of life. It was in that capacity that he was known to the Devonshire world; it was as such that he journeyed about with his humble carpet-bag, staying away from his parsonage a night or two at a time; it was in that character that he received now and again stray visitors in the single spare bedroom—not friends asked to see him and his girl because of their friendship—but men who knew something as to this buried stone, or that old land-mark. In all these things his daughter let him have his own way, assisting and encouraging him. That was his line of life, and therefore she respected it. But in all other matters she chose to be paramount at the parsonage.

Mr. Woolsworthy was a little man, who always wore, except on Sundays, grey clothes—clothes of so light a grey that they would hardly have been regarded as clerical in a district less remote. He had now reached a goodly age, being full seventy years old; but still he was wiry and active, and showed but few symptoms of decay. His head was bald, and the few remaining locks that surrounded it were nearly white. But there was a look of energy about his mouth, and a humour in his light grey eye, which forbade those who knew him to regard him altogether as an old man. As it was, he could walk from Oxney Colne to Priestown, fifteen long Devonshire miles across the moor; and he who could do that could hardly be regarded as too old for work.

But our present story will have more to do with his daughter than with him. A pretty girl, I have said, was Patience Woolsworthy; and one, too, in many ways remarkable. She had taken her outlook into life, weighing the things which she had and those which she had not, in a manner very unusual, and, as a rule, not always desirable for a young lady. The things which she had not were very many. She had not society; she had not a fortune; she had not any assurance of future means of livelihood; she had not high hope of procuring for herself a position in life by marriage; she had not that excitement and pleasure in life which she read of in such books as found their way down to Oxney Colne Parsonage. It would be easy to add to the list of the things which she had not; and this list against herself she made out with the utmost vigour. The things which she had, or those rather which she assured herself of having, were much more easily counted. She had the birth and education of a lady, the strength of a healthy woman, and a will of her own. Such was the list as she made it out for herself, and I protest that I assert no more than the truth in saying that she never added to it either beauty, wit, or talent.

I began these descriptions by saying that Oxney Colne would, of all places, be the best spot from which a tourist could visit those parts of Devonshire, but for the fact that he could obtain there none of the accommodation which tourists require. A brother antiquarian might, perhaps, in those days have done so, seeing that there was, as I have said, a spare bedroom at the parsonage. Any intimate friend of Miss Le Smyrger's might be as fortunate, for she was equally well provided at Oxney Combe, by which name her house was known. But Miss Le Smyrger was not given to extensive hospitality, and it was only to those who were bound to her, either by ties of blood or of very old friendship, that she delighted to open her doors. As her old friends were very few in number, as those few lived at a distance, and as her nearest relations were higher in the world than she was, and were said by herself to look down upon her, the visits made to Oxney Combe were few and far between.

But now, at the period of which I am writing, such a visit was about to be made. Miss Le Smyrger had a younger sister, who had inherited a property in the parish of Oxney Colne equal to that of the lady who now lived there; but this the younger sister had inherited beauty also, and she therefore, in early life, had found sundry lovers, one of whom became her husband. She had married a man even then well to do in the world, but now rich and almost mighty; a Member of Parliament, a lord of this and that board, a man who had a house in Eaton Square, and a park in the north of England; and in this way her course of life had been very much divided from that of our Miss Le Smyrger. But the Lord of the Government Board had been blessed with various children; and perhaps it was now thought expedient to look after Aunt Penelope's Devonshire acres. Aunt Penelope was empowered to leave them to whom she pleased; and though it was thought in Eaton Square that she must, as a matter of course, leave them to one of the family, nevertheless a little cousinly intercourse might make the thing more certain. I will not say that this was the sole cause of such a visit, but in these days a visit was to be made by Captain Broughton to his aunt. Now Captain John Broughton was the second son of Alfonso Broughton, of Clapham Park and Eaton Square, Member of Parliament, and Lord of the aforesaid Government Board.

"And what do you mean to do with him?" Patience Woolsworthy asked of Miss Le Smyrger when that lady walked over from the Combe to say that her nephew John was to arrive on the following morning.

"Do with him? Why I shall bring him over here to talk to your father."

"He'll be too fashionable for that; and papa won't trouble his head about him if he finds that he doesn't care for Dartmoor."

"Then he may fall in love with you, my dear."

"Well, yes; there's that resource at any rate, and for your sake I dare say I should be more civil to him than papa. But he'll soon get tired of making love, and what you'll do then I cannot imagine."

That Miss Woolsworthy felt no interest in the coming of the Captain I will not pretend to say. The advent of any stranger with whom she would be called on to associate must be matter of interest to her in that secluded place; and she was not so absolutely unlike other young ladies that the arrival of an unmarried young man would be the same to her as the advent of some patriarchal paterfamilias. In taking that outlook into life of which I have spoken, she had never said to herself that she despised those things from which other girls received the excitement, the joys, and the disappointment of their lives. She had simply given herself to understand that very little of such things would come her way, and that it behoved her to live—to live happily if such might be possible—without experiencing the need of them. She had heard, when there was no thought of any such visit to Oxney Colne, that John Broughton was a handsome, clever man—one who thought much of himself, and was thought much of by others—that there had been some talk of his marrying a great heiress, which marriage, however, had not taken place through unwillingness on his part, and that he was on the whole a man of more mark in the world than the ordinary captain of ordinary regiments.

Captain Broughton came to Oxney Combe, stayed there a fortnight,—the intended period for his projected visit having been fixed at three or four days,—and then went his way. He went his way back to his London haunts, the time of the year then being the close of the Easter holidays; but as he did so he told his aunt that he should assuredly return to her in the autumn.

"And assuredly I shall be happy to see you, John—if you come with a certain purpose. If you have no such purpose, you had better remain away."

"I shall assuredly come," the Captain had replied, and then he had gone on his journey.

The summer passed rapidly by, and very little was said between Miss Le Smyrger and Miss Woolsworthy about Captain Broughton. In many respects—nay, I may say, as to all ordinary matters, no two women could well be more intimate with each other than they were,—and more than that, they had the courage each to talk to the other with absolute truth as to things concerning themselves—a courage in which dear friends often fail. But nevertheless, very little was said between them about Captain John Broughton. All that was said may be here repeated.

"John says that he shall return here in August," Miss Le Smyrger said, as Patience was sitting with her in the parlour at Oxney Combe, on the morning after that gentleman's departure.

"He told me so himself," said Patience; and as she spoke her round dark eyes assumed a look of more than ordinary self-will. If Miss Le Smyrger had intended to carry the conversation any further, she changed her mind as she looked at her companion. Then, as I said, the summer ran by, and towards the close of the warm days of July, Miss Le Smyrger, sitting in the same chair in the same room, again took up the conversation.

"I got a letter from John this morning. He says that he shall be here on the third."

"Does he?"

"He is very punctual to the time he named."

"Yes; I fancy that he is a punctual man," said Patience.

"I hope that you will be glad to see him," said Miss Le Smyrger.

"Very glad to see him," said Patience, with a bold clear voice; and then the conversation was again dropped, and nothing further was said till after Captain Broughton's second arrival in the parish.

Four months had then passed since his departure, and during that time Miss Woolsworthy had performed all her usual daily duties in their accustomed course. No one could discover that she had been less careful in her household matters than had been her wont, less willing to go among her poor neighbours, or less assiduous in her attentions to her father. But not the less was there a feeling in the minds of those around her that some great change had come upon her. She would sit during the long summer evenings on a certain spot outside the parsonage orchard, at the top of a small sloping field in which their solitary cow was always pastured, with a book on her knees before her, but rarely reading. There she would sit, with the beautiful view down to the winding river below her, watching the setting sun, and thinking, thinking, thinking—thinking of something of which she had never spoken. Often would Miss Le Smyrger come upon her there, and sometimes would pass by her even without a word; but never—never once did she dare to ask her of the matter of her thoughts. But she knew the matter well enough. No confession was necessary to inform her that Patience Woolsworthy was in love with John Broughton—ay, in love, to the full and entire loss of her whole heart.

On one evening she was so sitting till the July sun had fallen and hidden himself for the night, when her father came upon her as he returned from one of his rambles on the moor. "Patty," he said, "you are always sitting there now. Is it not late? Will you not be cold?"

"No, papa," said she, "I shall not be cold."

"But won't you come to the house? I miss you when you come in so late that there's no time to say a word before we go to bed."

She got up and followed him into the parsonage, and when they were in the sitting-room together, and the door was closed, she came up to him and kissed him. "Papa," she said, "would it make you very unhappy if I were to leave you?"

"Leave me!" he said, startled by the serious and almost solemn tone of her voice. "Do you mean for always?"

"If I were to marry, papa?"

"Oh, marry! No; that would not make me unhappy. It would make me very happy, Patty, to see you married to a man you would love—very, very happy; though my days would be desolate without you."

"That is it, papa. What would you do if I went from you?"

"What would it matter, Patty? I should be free, at any rate, from a load which often presses heavy on me now. What will you do when I shall leave you? A few more years and all will be over with me. But who is it, love? Has anybody said anything to you?"

"It was only an idea, papa. I don't often think of such a thing; but I did think of it then." And so the subject was allowed to pass by. This had happened before the day of the second arrival had been absolutely fixed and made known to Miss Woolsworthy.

And then that second arrival took place. The reader may have understood from the words with which Miss Le Smyrger authorised her nephew to make his second visit to Oxney Combe that Miss Woolsworthy's passion was not altogether unauthorised. Captain Broughton had been told that he was not to come unless he came with a certain purpose; and having been so told, he still persisted in coming. There can be no doubt but that he well understood the purport to which his aunt alluded. "I shall assuredly come," he had said. And true to his word, he was now there.

Patience knew exactly the hour at which he must arrive at the station at Newton Abbot, and the time also which it would take to travel over those twelve uphill miles from the station to Oxney. It need hardly be said that she paid no visit to Miss Le Smyrger's house on that afternoon; but she might have known something of Captain Broughton's approach without going thither. His road to the Combe passed by the parsonage-gate, and had Patience sat even at her bedroom window she must have seen him. But on such a morning she would not sit at her bedroom window—she would do nothing which would force her to accuse herself of a restless longing for her lover's coming. It was for him to seek her. If he chose to do so, he knew the way to the parsonage.

Miss Le Smyrger—good, dear, honest, hearty Miss Le Smyrger, was in a fever of anxiety on behalf of her friend. It was not that she wished her nephew to marry Patience—or rather that she had entertained any such wish when he first came among them. She was not given to match-making, and moreover thought, or had thought within herself, that they of Oxney Colne could do very well without any admixture from Eaton Square. Her plan of life had been that, when old Mr. Woolsworthy was taken away from Dartmoor, Patience should live with her; and that when she also shuffled off her coil, then Patience Woolsworthy should be the maiden mistress of Oxney Combe—of Oxney Combe and Mr. Cloysey's farm—to the utter detriment of all the Broughtons. Such had been her plan before nephew John had come among them—a plan not to be spoken of till the coming of that dark day which should make Patience an orphan. But now her nephew had been there, and all was to be altered. Miss Le Smyrger's plan would have provided a companion for her old age; but that had not been her chief object. She had thought more of Patience than of herself, and now it seemed that a prospect of a higher happiness was opening for her friend.

"John," she said, as soon as the first greetings were over, "do you remember the last words that I said to you before you went away?" Now, for myself, I much admire Miss Le Smyrger's heartiness, but I do not think much of her discretion. It would have been better, perhaps, had she allowed things to take their course.

"I can't say that I do," said the Captain. At the same time the Captain did remember very well what those last words had been.

"I am so glad to see you, so delighted to see you, if—if—if—," and then she paused, for with all her courage she hardly dared to ask her nephew whether he had come there with the express purpose of asking Miss Woolsworthy to marry him.

To tell the truth, for there is no room for mystery within the limits of this short story,—to tell, I say, at a word the plain and simple truth, Captain Broughton had already asked that question. On the day before he left Oxney Combe, he had in set terms proposed to the parson's daughter, and indeed the words, the hot and frequent words, which previously to that had fallen like sweetest honey into the ears of Patience Woolsworthy, had made it imperative on him to do so. When a man in such a place as that has talked to a girl of love day after day, must not he talk of it to some definite purpose on the day on which he leaves her? Or if he do not, must he not submit to be regarded as false, selfish, and almost fraudulent? Captain Broughton, however, had asked the question honestly and truly. He had done so honestly and truly, but in words, or, perhaps, simply with a tone, that had hardly sufficed to satisfy the proud spirit of the girl he loved. She by that time had confessed to herself that she loved him with all her heart; but she had made no such confession to him. To him she had spoken no word, granted no favour, that any lover might rightfully regard as a token of love returned. She had listened to him as he spoke, and bade him keep such sayings for the drawing-rooms of his fashionable friends. Then he had spoken out and had asked for that hand,—not, perhaps, as a suitor tremulous with hope,—but as a rich man who knows that he can command that which he desires to purchase.

"You should think more of this," she had said to him at last. "If you would really have me for your wife, it will not be much to you to return here again when time for thinking of it shall have passed by." With these words she had dismissed him, and now he had again come back to Oxney Colne. But still she would not place herself at the window to look for him, nor dress herself in other than her simple morning country dress, nor omit one item of her daily work. If he wished to take her at all, he should wish to take her as she really was, in her plain country life, but he should take her also with full observance of all those privileges which maidens are allowed to claim from their lovers. He should contract no ceremonious observance because she was the daughter of a poor country parson who would come to him without a shilling, whereas he stood high in the world's books. He had asked her to give him all that she had, and that all she was ready to give, without stint. But the gift must be valued before it could be given or received. He also was to give her as much, and she would accept it as beyond all price. But she would not allow that that which was offered to her was in any degree the more precious because of his outward worldly standing.

She would not pretend to herself that she thought he would come to her that day, and therefore she busied herself in the kitchen and about the house, giving directions to her two maids as though the afternoon would pass as all other days did pass in that household. They usually dined at four, and she rarely in these summer months went far from the house before that hour. At four precisely she sat down with her father, and then said that she was going up as far as Helpholme after dinner. Helpholme was a solitary farmhouse in another parish, on the border of the moor, and Mr. Woolsworthy asked her whether he should accompany her.

"Do, papa," she said, "if you are not too tired." And yet she had thought how probable it might be that she should meet John Broughton on her walk. And so it was arranged; but just as dinner was over, Mr. Woolsworthy remembered himself.

"Gracious me," he said, "how my memory is going. Gribbles, from Ivybridge, and old John Poulter, from Bovey, are coming to meet here by appointment. You can't put Helpholme off till to-morrow?"

Patience, however, never put off anything, and therefore at six o'clock, when her father had finished his slender modicum of toddy, she tied on her hat and went on her walk. She started with a quick step, and left no word to say by which route she would go. As she passed up along the little lane which led towards Oxney Combe, she would not even look to see if he was coming towards her; and when she left the road, passing over a stone stile into a little path which ran first through the upland fields, and then across the moor ground towards Helpholme, she did not look back once, or listen for his coming step.

She paid her visit, remaining upwards of an hour with the old bedridden mother of the tenant of Helpholme. "God bless you, my darling!" said the old woman as she left her; "and send you some one to make your own path bright and happy through the world." These words were still ringing in her ears with all their significance as she saw John Broughton waiting for her at the first stile which she had to pass after leaving the farmer's haggard.

"Patty," he said, as he took her hand, and held it close within both his own, "what a chase I have had after you!"

"And who asked you, Captain Broughton?" she answered, smiling. "If the journey was too much for your poor London strength, could you not have waited till to-morrow morning, when you would have found me at the parsonage?" But she did not draw her hand away from him, or in any way pretend that he had not a right to accost her as a lover.

"No, I could not wait. I am more eager to see those I love than you seem to be."

"How do you know whom I love, or how eager I might be to see them? There is an old woman there whom I love, and I have thought nothing of this walk with the object of seeing her." And now, slowly drawing her hand away from him, she pointed to the farmhouse which she had left.

"Patty," he said, after a minute's pause, during which she had looked full into his face with all the force of her bright eyes; "I have come from London to-day, straight down here to Oxney, and from my aunt's house close upon your footsteps after you, to ask you that one question—Do you love me?"

"What a Hercules!" she said, again laughing. "Do you really mean that you left London only this morning? Why, you must have been five hours in a railway carriage and two in a postchaise, not to talk of the walk afterwards. You ought to take more care of yourself, Captain Broughton!"

He would have been angry with her—for he did not like to be quizzed—had she not put her hand on his arm as she spoke, and the softness of her touch had redeemed the offence of her words.

"All that I have done," said he, "that I may hear one word from you."

"That any word of mine should have such potency! But let us walk on, or my father will take us for some of the standing stones of the moor. How have you found your aunt? If you only knew the cares that have sat on her dear shoulders for the last week past, in order that your high mightiness might have a sufficiency to eat and drink in these desolate half-starved regions!"

"She might have saved herself such anxiety. No one can care less for such things than I do."

"And yet I think I have heard you boast of the cook of your club." And then again there was silence for a minute or two.

"Patty," said he, stopping again in the path; "answer my question. I have a right to demand an answer. Do you love me?"

"And what if I do? What if I have been so silly as to allow your perfections to be too many for my weak heart? What then, Captain Broughton?"

"It cannot be that you love me, or you would not joke now."

"Perhaps not, indeed," she said. It seemed as though she were resolved not to yield an inch in her own humour. And then again they walked on.

"Patty," he said once more, "I shall get an answer from you to-night,—this evening; now, during this walk, or I shall return to-morrow, and never revisit this spot again."

"Oh, Captain Broughton, how should we ever manage to live without you?"

"Very well," he said; "up to the end of this walk I can hear it all;—and one word spoken then will mend it all."

During the whole of this time she felt that she was ill-using him. She knew that she loved him with all her heart; that it would nearly kill her to part with him; that she had heard his renewed offer with an ecstasy of joy. She acknowledged to herself that he was giving proof of his devotion as strong as any which a girl could receive from her lover. And yet she could hardly bring herself to say the word he longed to hear. That word once said, and then she knew that she must succumb to her love for ever! That word once said, and there would be nothing for her but to spoil him with her idolatry! That word once said, and she must continue to repeat it into his ears, till perhaps he might be tired of hearing it! And now he had threatened her, and how could she speak after that? She certainly would not speak it unless he asked her again without such threat. And so they walked on in silence.

"Patty," he said at last. "By the heavens above us you shall answer me. Do you love me?"

She now stood still, and almost trembled as she looked up into his face. She stood opposite to him for a moment, and then placing her two hands on his shoulders, she answered him. "I do, I do, I do," she said, "with all my heart; with all my heart—with all my heart and strength." And then her head fell upon his breast.

———

Captain Broughton was almost as much surprised as delighted by the warmth of the acknowledgment made by the eager-hearted passionate girl whom he now held within his arms. She had said it now; the words had been spoken; and there was nothing for her but to swear to him over and over again with her sweetest oaths, that those words were true—true as her soul. And very sweet was the walk down from thence to the parsonage gate. He spoke no more of the distance of the ground, or the length of his day's journey. But he stopped her at every turn that he might press her arm the closer to his own, that he might look into the brightness of her eyes, and prolong his hour of delight. There were no more gibes now on her tongue, no raillery at his London finery, no laughing comments on his coming and going. With downright honesty she told him everything: how she had loved him before her heart was warranted in such a passion; how, with much thinking, she had resolved that it would be unwise to take him at his first word, and had thought it better that he should return to London, and then think over it; how she had almost repented of her courage when she had feared, during those long summer days, that he would forget her; and how her heart had leapt for joy when her old friend had told her that he was coming.

"And yet," said he, "you were not glad to see me!"

"Oh, was I not glad? You cannot understand the feelings of a girl who has lived secluded as I have done. Glad is no word for the joy I felt. But it was not seeing you that I cared for so much. It was the knowledge that you were near me once again. I almost wish now that I had not seen you till to-morrow." But as she spoke she pressed his arm, and this caress gave the lie to her last words.

"No, do not come in to-night," she said, when she reached the little wicket that led up to the parsonage. "Indeed, you shall not. I could not behave myself properly if you did."

"But I don't want you to behave properly."

"Oh! I am to keep that for London, am I? But, nevertheless, Captain Broughton, I will not invite you either to tea or to supper to-night."

"Surely I may shake hands with your father."

"Not to-night—not till—John, I may tell him, may I not? I must tell him at once."

"Certainly," said he.

"And then you shall see him to-morrow. Let me see—at what hour shall I bid you come?"

"To breakfast."

"No, indeed. What on earth would your aunt do with her broiled turkey and the cold pie? I have got no cold pie for you."

"I hate cold pie."

"What a pity! But, John, I should be forced to leave you directly after breakfast. Come down—come down at two, or three; and then I will go back with you to Aunt Penelope. I must see her to-morrow"; and so at last the matter was settled, and the happy Captain, as he left her, was hardly resisted in his attempt to press her lips to his own.

When she entered the parlour in which her father was sitting, there still were Gribbles and Poulter discussing some knotty point of Devon lore. So Patience took off her hat, and sat herself down, waiting till they should go. For full an hour she had to wait, and then Gribbles and Poulter did go. But it was not in such matters as this that Patience Woolsworthy was impatient. She could wait, and wait, and wait, curbing herself for weeks and months, while the thing waited for was in her eyes good; but she could not curb her hot thoughts or her hot words when things came to be discussed which she did not think to be good.

"Papa," she said, when Gribbles' long-drawn last word had been spoken at the door. "Do you remember how I asked you the other day what you would say if I were to leave you?"

"Yes, surely," he replied, looking up at her in astonishment.

"I am going to leave you now," she said. "Dear, dearest father, how am I to go from you?"

"Going to leave me," said he, thinking of her visit to Helpholme, and thinking of nothing else.

Now, there had been a story about Helpholme. That bedridden old lady there had a stalwart son, who was now the owner of the Helpholme pastures. But though owner in fee of all those wild acres, and of the cattle which they supported, he was not much above the farmers around him, either in manners or education. He had his merits, however; for he was honest, well-to-do in the world, and modest withal. How strong love had grown up, springing from neighbourly kindness, between our Patience and his mother, it needs not here to tell; but rising from it had come another love—or an ambition which might have grown to love. The young man, after much thought, had not dared to speak to Miss Woolsworthy, but he had sent a message by Miss Le Smyrger. If there could be any hope for him, he would present himself as a suitor—on trial. He did not owe a shilling in the world, and had money by him— saved. He wouldn't ask the parson for a shilling of fortune. Such had been the tenor of his message, and Miss Le Smyrger had delivered it faithfully. "He does not mean it," Patience had said with her stern voice. "Indeed he does, my dear. You may be sure he is in earnest," Miss Le Smyrger had replied; "and there is not an honester man in these parts."

"Tell him," said Patience, not attending to the latter portion of her friend's last speech, "that it cannot be—make him understand, you know—and tell him also that the matter shall be thought of no more." The matter had, at any rate, been spoken of no more, but the young farmer still remained a bachelor, and Helpholme still wanted a mistress. But all this came back upon the parson's mind when his daughter told him that she was about to leave him.

"Yes, dearest," she said; and as she spoke she now knelt at his knees. "I have been asked in marriage, and I have given myself away."

"Well, my love, if you will be happy—"

"I hope I shall; I think I shall. But you, papa?"

"You will not be far from us."

"Oh, yes; in London."

"In London?"

"Captain Broughton lives in London generally."

"And has Captain Broughton asked you to marry him?"

"Yes, papa—who else? Is he not good? Will you not love him? Oh, papa, do not say that I am wrong to love him?"

He never told her his mistake, or explained to her that he had not thought it possible that the high-placed son of the London great man should have fallen in love with his undowered daughter; but he embraced her, and told her, with all his enthusiasm, that he rejoiced in her joy, and would be happy in her happiness. "My own Patty," he said, "I have ever known that you were too good for this life of ours here." And then the evening wore away into the night, with many tears, but still with much happiness.

Captain Broughton, as he walked back to Oxney Combe, made up his mind that he would say nothing on the matter to his aunt till the next morning. He wanted to think over it all, and to think it over, if possible, by himself. He had taken a step in life, the most important that a man is ever called on to take, and he had to reflect whether or no he had taken it with wisdom.

"Have you seen her?" said Miss Le Smyrger, very anxiously, when he came into the drawing-room.

"Miss Woolsworthy you mean," said he. "Yes, I've seen her. As I found her out, I took a long walk, and happened to meet her. Do you know, aunt, I think I'll go to bed; I was up at five this morning, and have been on the move ever since."

Miss Le Smyrger perceived that she was to hear nothing that evening, so she handed him his candlestick and allowed him to go to his room.

But Captain Broughton did not immediately retire to bed, nor when he did so was he able to sleep at once. Had this step that he had taken been a wise one? He was not a man who, in worldly matters, had allowed things to arrange themselves for him, as is the case with so many men. He had formed views for himself, and had a theory of life. Money for money's sake he had declared to himself to be bad. Money, as a concomitant to things which were in themselves good, he had declared to himself to be good also. That concomitant in this affair of his marriage, he had now missed. Well; he had made up his mind to that, and would put up with the loss. He had means of living of his own, the means not so extensive as might have been desirable. That it would be well for him to become a married man, looking merely to the state of life as opposed to his present state, he had fully resolved. On that point, therefore, there was nothing to repent. That Patty Woolsworthy was good, affectionate, clever, and beautiful, he was sufficiently satisfied. It would be odd indeed if he were not so satisfied now, seeing that for the last four months he had so declared to himself daily with many inward asseverations. And yet though he repeated, now again, that he was satisfied, I do not think that he was so fully satisfied of it as he had been throughout the whole of those four months. It is sad to say so, but I fear—I fear that such was the case. When you have your plaything, how much of the anticipated pleasure vanishes, especially if it be won easily.

He had told none of his family what were his intentions in this second visit to Devonshire, and now he had to bethink himself whether they would be satisfied. What would his sister say, she who had married the Honourable Augustus Gumbleton, gold-stick-in-waiting to Her Majesty's Privy Council? Would she receive Patience with open arms, and make much of her about London? And then how far would London suit Patience, or would Patience suit London? There would be much for him to do in teaching her, and it would be well for him to set about the lesson without loss of time. So far he got that night, but when the morning came he went a step further, and began mentally to criticise her manner to himself. It had been very sweet, that warm, that full, that ready declaration of love. Yes; it had been very sweet; but—but—; when, after her little jokes, she did confess her love, had she not been a little too free for feminine excellence? A man likes to be told that he is loved, but he hardly wishes that the girl he is to marry should fling herself at his head!

Ah me! yes; it was thus he argued to himself as on that morning he went through the arrangements of his toilet. "Then he was a brute," you say, my pretty reader. I have never said that he was not a brute. But this I remark, that many such brutes are to be met with in the beaten paths of the world's highway. When Patience Woolsworthy had answered him coldly, bidding him go back to London and think over his love; while it seemed from her manner that at any rate as yet she did not care for him; while he was absent from her, and, therefore, longing for her, the possession of her charms, her talent and bright honesty of purpose had seemed to him a thing most desirable. Now they were his own. They had, in fact, been his own from the first. The heart of this country-bred girl had fallen at the first word from his mouth. Had she not so confessed to him? She was very nice—very nice indeed. He loved her dearly. But had he not sold himself too cheaply?

I by no means say that he was not a brute. But whether brute or no, he was an honest man, and had no remotest dream, either then, on that morning, or during the following days on which such thoughts pressed more quickly on his mind—of breaking away from his pledged word. At breakfast on that morning he told all to Miss Le Smyrger, and that lady, with warm and gracious intentions, confided to him her purpose regarding her property. "I have always regarded Patience as my heir," she said, "and shall do so still."

"Oh, indeed," said Captain Broughton.

"But it is a great, great pleasure to me to think that she will give back the little property to my sister's child. You will have your mother's, and thus it will all come together again."

"Ah!" said Captain Broughton. He had his own ideas about property, and did not, even under existing circumstances, like to hear that his aunt considered herself at liberty to leave the acres away to one who was by blood quite a stranger to the family.

"Does Patience know of this?" he asked.

"Not a word," said Miss Le Smyrger. And then nothing more was said upon the subject.

On that afternoon he went down and received the parson's benediction and congratulations with a good grace. Patience said very little on the occasion, and indeed was absent during the greater part of the interview. The two lovers then walked up to Oxney Combe, and there were more benedictions and more congratulations. "All went merry as a marriage bell," at any rate as far as Patience was concerned. Not a word had yet fallen from that dear mouth, not a look had yet come over that handsome face, which tended in any way to mar her bliss. Her first day of acknowledged love was a day altogether happy, and when she prayed for him as she knelt beside her bed there was no feeling in her mind that any fear need disturb her joy.

I will pass over the next three or four days very quickly, merely saying that Patience did not find them so pleasant as that first day after her engagement. There was something in her lover's manner—something which at first she could not define—which by degrees seemed to grate against her feelings.

He was sufficiently affectionate, that being a matter on which she did not require much demonstration; but joined to his affection there seemed to be—; she hardly liked to suggest to herself a harsh word, but could it be possible that he was beginning to think that she was not good enough for him? And then she asked herself the question—was she good enough for him? If there were doubt about that, the match should be broken off, though she tore her own heart out in the struggle. The truth, however, was this—that he had begun that teaching which he had already found to be so necessary. Now, had any one essayed to teach Patience German or mathematics, with that young lady's free consent, I believe that she would have been found a meek scholar. But it was not probable that she would be meek when she found a self-appointed tutor teaching her manners and conduct without her consent.

So matters went on for four or five days, and on the evening of the fifth day Captain Broughton and his aunt drank tea at the parsonage. Nothing very especial occurred; but as the parson and Miss Le Smyrger insisted on playing backgammon with devoted perseverance during the whole evening, Broughton had a good opportunity of saying a word or two about those changes in his lady-love which a life in London would require—and some word he said also— some single slight word as to the higher station in life to which he would exalt his bride. Patience bore it—for her father and Miss Le Smyrger were in the room—she bore it well, speaking no syllable of anger, and enduring, for the moment, the implied scorn of the old parsonage. Then the evening broke up, and Captain Broughton walked back to Oxney Combe with his aunt. "Patty," her father said to her before they went to bed, "he seems to me to be a most excellent young man." "Dear papa," she answered, kissing him. "And terribly deep in love," said Mr. Woolsworthy. "Oh, I don't know about that," she answered, as she left him with her sweetest smile. But though she could thus smile at her father's joke, she had already made up her mind that there was still something to be learned as to her promised husband before she could place herself altogether in his hands. She would ask him whether he thought himself liable to injury from this proposed marriage; and though he should deny any such thought, she would know from the manner of his denial what his true feelings were.

And he, too, on that night, during his silent walk with Miss Le Smyrger, had entertained some similar thoughts. "I fear she is obstinate," he said to himself; and then he had half accused her of being sullen also. "If that be her temper, what a life of misery I have before me!"

"Have you fixed a day yet?" his aunt asked him as they came near to her house.

"No, not yet; I don't know whether it will suit me to fix it before I leave."

"Why, it was but the other day you were in such a hurry."

"Ah—yes—I have thought more about it since then."

"I should have imagined that this would depend on what Patty thinks," said Miss Le Smyrger, standing up for the privileges of her sex. "It is presumed that the gentleman is always ready as soon as the lady will consent."

"Yes, in ordinary cases it is so; but when a girl is taken out of her own sphere—"

"Her own sphere! Let me caution you, Master John, not to talk to Patty about her own sphere."

"Aunt Penelope, as Patience is to be my wife and not yours, I must claim permission to speak to her on such subjects as may seem suitable to me." And then they parted—not in the best humour with each other.

On the following day Captain Broughton and Miss Woolsworthy did not meet till the evening. She had said, before those few ill-omened words had passed her lover's lips, that she would probably be at Miss Le Smyrger's house on the following morning. Those ill-omened words did pass her lover's lips, and then she remained at home. This did not come from sullenness, nor even from anger, but from a conviction that it would be well that she should think much before she met him again. Nor was he anxious to hurry a meeting. His thought—his base thought—was this; that she would be sure to come up to the Combe after him; but she did not come, and therefore in the evening he went down to her, and asked her to walk with him.

They went away by the path that led to Helpholme, and little was said between them till they had walked some mile together.

Patience, as she went along the path, remembered almost to the letter the sweet words which had greeted her ears as she came down that way with him on the night of his arrival; but he remembered nothing of that sweetness then. Had he not made an ass of himself during these last six months? That was the thought which very much had possession of his mind.

"Patience," he said at last, having hitherto spoken only an indifferent word now and again since they had left the parsonage, "Patience, I hope you realise the importance of the step which you and I are about to take?"

"Of course I do," she answered. "What an odd question that is for you to ask!"

"Because," said he, "sometimes I almost doubt it. It seems to me as though you thought you could remove yourself from here to your new home with no more trouble than when you go from home up to the Combe."

"Is that meant for a reproach, John?"

"No, not for a reproach, but for advice. Certainly not for a reproach."

"I am glad of that."

"But I should wish to make you think how great is the leap in the world which you are about to take." Then again they walked on for many steps before she answered him.

"Tell me, then, John," she said, when she had sufficiently considered what words she should speak; and as she spoke a bright colour suffused her face, and her eyes flashed almost with anger. "What leap do you mean? Do you mean a leap upwards?"

"Well, yes; I hope it will be so."

"In one sense, certainly, it would be a leap upwards. To be the wife of the man I loved; to have the privilege of holding his happiness in my hand; to know that I was his own—the companion whom he had chosen out of all the world—that would, indeed, be a leap upwards; a leap almost to heaven, if all that were so. But if you mean upwards in any other sense—"

"I was thinking of the social scale."

"Then, Captain Broughton, your thoughts were doing me dishonour."

"Doing you dishonour!"

"Yes, doing me dishonour. That your father is, in the world's esteem, a greater man than mine is doubtless true enough. That you, as a man, are richer than I am as a woman, is doubtless also true. But you dishonour me, and yourself also, if these things can weigh with you now."

"Patience,—I think you can hardly know what words you are saying to me."

"Pardon me, but I think I do. Nothing that you can give me—no gifts of that description—can weigh aught against that which I am giving you. If you had all the wealth and rank of the greatest lord in the land, it would count as nothing in such a scale. If—as I have not doubted—if in return for my heart you have given me yours, then—then—then you have paid me fully. But when gifts such as those are going, nothing else can count even as a make-weight."

"I do not quite understand you," he answered, after a pause. "I fear you are a little high-flown." And then, while the evening was still early, they walked back to the parsonage almost without another word.

Captain Broughton at this time had only one full day more to remain at Oxney Colne. On the afternoon following that he was to go as far as Exeter, and thence return to London. Of course, it was to be expected that the wedding day would be fixed before he went, and much had been said about it during the first day or two of his engagement. Then he had pressed for an early time, and Patience, with a girl's usual diffidence, had asked for some little delay. But now nothing was said on the subject; and how was it probable that such a matter could be settled after such a conversation as that which I have related? That evening, Miss Le Smyrger asked whether the day had been fixed. "No," said Captain Broughton, harshly; "nothing has been fixed." "But it will be arranged before you go?" "Probably not," he said; and then the subject was dropped for the time.

"John," she said, just before she went to bed, "if there be anything wrong between you and Patience, I conjure you to tell me."

"You had better ask her," he replied. "I can tell you nothing."

On the following morning he was much surprised by seeing Patience on the gravel path before Miss Le Smyrger's gate immediately after breakfast. He went to the door to open it for her, and she, as she gave him her hand, told him that she came up to speak to him. There was no hesitation in her manner, nor any look of anger in her face. But there was in her gait and form, in her voice and countenance, a fixedness of purpose which he had never seen before, or at any rate had never acknowledged.

"Certainly," said he. "Shall I come out with you, or will you come up stairs?"

"We can sit down in the summer-house," she said; and thither they both went.

"Captain Broughton," she said—and she began her task

the moment that they were both seated—"you and I have engaged ourselves as man and wife, but perhaps we have been over rash."

"How so?" said he.

"It may be—and indeed I will say more—it is the case that we have made this engagement without knowing enough of each other's character."

"I have not thought so."

"The time will perhaps come when you will so think, but for the sake of all that we most value, let it come before it is too late. What would be our fate—how terrible would be our misery—if such a thought should come to either of us after we have linked our lots together."

There was a solemnity about her as she thus spoke which almost repressed him,—which for a time did prevent him from taking that tone of authority which on such a subject he would choose to adopt. But he recovered himself. "I hardly think that this comes well from you," he said.

"From whom else should it come? Who else can fight my battle for me; and, John, who else can fight that same battle on your behalf? I tell you this, that with your mind standing towards me as it does stand at present, you could not give me your hand at the altar with true words and a happy conscience. Am I not true? You have half repented of your bargain already. Is it not so?"

He did not answer her; but getting up from his seat walked to the front of the summer-house, and stood there with his back turned upon her. It was not that he meant to be ungracious, but in truth he did not know how to answer her. He had half repented of his bargain.

"John," she said, getting up and following him, so that she could put her hand upon his arm, "I have been very angry with you."

"Angry with me!" he said, turning sharp upon her.

"Yes, angry with you. You would have treated me like a child. But that feeling has gone now. I am not angry now. There is my hand;—the hand of a friend. Let the words that have been spoken between us be as though they had not been spoken. Let us both be free."

"Do you mean it?"

"Certainly I mean it." As she spoke these words her eyes filled with tears, in spite of all the efforts she could make; but he was not looking at her, and her efforts had sufficed to prevent any sob from being audible.

"With all my heart," he said; and it was manifest from his tone that he had no thought of her happiness as he spoke. It was true that she had been angry with him—angry, as she had herself declared; but nevertheless, in what she had said and what she had done, she had thought more of his happiness than of her own. Now she was angry once again.

"With all your heart, Captain Broughton! Well, so be it. If with all your heart, then is the necessity so much the greater. You go to-morrow. Shall we say farewell now?"

"Patience, I am not going to be lectured."

"Certainly not by me. Shall we say farewell now?"

"Yes, if you are determined."

"I am determined. Farewell, Captain Broughton. You have all my wishes for your happiness." And she held out her hand to him.

"Patience!" he said. And he looked at her with a dark frown, as though he would strive to frighten her into submission. If so, he might have saved himself any such attempt.

"Farewell, Captain Broughton. Give me your hand, for I cannot stay." He gave her his hand, hardly knowing why he did so. She lifted it to her lips and kissed it, and then, leaving him, passed from the summer-house down through the wicket-gate, and straight home to the parsonage.

During the whole of that day she said no word to any one of what had occurred. When she was once more at home she went about her household affairs as she had done on that day of his arrival. When she sat down to dinner with her father he observed nothing to make him think that she was unhappy; nor during the evening was there any expression in her face, or any tone in her voice, which excited his attention. On the following morning Captain Broughton called at the parsonage, and the servant-girl brought word to her mistress that he was in the parlour. But she would not see him. "Laws, miss, you ain't a quarrelled with your beau?" the poor girl said. "No, not quarrelled," she said; "but give him that." It was a scrap of paper, containing a word or two in pencil. "It is better that we should not meet again. God bless you." And from that day to this, now more than ten years, they never have met.

"Papa," she said to her father that afternoon, "dear papa, do not be angry with me. It is all over between me and John Broughton. Dearest, you and I will not be separated." It would be useless here to tell how great was the old man's surprise and how true his sorrow. As the tale was told to him no cause was given for anger with any one. Not a word was spoken against the suitor who had on that day returned to London with a full conviction that now at least he was relieved from his engagement. "Patty, my darling child," he said, "may God grant that it be for the best!"

"It is for the best," she answered stoutly. "For this place I am fit; and I much doubt whether I am fit for any other."

On that day she did not see Miss Le Smyrger, but on the following morning, knowing that Captain Broughton had gone off, having heard the wheels of the carriage as they passed by the parsonage gate on his way to the station,—she walked up to the Combe.

"He has told you, I suppose?" said she.

"Yes," said Miss Le Smyrger. "And I will never see him again unless he asks your pardon on his knees. I have told him so. I would not even give him my hand as he went."

"But why so, thou kindest one? The fault was mine more than his."

"I understand. I have eyes in my head," said the old maid. "I have watched him for the last four or five days. If you could have kept the truth to yourself and bade him keep off from you, he would have been at your feet now, licking the dust from your shoes."

"But, dear friend, I do not want a man to lick dust from my shoes."

"Ah, you are a fool. You do not know the value of your own wealth."

"True; I have been a fool. I was a fool to think that one coming from such a life as he has led could be happy with such as I am. I know the truth now. I have bought the lesson dearly,—but perhaps not too dearly, seeing that it will never be forgotten."

There was but little more said about the matter between our three friends at Oxney Colne. What, indeed, could be said? Miss Le Smyrger for a year or two still expected that her nephew would return and claim his bride; but he has never done so, nor has there been any correspondence between them. Patience Woolsworthy had learned her lesson dearly. She had given her whole heart to the man; and, though she so bore herself that no one was aware of the violence of the struggle, nevertheless the struggle within her bosom was very violent. She never told herself that she had done wrong; she never regretted her loss; but yet—yet!—the loss was very hard to bear. He also had loved her, but he was not capable of a love which could much injure his daily peace. Her daily peace was gone for many a day to come.

Her father is still living; but there is a curate now in the parish. In conjunction with him and with Miss Le Smyrger she spends her time in the concerns of the parish. In her own eyes she is a confirmed old maid; and such is my opinion also. The romance of her life was played out in that summer. She never sits now lonely on the hill-side thinking how much she might do for one whom she really loved. But with a large heart she loves many, and, with no romance, she works hard to lighten the burdens of those she loves.

As for Captain Broughton, all the world know that he

did marry that great heiress with whom his name was once before connected, and that he is now a useful member of Parliament, working on committees three or four days a week with a zeal that is indefatigable. Sometimes, not often, as he thinks of Patience Woolsworthy, a gratified smile comes across his face.

MALACHI'S COVE

O N the northern coast of Cornwall, between Tintagel and Bossiney, down on the very margin of the sea, there lived not long since an old man who got his living by saving seaweed from the waves, and selling it for manure. The cliffs there are bold and fine, and the sea beats in upon them from the north with a grand violence. I doubt whether it be not the finest morsel of cliff scenery in England, though it is beaten by many portions of the west coast of Ireland, and perhaps also by spots in Wales and Scotland. Cliffs should be nearly precipitous, they should be broken in their outlines, and should barely admit here and there of an insecure passage from their summit to the sand at their feet. The sea should come, if not up to them, at least very near to them, and then, above all things, the water below them should be blue, and not of that dead leaden colour which is so familiar to us in England. At Tintagel all these requisites are there, except that bright blue colour which is so lovely. But the cliffs themselves are bold and well broken, and the margin of sand at high water is very narrow,— so narrow that at spring tides there is barely a footing there.

Close upon this margin was the cottage or hovel of Malachi Trenglos, the old man of whom I have spoken. But Malachi, or old Glos, as he was commonly called by the people around him, had not built his house absolutely upon the sand. There was a fissure in the rock so great that at the top it formed a narrow ravine, and so complete from the summit to the base that it afforded an opening for a steep and ragged track from the top of the rock to the bottom. This fissure was so wide at the bottom that it had afforded space for Trenglos to fix his habitation on a foundation of rock, and here he had lived for many years. It was told of him that in the early days of his trade he had always carried the weed in a basket on his back to the top, but latterly he had been possessed of a donkey which had been trained to go up and down the steep track with a single pannier over his loins, for the rocks would not admit of panniers hanging by his side; and for this assistant he had built a shed adjoining his own, and almost as large as that in which he himself resided.

But, as years went on, old Glos procured other assistance than that of the donkey, or, as I should rather say, Providence supplied him with other help; and, indeed, had it not been so, the old man must have given up his cabin and his independence and gone into the workhouse at Camelford. For rheumatism had afflicted him, old age had bowed him till he was nearly double, and by degrees he became unable to attend the donkey on its upward passage to the world above, or even to assist in rescuing the coveted weed from the waves.

At the time to which our story refers Trenglos had not been up the cliff for twelve months, and for the last six months he had done nothing towards the furtherance of his trade, except to take the money and keep it, if any of it was kept, and occasionally to shake down a bundle of fodder for the donkey. The real work of the business was done altogether by Mahala Trenglos, his grand-daughter.

Mally Trenglos was known to all the farmers round the coast, and to all the small tradespeople in Camelford. She was a wild-looking, almost unearthly creature, with wild-flowing, black, uncombed hair, small in stature, with small hands and bright black eyes; but people said that she was very strong, and the children around declared that she worked day and night, and knew nothing of fatigue. As to her age there were many doubts. Some said she was ten, and others five-and-twenty, but the reader may be allowed to know that at this time she had in truth passed her twentieth birthday. The old people spoke well of Mally, because she was so good to her grandfather; and it was said of her that though she carried to him a little gin and tobacco almost daily, she bought nothing for herself;—and as to the gin, no one who looked at her would accuse her of meddling with that. But she had no friends, and but few acquaintances among people of her own age. They said that she was fierce and ill-natured, that she had not a good word for anyone, and that she was, complete at all points, a thorough little vixen.

The young men did not care for her; for, as regarded dress, all days were alike with her. She never made herself smart on Sundays. She was generally without stockings, and seemed to care not at all to exercise any of those feminine attractions which might have been hers had she studied to attain them. All days were the same to her in regard to dress; and, indeed, till lately, all days had, I fear, been the same to her in other respects. Old Malachi had never been seen inside a place of worship since he had taken to live under the cliff.

But within the last two years Mally had submitted herself to the teaching of the clergyman at Tintagel, and had appeared at church on Sundays, if not absolutely with punctuality, at any rate so often that no one who knew the peculiarity of her residence was disposed to quarrel with her on that subject. But she made no difference in her dress on these occasions. She took her place in a low stone seat just inside the church door, clothed as usual in her thick red serge petticoat and loose brown serge jacket, such being the apparel which she had found to be best adapted for her hard and perilous work among the waters. She had pleaded to the clergyman when he attacked her on the subject of church attendance with vigour that she had got no church-going clothes. He had explained to her that she would be received there without distinction to her clothing. Mally had taken him at his word, and had gone, with a courage which certainly deserved admiration, though I doubt whether there was not mingled with it an obstinacy which was less admirable.

For people said that old Glos was rich, and that Mally might have proper clothes if she chose to buy them. Mr. Polwarth, the clergyman, who, as the old man could not come to him, went down the rocks to the old man, did make some hint on the matter in Mally's absence. But old Glos, who had been patient with him on other matters, turned upon him so angrily when he made an allusion to money, that Mr. Polwarth found himself obliged to give that matter up, and Mally continued to sit upon the stone bench in her short serge petticoat, with her long hair streaming down her face. She did so far sacrifice to decency as on such occasions to tie up her back hair with an old shoe-string. So tied it would remain through the Monday and Tuesday, but by Wednesday afternoon Mally's hair had generally managed to escape.

As to Mally's indefatigable industry there could be no manner of doubt, for the quantity of seaweed which she and the donkey amassed between them was very surprising. Old Glos, it was declared, had never collected half what Mally gathered together; but then the article was becoming cheaper, and it was necessary that the exertion should be greater. So Mally and the donkey toiled and toiled, and the seaweed came up in heaps which surprised those who looked at her little hands and light form. Was there not someone who helped her at nights, some fairy, or demon, or the like? Mally was so snappish in her answers to people that she had no right to be surprised if ill-natured things were said of her.

No one ever heard Mally Trenglos complain of her work, but about this time she was heard to make great and loud complaints of the treatment she received from some of her neighbours.

It was known that she went with her plaints to Mr. Polwarth; and when he could not help her, or did not give her such instant help as she needed, she went—ah, so foolishly!—to the office of a certain attorney at Camelford, who was not likely to prove himself a better friend than Mr. Polwarth.

Now the nature of her injury was as follows. The place in which she collected her seaweed was a little cove; the people had come to call it Malachi's Cove, from the name of the old man who lived there;—which was so formed that the margin of the sea therein could only be reached by the passage from the top down to Trenglos's hut. The breadth of the cove when the sea was out might perhaps be two hundred yards, and on each side the rocks ran out in such a way that both from north and south the domain of Trenglos was guarded from intruders. And this locality had been well chosen for its intended purpose.

There was a rush of the sea into the cove, which carried there large, drifting masses of seaweed, leaving them among the rocks when the tide was out. During the equinoctial winds of the spring and autumn the supply would never fail; and even when the sea was calm the long, soft, salt-bedewed, trailing masses of the weed could be gathered there when they could not be found elsewhere for miles along the coast. The task of getting the weed from the breakers was often difficult and dangerous,—so difficult that much of it was left to be carried away by the next incoming tide.

Mally doubtless did not gather half the crop that was there at her feet. What was taken by the returning waves she did not regret; but when interlopers came upon her cove, and gathered her wealth—her grandfather's wealth—beneath her eyes, then her heart was broken. It was this interloping, this intrusion, that drove poor Mally to the

Camelford attorney. But, alas, though the Camelford attorney took Mally's money, he could do nothing for her,
and her heart was broken!

She had an idea, in which no doubt her grandfather
shared, that the path to the cove was, at any rate, their
property. When she was told that the cove, and sea running
into the cove, were not the freeholds of her grandfather, she
understood that the statement might be true. But what
then as to the use of the path? Who had made the path
what it was? Had she not painfully, wearily, with exceeding
toil, carried up bits of rock with her own little hands, that
her grandfather's donkey might have footing for his feet?
Had she not scraped together crumbs of earth along the
face of the cliff that she might make easier to the animal the
track of that rugged way? And now, when she saw big farmers' lads coming down with other donkeys,— and, indeed,
there was one who came with a pony; no boy, but a young
man, old enough to know better than rob a poor old man
and a young girl,—she reviled the whole human race, and
swore that the Camelford attorney was a fool.

Any attempt to explain to her that there was still weed
enough for her was worse than useless. Was it not all hers
and his, or, at any rate, was not the sole way to it his and
hers? And was not her trade stopped and impeded? Had
she not been forced to back her laden donkey down, twenty
yards she said, but it had, in truth, been five, because
Farmer Gunliffe's son had been in the way with his thieving
pony? Farmer Gunliffe had wanted to buy her weed at his
own price, and because she had refused he had set on his
thieving son to destroy her in this wicked way.

"I'll hamstring the beast the next time as he's down here!" said Mally to old Glos, while the angry fire literally streamed from her eyes.

Farmer Gunliffe's small homestead—he held about fifty acres of land—was close by the village of Tintagel, and not a mile from the cliff. The sea-wrack, as they call it, was pretty well the only manure within his reach, and no doubt he thought it hard that he should be kept from using it by Mally Trenglos and her obstinacy.

"There's heaps of other coves, Barty," said Mally to Barty Gunliffe, the farmer's son.

"But none so nigh, Mally, nor yet none that fills 'emselves as this place."

Then he explained to her that he would not take the weed that came up close to hand. He was bigger than she was, and stronger, and would get it from the outer rocks, with which she never meddled. Then, with scorn in her eye, she swore that she could get it where he durst not venture, and repeated her threat of hamstringing the pony. Barty laughed at her wrath, jeered her because of her wild hair, and called her a mermaid.

"I'll mermaid you!" she cried. "Mermaid, indeed! I wouldn't be a man to come and rob a poor girl and an old cripple. But you're no man, Barty Gunliffe! You're not half a man."

Nevertheless, Bartholomew Gunliffe was a very fine young fellow, as far as the eye went. He was about five feet eight inches high, with strong arms and legs, with light curly brown hair and blue eyes. His father was but in a small way as a farmer, but, nevertheless, Barty Gunliffe was well thought of among the girls around. Everybody liked Barty,—excepting only Mally Trenglos, and she hated him like poison.

Barty, when he was asked why so good-natured a lad as he persecuted a poor girl and an old man, threw himself upon the justice of the thing. It wouldn't do at all, according to his view, that any single person should take upon himself to own that which God Almighty sent as the common property of all. He would do Mally no harm, and so he had told her. But Mally was a vixen,—a wicked little vixen; and she must be taught to have a civil tongue in her head. When once Mally would speak him civil as he went for weed, he would get his father to pay the old man some sort of toll for the use of the path.

"Speak him civil!" said Mally. "Never; not while I have a tongue in my mouth!" And I fear old Glos encouraged her rather than otherwise in her view of the matter.

But her grandfather did not encourage her to hamstring the pony. Hamstringing a pony would be a serious thing, and old Glos thought it might be very awkward for both of them if Mally were put into prison. He suggested, therefore, that all manner of impediments should be put in the way of the pony's feet, surmising that the well-trained donkey might be able to work in spite of them. And Barty Gunliffe, on his next descent, did find the passage very awkward when he came near to Malachi's hut, but he made his way down, and poor Mally saw the lumps of rock at which she had laboured so hard pushed on one side or rolled out of the way with a steady persistency of injury towards herself that almost drove her frantic.

"Well, Barty, you're a nice boy," said old Glos, sitting in the doorway of the hut, as he watched the intruder.

"I ain't a doing no harm to none as doesn't harm me," said Barty. "The sea's free to all, Malachi."

"And the sky's free to all, but I mustn't get up on the top of your big barn to look at it," said Mally, who was standing among the rocks with a long hook in her hand. The long hook was the tool with which she worked in dragging the weed from the waves. "But you ain't got no justice nor yet no sperrit, or you wouldn't come here to vex an old man like he."

"I didn't want to vex him, nor yet to vex you, Mally. You let me be for a while, and we'll be friends yet."

"Friends!" exclaimed Mally. "Who'd have the likes of you for a friend? What are you moving them stones for? Them stones belongs to grandfather." And in her wrath she made a movement as though she were going to fly at him.

"Let him be, Mally," said the old man; "let him be. He'll get his punishment. He'll come to be drowned some day if he comes down here when the wind is in shore."

"That he may be drowned then!" said Mally, in her anger. "If he was in the big hole there among the rocks, and the sea running in at half tide, I wouldn't lift a hand to help him out."

"Yes, you would, Mally; you'd fish me up with your hook like a big stick of seaweed."

She turned from him with scorn as he said this, and went into the hut. It was time for her to get ready for her work, and one of the great injuries done her lay in this,—

that such a one as Barty Gunliffe should come and look at her during her toil among the breakers.

It was an afternoon in April, and the hour was something after four o'clock. There had been a heavy wind from the north-west all the morning, with gusts of rain, and the seagulls had been in and out of the cove all the day, which was a sure sign to Mally that the incoming tide would cover the rocks with weed. The quick waves were now returning with wonderful celerity over the low reefs, and the time had come at which the treasure must be seized if it was to be garnered on that day. By seven o'clock it would be growing dark, at nine it would be high water, and before daylight the crop would be carried out again if not collected. All this Mally understood very well, and some of this Barty was beginning to understand also.

As Mally came down with her bare feet, bearing her long hook in her hand, she saw Barty's pony standing patiently on the sand, and in her heart she longed to attack the brute. Barty at this moment, with a common three-pronged fork in his hand, was standing down on a large rock, gazing forth towards the waters. He had declared that he would gather the weed only at places which were inaccessible to Mally, and he was looking out that he might settle where he would begin.

"Let 'un be, let 'un be," shouted the old man to Mally, as he saw her take a step towards the beast, which she hated almost as much as she hated the man.

Hearing her grandfather's voice through the wind, she desisted from her purpose, if any purpose she had had, and went forth to her work. As she passed down the cove, and scrambled in among the rocks, she saw Barty still standing on his perch; out beyond, the white-curling waves were cresting and breaking themselves with violence, and the wind was howling among the caverns and abutments of the cliff.

Every now and then there came a squall of rain, and though there was sufficient light, the heavens were black with clouds. A scene more beautiful might hardly be found by those who love the glories of the coast. The light for such objects was perfect. Nothing could exceed the grandeur of the colours,—the blue of the open sea, the white of the breaking waves, the yellow sands, or the streaks of red and brown which gave such richness to the cliff.

But neither Mally nor Barty were thinking of such things as these. Indeed, they were hardly thinking of their trade after its ordinary forms. Barty was meditating how he might best accomplish his purpose of working beyond the reach of Mally's feminine powers, and Mally was resolving that wherever Barty went she would go father.

And, in many respects, Mally had the advantage. She knew every rock in the spot, and was sure of those which gave a good foothold, and sure also of those which did not. And then her activity had been made perfect by practice for the purpose to which it was to be devoted. Barty, no doubt, was stronger than she, and quite as active. But Barty could not jump among the waves from one stone to another as she could do, nor was he as yet able to get aid in his work from the very force of the water as she could get it. She had been hunting seaweed in that cove since she had been an urchin of six years old, and she knew every hole and corner and every spot of vantage. The waves were her friends, and she could use them. She could measure their strength, and knew when and where it would cease.

Mally was great down in the salt pools of her own cove,—great, and very fearless. As she watched Barty make his way forward from rock to rock, she told herself, gleefully, that he was going astray. The curl of the wind as it blew into the cove would not carry the weed up to the northern buttresses of the cove; and then there was the great hole just there,—the great hole of which she had spoken when she wished him evil.

And now she went to work, hooking up the dishevelled hairs of the ocean, and landing many a cargo on the extreme margin of the sand, from whence she would be able in the evening to drag it back before the invading waters would return to reclaim the spoil.

And on his side also Barty made his heap up against the northern buttresses of which I have spoken. Barty's heap became big and still bigger, so that he knew, let the pony work as he might, he could not take it all up that evening. But still it was not as large as Mally's heap. Mally's hook was better than his fork, and Mally's skill was better than his strength. And when he failed in some haul Mally would jeer him with a wild, weird laughter, and shriek to him through the wind that he was not half a man. At first he answered her with laughing words, but before long, as she boasted of her success and pointed to his failure, he became angry, and then he answered her no more. He became angry with himself, in that he missed so much of the plunder before him.

The broken sea was full of the long straggling growth which the waves had torn up from the bottom of the ocean, but the masses were carried past him, away from him,—nay, once or twice over him; and then Mally's weird voice would sound in his ear, jeering him. The gloom among the rocks was now becoming thicker and thicker, the tide was beating in with increased strength, and the gusts of wind came with quicker and greater violence. But still he worked on. While Mally worked he would work, and he would work for some time after she was driven in. He would not be beaten by a girl.

The great hole was now full of water, but of water which seemed to be boiling as though in a pot. And the pot was full of floating masses,— large treasures of seaweed which were thrown to and fro upon its surface, but lying there so thick that one would seem almost able to rest upon it without sinking.

Mally knew well how useless it was to attempt to rescue aught from the fury of that boiling caldron. The hole went in under the rocks, and the side of it towards the shore lay high, slippery, and steep. The hole, even at low water, was never empty; and Mally believed that there was no bottom to it. Fish thrown in there could escape out to the ocean, miles away,—so Mally in her softer moods would tell the visitors to the cove. She knew the hole well. Poulnadioul she was accustomed to call it; which was supposed, when translated, to mean that this was the hole of the Evil One.

Never did Mally attempt to make her own of weed which had found its way into that pot.

But Barty Gunliffe knew no better, and she watched him as he endeavoured to steady himself on the treacherously slippery edge of the pool. He fixed himself there and made a haul, with some small success. How he managed it she hardly knew, but she stood still for a while watching him anxiously, and then she saw him slip. He slipped, and recovered himself;—slipped again, and again recovered himself.

"Barty, you fool!" she screamed; "if you get yourself pitched in there, you'll never come out no more."

Whether she simply wished to frighten him, or whether her heart relented and she had thought of his danger with dismay, who shall say? She could not have told herself. She hated him as much as ever,—but she could hardly have wished to see him drowned before her eyes.

"You go on, and don't mind me," said he, speaking in a hoarse, angry tone.

"Mind you!—Who minds you?" retorted the girl. And then she again prepared herself for her work.

But as she went down over the rocks with her long hook balanced in her hands she suddenly heard a splash, and, turning quickly round, saw the body of her enemy tumbling amidst the eddying waves in the pool. The tide had now come up so far that every succeeding wave washed into it and over it from the side nearest to the sea, and then ran down again back from the rocks, as the rolling wave receded, with a noise like the fall of a cataract. And then, when the surplus water had retreated for a moment, the surface of the pool would be partly calm, though the fretting bubbles would still boil up and down, and there was ever a simmer on the surface, as though, in truth, the caldron were heated. But this time of comparative rest was but a moment, for the succeeding breaker would come up almost as soon as the foam of the preceding one had gone, and then again the waters would be dashed upon the rocks, and the sides would echo with the roar of the angry wave.

Instantly Mally hurried across to the edge of the pool, crouching down upon her hands and knees for security as she did so. As a wave receded, Barty's head and face was carried near to her, and she could see that his forehead was covered with blood. Whether he were alive or dead she did not know. She had seen nothing but his blood, and the light-coloured hair of his head lying amidst the foam. Then his body was drawn along by the suction of the retreating wave; but the mass of water that escaped was not on this occasion large enough to carry the man out with it.

Instantly Mally was at work with her hook, and getting it fixed into his coat, dragged him towards the spot on which she was kneeling. During the half minute of repose she got him so close that she could touch his shoulder. Straining herself down, laying herself over the long bending handle of the hook, she strove to grasp him with her right hand. But she could not do it; she could only touch him.

Then came the next breaker, forcing itself on with a roar, looking to Mally as though it must certainly knock her from her resting-place and destroy them both. But she had nothing for it but to kneel and hold by her hook.

What prayer passed through her mind at that moment

for herself or for him, or for that old man who was sitting unconsciously up at the cabin, who can say? The great wave came and rushed over her as she lay almost prostrate, and when the water was gone from her eyes, and the tumult of the foam, and the violence of the roaring breaker had passed by her, she found herself at her length upon the rock, while his body had been lifted up, free from her hook, and was lying upon the slippery ledge, half in the water and half out of it. As she looked at him, in that instant, she could see that his eyes were open and that he was struggling with his hands.

"Hold by the hook, Barty," she cried, pushing the stick of it before him, while she seized the collar of his coat in her hands.

Had he been her brother, her lover, her father, she could not have clung to him with more of the energy of despair. He did contrive to hold by the stick which she had given him, and when the succeeding wave had passed by he was still on the ledge. In the next moment she was seated a yard or two above the hole, in comparative safety, while Barty lay upon the rocks with his still bleeding head resting upon her lap.

What could she do now? She could not carry him; and in fifteen minutes the sea would be up where she was sitting. He was quite insensible and very pale, and the blood was coming slowly—very slowly—from the wound on his forehead. Ever so gently she put her hand upon his hair to move it back from his face; and then she bent over his mouth to see if he breathed, and as she looked at him she knew that he was beautiful.

What would she not give that he might live? Nothing now was so precious to her as his life,—as this life which she had so far rescued from the waters. But what could she do? Her grandfather could scarcely get himself down over the rocks, if indeed he could succeed in doing so much as that. Could she drag the wounded man backwards, if it were only a few feet, that he might lie above the reach of the waves till further assistance could be procured?

She set herself to work and she moved him, almost lifting him. As she did so she wondered at her own strength, but she was very strong at that moment. Slowly, tenderly, falling on the rocks herself so that he might fall on her, she got him back to the margin of the sand, to a spot which the waters would not reach for the next two hours.

Here her grandfather met them, having seen at last what had happened from the door.

"Dada," she said, "he fell into the pool yonder, and was battered against the rocks. See there at his forehead."

"Mally, I'm thinking that he's dead already," said old Glos, peering down over the body.

"No, Dada, he is not dead; but mayhap he's dying. But I'll go at once up to the farm."

"Mally," said the old man, "look at his head. They'll say we murdered him."

"Who'll say so? Who'll lie like that? Didn't I pull him out of the hole?"

"What matters that? His father'll say we killed him."

It was manifest to Mally that whatever anyone might say hereafter her present course was plain before her. She must run up the path to Gunliffe's farm and get necessary assistance. If the world were as bad as her grandfather said, it would be so bad that she would not care to live longer in it. But be that as it might, there was no doubt as to what she must do now.

So away she went as fast as her naked feet could carry her up the cliff. When at the top she looked round to see if any person might be within ken, but she saw no one. So she ran with all her speed along the headland of the corn-field which led in the direction of old Gunliffe's house, and as she drew near to the homestead she saw that Barty's mother was leaning on the gate. As she approached she attempted to call, but her breath failed her for any purpose of loud speech, so she ran on till she was able to grasp Mrs. Gunliffe by the arm.

"Where's himself?" she said, holding her hand upon her beating heart that she might husband her breath.

"Who is it you mean?" said Mrs. Gunliffe, who participated in the family feud against Trenglos and his granddaughter. "What does the girl clutch me for in that way?"

"He's dying then, that's all."

"Who is dying? Is it old Malachi? If the old man's bad, we'll send some one down."

"It ain't Dada, it's Barty! Where's himself? Where's the master?"

But by this time Mrs. Gunliffe was in an agony of despair, and was calling out for assistance lustily. Happily Gunliffe, the father, was at hand, and with him a man from the neighbouring village.

"Will you not send for the doctor?" said Mally. "Oh, man, you should send for the doctor!"

Whether any orders were given for the doctor she did not know, but in a very few minutes she was hurrying across the field again towards the path to the cove, and Gunliffe with the other man and his wife were following her.

As Mally went along she recovered her voice, for their step was not so quick as hers, and that which to them was a hurried movement allowed her to get her breath again. And as she went, she tried to explain to the father what had happened, saying but little, however, of her own doings in the matter. The wife hung behind listening, exclaiming every now and again that her boy was killed, and then asking wild questions as to his being yet alive. The father, as he went, said little. He was known as a silent, sober man, well spoken of for diligence and general conduct, but supposed to be stern and very hard when angered.

As they drew near to the top of the path the other man whispered something to him, and then he turned round upon Mally and stopped her.

"If he has come by his death between you, your blood shall be taken for his," said he.

Then the wife shrieked out that her child had been murdered, and Mally, looking round into the faces of the three, saw that her grandfather's words had come true. They suspected her of having taken the life in saving which she had nearly lost her own.

She looked round at them with awe in her face, and then, without saying a word, preceded them down the path. What had she to answer when such a charge as that was made against her? If they chose to say that she pushed him into the pool, and hit him with her hook as he lay amidst the waters, how could she show that it was not so?

Poor Mally knew little of the law of evidence, and it seemed to her that she was in their hands. But as she went down the steep track with a hurried step,—a step so quick that they could not keep up with her,—her heart was very full,—very full and very high. She had striven for the man's life as though he had been her brother. The blood was yet not dry on her own legs and arms, where she had torn them in his service. At one moment she had felt sure that she would die with him in that pool. And now they said that she had murdered him! It may be that he was not dead, and what would he say if ever he should speak again? Then she thought of that moment when his eyes had opened, and he had seemed to see her. She had no fear for herself, for her heart was very high. But it was full also,—full of scorn, disdain, and wrath.

When she had reached the bottom she stood close to the door of the hut waiting for them, so that they might precede her to the other group, which was there in front of them, at a little distance on the sand.

"He is there, and Dada is with him. Go and look at him," said Mally.

The father and mother ran on stumbling over the stones, but Mally remained behind by the door of the hut.

Barty Gunliffe was lying on the sand where Mally had left him, and old Malachi Trenglos was standing over him, resting himself with difficulty upon a stick.

"Not a move he's moved since she left him," said he, "not a move. I put his head on the old rug as you see, and I tried 'un with a drop of gin, but he wouldn't take it,—he wouldn't take it."

"Oh, my boy! my boy!" said the mother, throwing herself beside her son upon the sand.

"Haud your tongue, woman," said the father, kneeling down slowly by the lad's head, "whimpering that way will do 'un no good."

Then having gazed for a minute or two upon the pale face beneath him, he looked up sternly into that of Malachi Trenglos.

The old man hardly knew how to bear this terrible inquisition.

"He would come," said Malachi; "he brought it all upon hisself."

"Who was it struck him?" said the father.

"Sure he struck hisself, as he fell among the breakers."

"Liar!" said the father, looking up at the old man.

"They have murdered him!—They have murdered him!" shrieked the mother.

"Haud your peace, woman!" said the husband again. "They shall give us blood for blood."

Mally, leaning against the corner of the hovel, heard it all, but did not stir. They might say what they liked. They might make it out to be murder. They might drag her and her grandfather to Camelford gaol, and then to Bodmin, and the gallows; but they could not take from her the conscious feeling that was her own. She had done her best to save him,—her very best. And she had saved him!

She remembered her threat to him before they had gone down on the rocks together, and her evil wish. Those words had been very wicked; but since that she had risked her life to save his. They might say what they pleased of her, and do what they pleased. She knew what she knew.

Then the father raised his son's head and shoulders in his arms, and called on the others to assist him in carrying Barty towards the path. They raised him between them carefully and tenderly, and lifted their burden on towards the spot at which Mally was standing. She never moved, but watched them at their work; and the old man followed them, hobbling after them with his crutch.

When they had reached the end of the hut she looked upon Barty's face, and saw that it was very pale. There was no longer blood upon the forehead, but the great gash was to be seen there plainly, with its jagged cut, and the skin livid and blue round the orifice. His light brown hair was hanging back, as she had made it to hang when she had gathered it with her hand after the big wave had passed over them. Ah, how beautiful he was in Mally's eyes with that pale face, and the sad scar upon his brow! She turned her face away, that they might not see her tears; but she did not move, nor did she speak.

But now, when they had passed the end of the hut, shuffling along with their burden, she heard a sound which stirred her. She roused herself quickly from her leaning posture, and stretched forth her head as though to listen; then she moved to follow them. Yes, they had stopped at the bottom of the path, and had again laid the body on the rocks. She heard that sound again, as of a long, long sigh, and then, regardless of any of them, she ran to the wounded man's head.

"He is not dead," she said. "There; he is not dead."

As she spoke Barty's eyes opened, and he looked about him.

"Barty, my boy, speak to me," said the mother.

Barty turned his face upon his mother, smiled, and then stared about him wildly.

"How is it with thee, lad?" said his father. Then Barty turned his face again to the latter voice, and as he did so his eyes fell upon Mally.

"Mally!" he said, "Mally!"

It could have wanted nothing further to any of those present to teach them that, according to Barty's own view of the case, Mally had not been his enemy; and, in truth, Mally herself wanted no further triumph. That word had vindicated her, and she withdrew back to the hut.

"Dada," she said, "Barty is not dead, and I'm thinking they won't say anything more about our hurting him."

Old Glos shook his head. He was glad the lad hadn't met his death there; he didn't want the young man's blood, but he knew what folk would say. The poorer he was the more sure the world would be to trample on him. Mally said what she could to comfort him, being full of comfort herself.

She would have crept up to the farm if she dared, to ask how Barty was. But her courage failed her when she thought of that, so she went to work again, dragging back the weed she had saved to the spot at which on the morrow she would load the donkey. As she did this she saw Barty's pony still standing patiently under the rock, so she got a lock of fodder and threw it down before the beast.

It had become dark down in the cove, but she was still dragging back the seaweed when she saw the glimmer of a lantern coming down the pathway. It was a most unusual sight, for lanterns were not common down in Malachi's Cove. Down came the lantern rather slowly— much more slowly than she was in the habit of descending; and then through the gloom she saw the figure of a man standing at the bottom of the path. She went up to him, and saw that it was Mr. Gunliffe, the father.

"Is that Mally?" said Gunliffe.

"Yes, it is Mally; and how is Barty, Mr. Gunliffe?"

"You must come to 'un yourself, now at once," said the farmer. "He won't sleep a wink till he's seed you. You must not say but you'll come."

"Sure I'll come if I'm wanted," said Mally.

Gunliffe waited a moment, thinking that Mally might have to prepare herself, but Mally needed no preparation. She was dripping with salt water from the weed which she had been dragging, and her elfin locks were streaming wildly from her head; but, such as she was, she was ready.

"Dada's in bed," she said, "and I can go now, if you please."

Then Gunliffe turned round and followed her up the path, wondering at the life which this girl led so far away from all her sex. It was now dark night, and he had found her working at the very edge of the rolling waves by herself, in the darkness, while the only human being who might seem to be her protector had already gone to his bed.

When they were at the top of the cliff, Gunliffe took her by her hand and led her along. She did not comprehend this, but she made no attempt to take her hand from his. Something he said about falling on the cliffs, but it was muttered so lowly that Mally hardly understood him. But, in truth, the man knew that she had saved his boy's life, and that he had injured her instead of thanking her. He was now taking her to his heart, and as words were wanting to him, he was showing his love after this silent fashion. He held her by the hand as though she were a child, and Mally tripped along at his side asking him no questions.

When they were at the farmyard gate he stopped there for a moment.

"Mally, my girl," he said, "he'll not be content till he sees thee, but thou must not stay long wi' him, lass. Doctor says he's weak like, and wants sleep badly."

Mally merely nodded her head, and then they entered the house. Mally had never been within it before, and looked about with wondering eyes at the furniture of the big kitchen. Did any idea of her future destiny flash upon her then, I wonder? But she did not pause here a moment, but was led up to the bedroom above stairs, where Barty was lying on his mother's bed.

"Is it Mally herself?" said the voice of the weak youth.

"It's Mally herself," said the mother, "so now you can say what you please."

"Mally," said he, "Mally, it's along of you that I'm alive this moment."

"I'll not forget it on her," said the father, with his eyes turned away from her. "I'll never forget it on her."

"We hadn't a one but only him," said the mother, with her apron up to her face.

"Mally, you'll be friends with me now?" said Barty.

To have been made lady of the manor of the cove for ever, Mally couldn't have spoken a word now. It was not only that the words and presence of the people there cowed her and made her speechless, but the big bed, and the looking-glass, and the unheard-of wonders of the chamber, made her feel her own insignificance. But she crept up to Barty's side, and put her hand upon his.

"I'll come and get the weed, Mally; but it shall all be for you," said Barty.

"Indeed, you won't then, Barty dear," said the mother; "you'll never go near the awesome place again. What would we do if you were took from us?"

"He mustn't go near the hole if he does," said Mally, speaking at last in a solemn voice, and imparting the knowledge which she had kept to herself while Barty was her enemy; " 'specially not if the wind's any way from the nor'ard."

"She'd better go down now," said the father.

Barty kissed the hand which he held, and Mally, looking at him as he did so, thought that he was like an angel.

"You'll come and see us to-morrow, Mally," said he.

To this she made no answer, but followed Mrs. Gunliffe out of the room. When they were down in the kitchen the mother had tea for her, and thick milk, and a hot cake,—all the delicacies which the farm could afford. I don't know that Mally cared much for the eating and drinking that night, but she began to think that the Gunliffes were good people,—very good people. It was better thus, at any rate, than being accused of murder and carried off to Camelford prison.

"I'll never forget it on her—never," the father had said.

Those words stuck to her from that moment, and seemed to sound in her ears all the night. How glad she was that Barty had come down to the cove,—oh, yes, how glad! There was no question of his dying now, and as for the blow on his forehead, what harm was that to a lad like him?

"But Father shall go with you," said Mrs. Gunliffe, when Mally prepared to start for the cove by herself. Mally, however, would not hear of this. She could find her way to the cove whether it was light or dark.

"Mally, thou art my child now, and I shall think of thee so," said the mother, as the girl went off by herself.

Mally thought of this, too, as she walked home. How could she become Mrs. Gunliffe's child; ah, how?

I need not, I think, tell the tale any further. That Mally did become Mrs. Gunliffe's child, and how she became so the reader will understand; and in process of time the big kitchen and all the wonders of the farmhouse were her own. The people said that Barty Gunliffe had married a mermaid out of the sea; but when it was said in Mally's hearing, I doubt whether she liked it; and when Barty himself would call her a mermaid, she would frown at him, and throw about her black hair, and pretend to cuff him with her little hand.

Old Glos was brought up to the top of the cliff, and lived his few remaining days under the roof of Mr. Gunliffe's house; and as for the cove and the right of seaweed, from that time forth all that has been supposed to attach itself to Gunliffe's farm, and I do not know that any of the neighbours are prepared to dispute the right.

MISS OPHELIA GLEDD

WHO can say what is a lady? My intelligent and well-bred reader of either sex will at once declare that he and she know very well who is a lady. So, I hope, do I. But the present question goes further than that. What is it, and whence does it come? Education does not give it, nor intelligence, nor birth, not even the highest. The thing, which in its presence or absence is so well known and understood, may be wanting to the most polished manners, to the sweetest disposition, to the truest heart. There are thousands among us who know it at a glance, and recognise its presence from the sound of a dozen words, but there is not one among us who can tell us what it is.

Miss Ophelia Gledd was a young lady of Boston, Massachusetts, and I should be glad to know whether, in the estimation of my countrymen and countrywomen, she is to be esteemed a lady.

An Englishman, even of the best class, is often at a loss to judge of the "ladyship" of a foreigner, unless he has really lived in foreign cities and foreign society; but I do not know that he is ever so much puzzled in this matter by any nationality as he is by the American.

American women speak his own language, read his own literature, and in many respects think his own thoughts;

but there have crept into American society so many little social ways at variance with our social ways, there have been wafted thither so many social atoms which there fit into their places, but which with us would clog the wheels, that the words, and habits, and social carriage, of an American woman of the best class, too often offend the taste of an Englishman; as do, quite as strongly, those of the Englishwoman offend the American.

There are those who declare that there are no American ladies; but these are people who would probably declare the same of the French and the Italians, if the languages of France and Italy were as familiar to their ears as is the language of the States. They mean that American women do not grow up to be English ladies,—not bethinking themselves that such a growth was hardly to be expected. Now I will tell my story, and ask my readers to answer this question,—Was Miss Ophelia Gledd a lady?

When I knew her she was at any rate great in the society of Boston, Massachusetts, in which city she had been as well known for the last four or five years as the yellow dome of the State House. She was as pure and perfect a specimen of a Yankee girl as ever it was my fortune to know.

Standing about five feet eight, she seemed to be very tall, because she always carried herself at her full height. She was thin too, and rather narrower at the shoulders than the strictest rules of symmetry would have made her. Her waist was very slight; so much so, that to the eye it would seem that some unjust and injurious force had created its slender compass; but I have fair ground for stating my belief that no such force had been employed. But yet, though she was slight and thin, and even narrow, there was a vivacity and quickness about all her movements, and an easiness in her mode of moving which made it impossible to deny to her the merit of a pleasing figure.

No man would, I think, at first sight, declare her to be pretty, and certainly no woman would do so; and yet I have seldom known a face in the close presence of which it was more gratifying to sit, and talk, and listen. Her brown hair was always brushed close off from her forehead. Her brow was high, and her face narrow and thin; but that face was ever bright with motion, and her clear, deep, gray eyes, full of life and light, were always ready for some combat or some enterprise. Her nose and mouth were the best features in her face, and her teeth were perfect,—miracles of perfection; but her lips were too thin for feminine beauty; and indeed such personal charms as she had were not the charms which men love most,—sweet changing colour, soft full flowing lines of grace, and womanly gentleness in every movement. Ophelia Gledd had none of these. She was hard and sharp in shape, of a good brown steady colour, hard and sharp also in her gait; with no full flowing lines, with no softness; but she was bright as burnished steel.

And yet she was the belle of Boston. I do not know that any man of Boston,—or any stranger knowing Boston, would have ever declared that she was the prettiest girl in the city; but this was certain almost to all,—that she received more of that admiration which is generally given to beauty than did any other lady there; and that the upper social world of Boston had become so used to her appearance, such as it was, that no one ever seemed to question the fact of her being a beauty. She had been passed as a beauty by examiners whose certificate in that matter was held to be good, and had received high rank as a beauty in the drawing-rooms at Boston.

The fact was never questioned now, unless by some passing stranger who would be told in flat terms that he was wrong.

"Yes, Sir; you'll find you're wrong; you'll find you aire, if you'll bide here awhile."

I did bide there awhile, and did find that I was wrong. Before I left I was prepared to allow that Miss Ophelia Gledd was a beauty. And moreover, which was more singular, all the women allowed it.

Ophelia Gledd, though the belle of Boston, was not hated by the other belles. The female feeling with regard to her was, I think, this, that the time had arrived in which she should choose her husband and settle down, so as to leave room for others less attractive than herself.

When I knew her she was very fond of men's society; but I doubt if anyone could fairly say that Miss Gledd ever flirted. In the proper sense of the word she certainly never flirted. Interesting conversations with interesting young men at which none but themselves were present she had by the dozen. It was as common for her to walk up and down Beacon Street,—the parade of Boston,—with young Jones, or Smith, or more probably with young Mr. Optimus M. Opie, or young Mr. Hannibal H. Hoskins, as it is for our young Joneses, and young Smiths, and young Hoskinses, to saunter out together.

That is the way of the country, and no one took wider advantage of the ways of her own country than did Miss Ophelia Gledd. She told young men also when to call upon her, if she liked them, and in seeking or in avoiding their society, did very much as she pleased.

But these practices are right or wrong, not in accordance with a fixed rule of morality prevailing over all the earth,— such a rule, for instance, as that which orders men not to steal; but they are right or wrong according to the usages of the country in which they are practised.

In Boston it is right that Miss Ophelia Gledd should walk up Beacon Street with Hannibal Hoskins the morning after she has met him at a ball, and that she should invite him to call upon her at twelve o'clock on the following day.

She had certainly a nasal twang in speaking. Before my intercourse with her was over, her voice had become pleasant in my ears, and it may be that that nasal twang which had at first been so detestable to me, had recommended itself to my sense of hearing. At different periods of my life I have learned to love an Irish brogue and a northern burr.

Be that as it may, I must acknowledge that Miss Ophelia Gledd spoke with a certain nasal twang. But then such is the manner of speech at Boston; and she only did that which the Joneses and Smiths, the Opies and Hoskinses, were doing around her.

Ophelia Gledd's mother was, for a living being, the nearest thing to a nonentity that I ever met. Whether within her own house in Chestnut Street she exerted herself in her domestic duties and held authority over her maidens I cannot say, but neither in her dining parlour nor in her draw-ing-room did she hold any authority. Indeed, throughout the house, Ophelia was paramount, and it seemed as though her mother could not venture on a hint in opposi-tion to her daughter's behests.

Mrs. Gledd never went out, but her daughter frequented all balls, dinners, and assemblies, which she chose to hon-our. To all these she went alone, and had done since she was eighteen years of age. She went also to lectures, to meetings of wise men, for which the Western Athens is much noted, to political debates, and wherever her enterprising heart and enquiring head chose to carry her. But her mother never went anywhere; and it always seemed to me that Mrs. Gledd's intercourse with her domestics must have been nearer, closer, and almost dearer to her, than any that she could have with her daughter.

Mr. Gledd had been a merchant all his life. When Oph-elia Gledd first came before the Boston world he had been a rich merchant; and as she was an only child she had opened her campaign with all the advantages which attach to an heiress. But now, in these days, Mr. Gledd was known to be a merchant without riches. He still kept the same house, and lived apparently as he had always lived; but the world knew that he had been a broken merchant and was now again struggling. That Miss Gledd felt the disadvan-tage of this no one can, I suppose, doubt. But she never showed that she felt it. She spoke openly of her father's poverty as of a thing that was known, and of her own. Where she had been *exigeante* before, she was *exigeante* now. Those she disliked when rich she disliked now that she was poor. Where she had been patronising before, she patronised now. Where she had loved, she still loved. In former days she had a carriage, and now she had none. Where she had worn silk, she now wore cotton. In her gloves, her laces, her little belongings, there was all the difference which money makes or the want of money; but in her manner there was none.

Nor was there any difference in the manner of others to her. The loss of wealth seemed to entail on Miss Gledd no other discomfort than the actual want of those things which hard money buys. To go in a coach might have been a luxury to her, and that she had lost; but she had lost none of her ascendency, none of her position, none of her sovereignty.

I remember well where, when, and how, I first met Miss Gledd. At that time her father's fortune was probably already gone; but if so, she did not then know that it was gone.

It was in winter,—towards the end of winter,—when the passion for sleighing became ecstatic. I expect all my readers to know that sleighing is the grand winter amusement of Boston. And indeed it is not bad fun. There is the fashionable course for sleighing,—the Brighton Road,—and along that you drive, seated among furs, with a young lady beside you if you can get one to trust you; your horse or horses carry little bells, which add to the charms; the motion is rapid and pleasant, and, which is the great thing, you see and are seen by everybody. Of course it is expedient that the frost should be sound and perfect, so that the sleigh should run over a dry, smooth surface. But as the season draws to an end, and when sleighing intimacies have become close and warm, the horses are made to travel through slush and wet, and the scene becomes one of peril and discomfort, though one also of excitement, and not unfrequently of love.

Sleighing was fairly over at the time of which I now speak, so that the Brighton Road was deserted in its slush and sloppiness. Nevertheless, there was a possibility of sleighing; and as I was a stranger newly arrived, a young friend of mine took me—or rather allowed me to take him—out, so that the glory of the charioteer might be mine.

"I guess we're not alone," said he, after we had passed the bridge out of the town. "There's young Hoskins with Pheely Gledd just ahead of us."

That was the first I had ever heard of Ophelia, and then as I pushed along after her, instigated by a foolish Briton's ambition to pass the Yankee whip, I did hear a good deal about her; and in addition to what has already been told, I then heard that this Mr. Hannibal Hoskins, to pass whom on the road was now my only earthly desire, was Miss Gledd's professed admirer;—in point of fact, that it was known to all Boston that he had offered his hand to her more than once already.

"She has accepted him now, at any rate," said I, looking at their close contiguity on the sleigh before me. But my friend explained to me that such was by no means probable;—that Miss Gledd had twenty hangers-on of the same description, with any one of whom she might be seen sleighing, walking, or dancing; but that no argument as to any further purpose on her part was to be deduced from any such practice. "Our girls," said my friend, "don't go about tied to their mothers' aprons, as girls do in the old country. Our free institutions—&c. &c. &c." I confessed my blunder, and acknowledged that a wide and perhaps salutary latitude was allowed to the feminine creation on his side of the Atlantic.

But, do what I would, I couldn't pass Hannibal Hoskins. Whether he guessed that I was an ambitious Englishman, or whether he had a general dislike to be passed on the road, I don't know; but he raised his whip to his horses and went away from us suddenly and very quickly through the slush. The snow was half gone, and hard ridges of it remained across the road, so that his sleigh was bumped about most uncomfortably. I soon saw that his horses were running away, and that Hannibal Hoskins was in a fix. He was standing up, pulling at them with all his strength and weight, and the carriage was yawing about and across the road in a manner that made us fear it would go to pieces. Miss Ophelia Gledd, however, kept her seat, and there was no shrieking. In about five minutes they were well planted into a ditch, and we were alongside of them.

"You fixed that pretty straight, Hoskins," said my friend.

"Darn them for horses," said Hoskins, as he wiped the perspiration from his brow and looked down upon the fiercest of the quadrupeds, sprawling up to his withers in the snow. Then he turned to Miss Gledd, who was endeavouring to unroll herself from her furs.

"Oh, Miss Gledd, I am so sorry. What am I to say?"

"You'd better say that the horses ran away, I think," said

Miss Gledd. Then she stepped carefully out, on to a buf-
falo-robe, and moved across from that, quite dryfooted, on
to our sleigh. As my friend and Hoskins were very intimate, and could, as I thought, get on very well by themselves with the débris in the ditch, I offered to drive Miss
Gledd back to town. She looked at me with eyes which
gave me, as I thought, no peculiar thanks, and then remarked that she had come out with Mr. Hoskins, and that
she would go back with him.

"Oh, don't mind me," said Hoskins, who was at that
time up to his middle in snow.

"Ah, but I do mind you," said Ophelia. "Don't you think
we could go back and send some people to help these
gentlemen?"

It was the coolest proposition that I had ever heard, but
in two minutes Miss Gledd was putting it into execution.
Hannibal Hoskins was driving her back in the sleigh which
I had hired, and I was left with my friend to extricate those
other two brutes from the ditch.

"That's so like Pheely Gledd," said my friend. "She always has her own way."

Then it was that I questioned Miss Gledd's beauty, and
was told that before long I should find myself to be wrong.
I had almost acknowledged myself to be wrong before that
night was over.

I was at a tea-party that same evening at which Miss
Gledd was present;—it was called a tea-party, though I saw
no tea. I did, however, see a large hot supper, and a very
large assortment of long-necked bottles. I was standing
rather listlessly near the door, being short of acquaintance,

when young Yankee dandy, with a very stiff neck, informed me that Miss Gledd wanted to speak to me. Having given me this intimation he took himself off, with an air of disgust, among the long-necked bottles.

"Mr. Green," she said,—I had just been introduced to her as she was being whisked away by Hoskins in my sleigh—"Mr. Green, I believe I owe you an apology. When I took your sleigh from you I didn't know you were a Britisher,—I didn't, indeed."

I was a little nettled, and endeavoured to explain to her that an Englishman would be just as ready to give up his carriage to a lady as any American.

"Oh, dear, yes; of course," she said. "I didn't mean that; and now I've put my foot into it worse than ever; I thought you were at home here, and knew our ways, and if so you wouldn't mind being left with a broken sleigh."

I told her that I didn't mind it. That what I had minded was the being robbed of the privilege of driving her home, which I had thought to be justly mine.

"Yes," said she, "and I was to leave my friend in the ditch! That's what I never do. You didn't suffer any disgrace by remaining there till the men came."

"I didn't remain there till any men came. I got it out and drove it home."

"What a wonderful man! But then you're English. However, you can understand that if I had left my driver he would have been disgraced. If ever I go out anywhere with you, Mr. Green, I'll come home with you. At any rate it sha'n't be my fault if I don't." After that I couldn't be angry with her, and so we became great friends.

Shortly afterwards the crash came; but Miss Gledd seemed to disregard the crash altogether, and held her own in Boston. As far as I could see there were just as many men desirous of marrying her as ever, and among the number Hannibal H. Hoskins was certainly no defaulter.

My acquaintance with Boston had become intimate; but, after awhile, I went away for twelve months, and when I returned, Miss Gledd was still Miss Gledd. "And what of Hoskins?" I said to my friend,—the same friend who had been with me in the sleighing expedition.

"He's just on the old tack. I believe he proposes once a-year regularly. But they say now that she's going to marry an Englishman."

It was not long before I had an opportunity of renewing my friendship with Miss Gledd,—for our acquaintance had latterly amounted to a friendship,—and of seeing the Englishman with her. As it happened, he also was a friend of my own,—an old friend, and the last man in the world whom I should have picked out as a husband for Ophelia. He was a literary man of some mark, fifteen years her senior, very sedate in his habits, not much given to love-making, and possessed of a small fortune sufficient for his own wants, but not sufficient to enable him to marry with what he would consider comfort. Such was Mr. Pryor, and I was given to understand that Mr. Pryor was a suppliant at the feet of Ophelia. He was a suppliant, too, with so much hope, that Hannibal Hoskins and the other suitors were up in arms against him. I saw them together at some evening assembly, and on the next morning I chanced to be in Miss Gledd's drawing-room. On my entrance there were others there, but the first moment that we were alone, she turned round sharp upon me with a question,—"You know your countryman, Mr. Pryor; what sort of a man is he?"

"But you know him also," I answered. "If the rumours in Boston are true, he is already a favourite in Chestnut Street."

"Well, then, for once in a way the rumours in Boston are true, for he is a favourite. But that is no reason you shouldn't tell me what sort of a man he is. You've known him these ten years."

"Pretty nearly twenty," I said. I had known him ten or twelve.

"Ah," said she, "you want to make him out to be older than he is. I knew his age to-day."

"And does he know yours?"

"He may if he wishes it. Everybody in Boston knows it,—including yourself. Now tell me; what sort of man is Mr. Pryor?"

"He is a man highly esteemed in his own country."

"So much I knew before; and he is highly esteemed here also. But I hardly understand what high estimation means in your country."

"It is much the same thing in all countries, as I take it," said I.

"There you are absolutely wrong. Here in the States, if a man be highly esteemed it amounts almost to everything; such estimation will carry him everywhere,—and will carry his wife everywhere too, so as to give her a chance of making standing ground for herself."

"But Mr. Pryor has not got a wife."

"Don't be stupid. Of course he hasn't got a wife, and of course you know what I mean."

But I did not know what she meant. I knew that she was meditating whether or no it would be good for her to become Mrs. Pryor, and that she was endeavouring to get from me some information which might assist her in coming to a decision on that matter; but I did not understand the exact gist and point of her enquiry.

"You have so many prejudices of which we know nothing," she continued. "Now don't put your back up and fight for that blessed old country of yours, as though I were attacking it."

"It is a blessed old country," said I, patriotically.

"Quite so; very blessed, and very old,—and very nice too, I'm sure. But you must admit that you have prejudices. You are very much the better, perhaps, for having them. I often wish that we had a few." Then she stopped her tongue, and asked no further question about Mr. Pryor; but it seemed to me that she wanted me to go on with the conversation.

"I hate discussing the relative merits of the two countries," said I; "and I especially hate to discuss them with you. You always begin as though you meant to be fair, and end by an amount of unfairness, that— that—"

"Which would be insolent if I were not a woman, and which is pert as I am one. That is what you mean."

"Something like it."

"And yet I love your country so dearly, that I would sooner live there than in any other land in the world, if only I thought that I could be accepted. You English people," she continued, "are certainly wanting in intelligence, or you would read in the anxiety of all we say about England how much we all think of you. What will England say of us?—what will England think of us? —what will England do in this or that matter as it concerns us? —that is our first thought as to every matter that is of importance to us. We abuse you, and admire you. You abuse us, and despise us. That is the difference. So you won't tell me anything about Mr. Pryor? Well, I sha'n't ask you again!—I never again ask a favour that has been refused." Then she turned away to some old gentleman that was talking to her mother, and the conversation was at an end.

I must confess that as I walked away from Chestnut Street into Beacon Street, and across the common, my anxiety was more keen with regard to Mr. Pryor than as concerned Miss Gledd. He was an Englishman and an old friend, and being also a man not much younger than myself, he was one regarding whom I might, perhaps, form some correct judgment as to what would and what would not suit him. Would he do well in taking Ophelia Gledd home to England with him as his wife? Would she be accepted there, as she herself had phrased it,—accepted in such fashion as to make him contented? She was intelligent,—so intelligent that few women whom she would meet in her proposed new country could beat her there; she was pleasant, good-humoured, true, as I believed; but would she be accepted in London? There was a freedom and easiness about her, a readiness to say anything that came into her mind, an absence of all reticence, which would go very hard with her in London. But I never had heard her say anything that she should not have said. Perhaps, after all, we have got our prejudices in England. When next I met Pryor, I spoke to him about Miss Gledd.

"The long and the short of it is," I said, "that people say that you are going to marry her."

"What sort of people?"

"They were backing you against Hannibal Hoskins the other night at the club, and it seemed clear that you were the favourite."

"The vulgarity of these people surpasses anything that I ever dreamed of," said Pryor. "That is, of some of them. It's all very well for you to talk, but could such a bet as that be proposed in the open room of any club in London?"

"The clubs in London are too big, but I dare say it might down in the country. It would be just the thing for Little Pedlington."

"But Boston is not Little Pedlington. Boston assumes to be the Athens of the States. I shall go home by the first boat next month." He had said nothing to me about Miss Gledd, but it was clear that if he went home by the first boat next month, he would go home without a wife; and as I certainly thought that the suggested marriage was undesirable, I said nothing to persuade him to remain at Boston.

It was again sleighing time, and some few days after my meeting with Pryor I was out upon the Brighton Road in the thick of the crowd. Presently I saw the hat and back of Hannibal Hoskins, and by his side was Ophelia Gledd. Now, it must be understood that Hannibal Hoskins, though he was in many respects most unlike an English gentleman, was neither a fool nor a bad fellow. A fool he certainly was not. He had read much. He could speak glibly, as is the case with all Americans. He was scientific, classical, and poetical,— probably not to any great depth. And he knew how to earn a large income with the full approbation of his fellow-citizens. I had always hated him since the day on which he had driven Miss Gledd home; but I had generally attributed my hatred to the manner in which he wore his hat on one side. I confess I had often felt amazed that Miss Gledd should have so far encouraged him. I think I may at any rate declare that he would not have been accepted in London,—not accepted for much! And yet Hannibal Hoskins was not a bad fellow. His true devotion to Ophelia Gledd proved that.

"Miss Gledd," said I, speaking to her from my sleigh, "do you remember your calamity? There is the very ditch not a hundred yards ahead of you."

"And here is the very knight that took me home in your sleigh," said she, laughing.

Hoskins sat bolt upright and took off his hat. Why he took off his hat I don't know, unless that thereby he got an opportunity of putting it on again a little more on one side.

"Mr. Hoskins would not have the goodness to upset you again, I suppose?" said I.

"No, Sir," said Hoskins; and he raised the reins and squared up his elbows, meaning to look like a knowing charioteer. "I guess we'll go back; eh, Miss Gledd?"

"I guess we will," said she. "But, Mr. Green, don't you remember that I once told you if you'd take me out, I'd be sure to come home with you? You never tried me, and I take it bad of you." So encouraged I made an engagement with her, and in two or three days' time from that I had her beside me in my sleigh on the same road.

By this time I had quite become a convert to the general opinion, and was ready to confess in any presence, that Miss Gledd was a beauty. As I started with her out of the city warmly enveloped in buffalo furs, I could not but think how nice it would be to drive on and on, so that nobody should ever catch us. There was a sense of companionship about her in which no woman that I have ever known excelled her. She had a way of adapting herself to the friend of the moment which was beyond anything winning. Her voice was decidedly very pleasant; and as to that nasal twang I am not sure that I was ever right about it. I wasn't in love with her myself, and didn't want to fall in love with her. But I felt that I should have liked to cross the Rocky Mountains with her, over to the Pacific, and to have come home round by California, Peru, and the Pampas. And for such a journey I should not at all have desired to hamper the party with the society either of Hannibal Hoskins or of Mr. Pryor!

"I hope you feel that you're having your revenge," said she.

"But I don't mean to upset you."

"I almost wish you would, so as to make it even. And my poor friend Mr. Hoskins would feel himself so satisfied. He says you Englishmen are conceited about your driving."

"No doubt he thinks we are conceited about everything."

"So you are, and so you should be. Poor Hannibal! He is wild with despair, because—"

"Because what?"

"Oh, never mind. He is an excellent fellow, but I know you hate him."

"Indeed, I don't."

"Yes, you do; and so does Mr. Pryor. But he is so good! You can't either understand or appreciate the kind of goodness which our young men have. Because he pulls his hat about, and can't wear his gloves without looking stiff, you won't remember that out of his hard earnings he gives his mother and sisters everything that they want."

"I didn't know anything of his mother and sisters."

"No, of course you didn't. But you know a great deal about his hat and gloves. You are too hard, and polished, and well-mannered in England to know anything about anybody's mother or sisters,—or indeed to know anything about anybody's anything. It is nothing to you whether a man be moral, or affectionate, or industrious, or good-tempered. As long as he can wear his hat properly, and speak as though nothing on the earth, or over the earth, or under the earth, could ever move him,—that is sufficient."

"And yet I thought you were so fond of England?"

"So I am. I too like,—nay love that ease of manner which you all possess and which I cannot reach."

Then there was silence between us for perhaps half a mile, and yet I was driving slow, as I did not wish to bring our journey to an end. I had fully made up my mind that it would be in every way better for my friend Pryor that he should give up all thoughts of this Western Aspasia, and yet I was anxious to talk to her about him as though such a marriage were still on the cards. It had seemed that lately she had thrown herself much into an intimacy with myself, and that she was anxious to speak openly to me if I would only allow it. But she had already declared, on a former occasion, that she would ask me no further question about Mr. Pryor. At last I plucked up courage, and put to her a direct proposition about the future tenor of her life.

"After all that you have said about Mr. Hoskins, I suppose I may expect to hear that you have at last accepted him?"

I could not have asked such a question of any English girl that I ever knew,—not even of my own sister in these plain terms. And yet she took it not only without anger, but even without surprise. And she answered it, as though I had asked her the most ordinary question in the world.

"I wish I had," she said. "That is, I think I wish I had. It is certainly what I ought to do."

"Then why do you not do it?"

"Ah ! why do I not? Why do we not all do just what we ought to do? But why am I to be cross-questioned by you? You would not answer me a question when I asked you the other day."

"You tell me that you wish you had accepted Mr. Hoskins. Why do you not do so?" said I, continuing my cross-examination.

"Because I have a vain ambition,—a foolish ambition,— a silly, moth-like ambition,—by which, if I indulge it, I shall only burn my wings. Because I am such an utter ass that I would fain make myself an Englishwoman."

"I don't see that you need burn your wings!"

"Yes; should I go there I shall find myself to be nobody, whereas here I am in good repute. Here I could make my husband a man of mark by dint of my own power. There I doubt whether even his esteem would so shield and cover me as to make me endurable. Do you think that I do not know the difference; that I am not aware of what makes social excellence there? And yet, though I know it all, and covet it, I despise it. Social distinction with us is given on sounder terms than it is with you, and is more frequently the deserved reward of merit. Tell me; if I go to London they will ask who was my grandfather?"

"Indeed, no; they will not ask even of your father unless you speak of him."

"No; their manners are too good. But they will speak of their fathers, and how shall I talk with them? Not but what my grandfather was a good man; and you are not to suppose that I am ashamed of him because he stood in a store and sold leather with his own hands. Or rather, I am ashamed of it. I should tell my husband's old friends and my new acquaintances that it was so because I am not a coward; and yet, as I told them, I should be ashamed. His brother is what you call a baronet."

"Just so."

"And what would the baronet's wife say to me with all my sharp Boston notions? Can't you see her looking at me over the length of the drawing-room? And can't you fancy how pert I should be, and what snappish words I should say to the she baronet? Upon the whole, don't you think I should do better with Mr. Hoskins?"

Again I sat silent for some time. She had now asked me a question to which I was bound to give her a true answer,— an answer that should be true as to herself without reference to Pryor. She was sitting back in the sleigh, tamed as it were by her own thoughts, and she had looked at me as though she had really wanted counsel. "If I am to answer you in truth,—" I said.

"You are to answer me in truth."

"Then," said I, "I can only bid you take him of the two whom you love; that is, if it be the case that you love either."

"Love!" she said.

"And if it be the case," I continued, "that you love neither, then leave them both as they are."

"I am not then to think of the man's happiness?"

"Certainly not by marrying him without affection."

"Ah! but I may regret him,—with affection."

"And for which of them do you feel affection?" I asked. And as I asked, we were already within the streets of Boston.

She again remained silent, almost till I had placed her at her own door; then she looked at me with eyes full, not only of meaning, but of love also;—with that in her eyes for which I had not hitherto given her credit.

"You know the two men," she said, "and do you ask me that?" When these words were spoken, she jumped from the sleigh, and hurried up the steps to her father's door. In very truth, the hat and gloves of Hannibal Hoskins had influenced her as they had influenced me, and they had done so although she knew how devoted he was as a son and a brother.

For a full month after that I had no further conversation with Miss Gledd or with Mr. Pryor on the subject. At this time I was living in habits of daily intimacy with Pryor, but as he did not speak to me about Ophelia, I did not often mention her name to him. I was aware that he was often with her,—or at any rate often in her company. But I did not believe that he had any daily habit of going to the house, as he would have done had he been her accepted suitor. And indeed I believed him to be a man who would be very persevering in offering his love; but who, if persistently refused, would not probably tender it again. He still talked of returning to England, though he had fixed no day. I myself purposed doing so early in May, and used such influence as I had in endeavouring to keep him at Boston till that time. Miss Gledd, also, I constantly saw. Indeed, one could not live in the society of Boston without seeing her almost daily, and I was aware that Mr. Hoskins was frequently with her. But, as regarded her, this betokened nothing, as I have before endeavoured to explain. She never deserted a friend, and had no idea of being reserved in her manners with a man because it was reported that such man was her lover. She would be very gracious to Hannibal in Mr. Pryor's presence; and yet it was evident, at any rate to me, that in doing so, she had no thought of grieving her English admirer.

I was one day seated in my room at the hotel when a servant brought me up a card. "Misther Hoskins; he's a waiting below, and wants to see yer honour very partickler," said the raw Irishman. Mr. Hoskins had never done me the honour of calling on me before, nor had I ever become intimate with him even at the club; but, nevertheless, as he had come to me, of course I was willing to see him, and so he was shown up into my room. When he entered, his hat was, I suppose, in his hand; but it looked as though it had been on one side of his head the moment before, and as though it would be on one side again the moment he left me.

"I beg your pardon, Mr. Green," said he. "Perhaps I ought not to intrude upon you here."

"No intrusion at all. Won't you take a chair, and put your hat down?" He did take a chair, but he wouldn't put his hat down. I confess that I had been actuated by a foolish desire to see it placed for a few minutes in a properly perpendicular position.

"I've just come,—I'll tell you why I've come. There are some things, Mr. Green, in which a man doesn't like to be interfered with." I could not but agree with this, but in doing so I expressed a hope that Mr. Hoskins had not been interfered with to any very disagreeable extent. "Well!" I scorn to say that the Boston dandy said "wa'all," but if this story were written by any Englishman less conscientious than myself, that latter form of letters is the one which he would adopt in his endeavour to convey the sound as uttered by Mr. Hoskins. "Well, I don't quite know about that. Now, Mr. Green, I'm not a quarrelsome man. I don't go about with six-shooters in my pocket, and I don't want to fight, nohow, if I can help it."

In answer to this I was obliged to tell him that I sincerely hoped that he would not have to fight; but that if fighting became necessary to him, I trusted that his fighting propensities would not be directed against any friend of mine.

"We don't do much in that way on our side of the water," said I.

"I am well aware of that," said he. "I don't want any one to teach me what are usages of genteel life in England. I was there the whole fall, two years ago."

"As regards myself," said I, "I don't think much good was ever done by duelling."

"That depends, Sir, on how things eventuate. But, Mr. Green, satisfaction of that description is not what I desiderate on the present occasion. I wish to know whether Mr. Pryor is, or is not, engaged to marry Miss Ophelia Gledd."

"If he is, Mr. Hoskins, I don't know it."

"But, Sir, you are his friend."

This I admitted; but again assured Mr. Hoskins that I knew nothing of any such engagement. He pleaded also that I was her friend as well as his. This, too, I admitted, but again declared that from neither side had I been made aware of the fact of any such engagement.

"Then, Mr. Green," said he, "may I ask you for your own private opinion?"

Upon the whole I was inclined to think that he might not, and so I told him in what most courteous words I could find for the occasion. His back at first grew very long and stiff, and his hat became more and still more sloped as he held it. I began to fear that, though he might not have a six-shooter in his pocket, he had nevertheless some kind of pistol in his thoughts. At last he started up on his feet and confronted me, as I thought, with a look of great anger. But his words when they came were no longer angry.

"Mr. Green," said he, "if you knew all that I've done to get that girl!"

My heart was instantly softened to him.

"For aught that I know," said I, "you may have her this moment for asking."

"No," said he; "no." His voice was very melancholy, and as he spoke he looked into his sloping hat. "No; I've just come from Chestnut Street, and I think she's rather more turned against me than ever."

He was a tall man, good-looking after a fashion, dark, with thick black shiny hair, and huge bold moustachios. I myself do not like his style of appearance, but he certainly had a manly bearing. And in the society of Boston generally he was regarded as a stout fellow, well able to hold his own; as a man, by no means soft, or green, or feminine. And yet now, in the presence of me, a stranger to him, he was almost crying about his lady love. In England no man tells another that he has been rejected; but then in England so few men tell to others anything of their real feeling. As Ophelia had said to me, we are hard and polished, and nobody knows anything about anybody's anything. What could I say to him? I did say something. I went so far as to assure him that I had heard Miss Gledd speak of him in the highest language; and at last perhaps I hinted,— though I don't think I did quite hint it,—that if Pryor were out of the way, Hoskins might find the lady more kind. He soon became quite confidential, as though I were his bosom friend. He perceived, I think, that I was not anxious that Pryor should carry off the prize, and he wished me to teach Pryor that the prize was not such a prize as would suit him.

"She's the very girl for Boston," he said, in his energy;

"but, I put it to you, Mr. Green, she hasn't the gait of going that would suit London."

Whether her gait of going would or would not suit our metropolis, I did not undertake to say in the presence of Mr. Hoskins, but I did at last say that I would speak to Pryor, so that the field might be left open for others if he had no intention of running for the cup himself.

I could not but be taken, and indeed charmed, by the honest strength of affection which Hannibal Hoskins felt for the object of his adoration. He had come into my room determined to display himself as a man of will, of courage, and of fashion. But he had broken down in all that, under his extreme desire to obtain assistance in getting the one thing which he wanted. When he parted with me he shook hands almost boisterously, while he offered me most exuberant thanks. And yet I had not suggested that I could do anything for him. I did think that Ophelia Gledd would accept his offer as soon as Pryor was gone; but I had not told him that I thought so.

About two days afterwards I had a very long and a very serious conversation with Pryor, and at that time I do not think that he had made up his mind as to what he intended to do. He was the very opposite to Hoskins in all his ways and all his moods. There was not only no swagger with him, but a propriety and quiescence of demeanour the very opposite to swagger. In conversation his most violent opposition was conveyed by a smile. He displayed no other energy than what might be shown in the slight curl of his upper lip. If he reproved you he did it by silence. There could be no greater contrast than that between him and

Hoskins, and there could be no doubt which man would recommend himself most to our English world by his gait and demeanour. But I think there may be a doubt as to which was the best man, and a doubt also as to which would make the best husband. That my friend was not then engaged to Miss Gledd I did learn,—but I learned nothing further,—except this, that he would take his departure with me the first week in May, unless anything special occurred to keep him in Boston.

It was some time early in April that I got a note from Miss Gledd, asking me to call on her.

"Come at once," she said, "as I want your advice above all things." And she signed herself, "Yours in all truth, O. G."

I had had many notes from her, but none written in this strain; and therefore, feeling that there was some circumstance to justify such instant notice, I got up and went to her then, at ten o'clock in the morning. She jumped up to meet me, giving me both her hands.

"Oh, Mr. Green," she said to me, "I'm so glad you have come to me. It is all over."

"What is over?" said I.

"My chance of escape from the she baronet. I gave in last night. Pray tell me that I was right. Yet I want you to tell me the truth. And yet, above all things, you must not tell me that I have been wrong."

"Then you have accepted Mr. Pryor?"

"I could not help it," she said. "The temptation was too much for me. I love the very cut of his coat, the turn of his lip, the tone of his voice. The very sound which he makes as he closes the door behind him is too much for me. I believe that I ought to have let him go,—but I could not do it."

"And what will Mr. Hoskins do?"

"I wrote to him immediately and told him everything. Of course I had John's leave for doing so."

This calling of my sedate friend by the name of John was, to my feeling, a most wonderful breaking down of all proprieties.

"I told him the exact truth. This morning I got an answer from him saying that he should visit Russia. I am so sorry because of his mother and sisters."

"And when is it to be?"

"Oh! at once; immediately. So John says. When we resolve on doing these things here, on taking the plunge, we never stand shilly-shallying on the brink as your girls do in England. And that is one reason why I have sent for you. You must promise to go over with us. Do you know I am half afraid of him,—much more afraid of him than I am of you."

They were to be married very early in May, and of course I promised to put off my return for a week or two to suit them.

"And then for the she baronet," she said, "and for all the terrible grandeur of London!"

When I endeavoured to explain to her that she would encounter no great grandeur, she very quickly corrected me.

"It is not grandeur of that sort, but the grandeur of coldness that I mean;—I fear that I shall not do for them. But, Mr. Green, I must tell you one thing. I have not cut off from myself all means of retreat."

"Why, what do you mean? You have resolved to marry him."

"Yes, I have promised to do so; but I did not promise till he had said that if I could not be made to suit his people in Old England, he would return here with me and teach himself to suit my people in New England. The task will be very much easier."

They were married in Boston, not without some considerable splendour of ceremony,—as far as the splendour of Boston went. She was so unusual a favourite that everyone wished to be at her wedding, and she had no idea of giving herself airs and denying her friends a favour. She was married with much éclat, and, as far as I could judge, seemed to enjoy the marriage herself.

Now comes the question: Will she or will she not be received in London as a lady,—as such a lady as my friend Pryor might have been expected to take for his wife?

THE O'CONORS OF CASTLE CONOR, COUNTY MAYO

I SHALL never forget my first introduction to country life in Ireland, my first day's hunting there, or the manner in which I passed the evening afterwards. Nor shall I ever cease to be grateful for the hospitality which I received from the O'Conors of Castle Conor. My acquaintance with the family was first made in the following manner. But before I begin my story, let me inform my reader that my name is Archibald Green.

I had been for a fortnight in Dublin, and was about to proceed into county Mayo on business which would occupy me there for some weeks. My head-quarters would, I found, be at the town of Ballyglass; and I soon learned that Ballyglass was not a place in which I should find hotel accommodation of a luxurious kind, or much congenial society indigenous to the place itself.

"But you are a hunting man, you say," said old Sir P— C—; "and in that case you will soon know Tom O'Conor. Tom won't let you be dull. I'd write you a letter to Tom, only he'll certainly make you out without my taking the trouble."

I did think at the time that the old baronet might have

written the letter for me, as he had been a friend of my father's in former days; but he did not, and I started for Ballyglass with no other introduction to any one in the county than that contained in Sir P—'s promise that I should soon know Mr. Thomas O'Conor.

I had already provided myself with a horse, groom, saddle, and bridle, and these I sent down, *en avant*, that the Ballyglassians might know that I was somebody. Perhaps before I arrived Tom O'Conor might learn that a hunting man was coming into the neighbourhood, and I might find at the inn a polite note intimating that a bed was at my service at Castle Conor. I had heard so much of the free hospitality of the Irish gentry as to imagine that such a thing might be possible.

But I found nothing of the kind. Hunting gentlemen in those days were very common in county Mayo, and one horse was no great evidence of a man's standing in the world. Men there, as I learnt afterwards, are sought for themselves quite as much as they are elsewhere; and though my groom's top-boots were neat, and my horse a very tidy animal, my entry into Ballyglass created no sensation whatever.

In about four days after my arrival, when I was already infinitely disgusted with the little pot-house in which I was forced to stay, and had made up my mind that the people in county Mayo were a churlish set, I sent my horse on to a meet of the fox-hounds, and followed after myself on an open car.

No one but an erratic fox-hunter such as I am,—a fox-hunter, I mean, whose lot it has been to wander about from one pack of hounds to another,—can understand the melancholy feeling which a man has when he first intrudes himself, unknown by any one, among an entirely new set of sportsmen. When a stranger falls thus as it were out of the moon into a hunt, it is impossible that men should not stare at him and ask who he is. And it is so disagreeable to be stared at, and to have such questions asked! This feeling does not come upon a man in Leicestershire or Gloucestershire where the numbers are large, and a stranger or two will always be overlooked, but in small hunting fields it is so painful that a man has to pluck up much courage before he encounters it.

We met on the morning in question at Bingham's Grove. There were not above twelve or fifteen men out, all of whom, or nearly all, were cousins to each other. They seemed to be all Toms, and Pats, and Larrys, and Micks. I was done up very knowingly in pink, and thought that I looked quite the thing, but for two or three hours nobody noticed me.

I had my eyes about me, however, and soon found out which of them was Tom O'Conor. He was a fine-looking fellow, thin and tall, but not largely made, with a piercing gray eye, and a beautiful voice for speaking to a hound. He had two sons there also, short, slight fellows, but exquisite horsemen. I already felt that I had a kind of acquaintance with the father, but I hardly knew on what ground to put in my claim.

We had no sport early in the morning. It was a cold bleak February day, with occasional storms of sleet. We rode from cover to cover, but all in vain. "I am sorry, sir, that we are to have such a bad day, as you are a stranger here," said one gentleman to me. This was Jack O'Conor, Tom's eldest son, my bosom friend for many a year after. Poor Jack! I fear that the Encumbered Estates Court sent him altogether adrift upon the world.

"We may still have a run from Poulnaroe, if the gentleman chooses to come on," said a voice coming from behind with a sharp trot. It was Tom O'Conor.

"Wherever the hounds go, I'll follow," said I.

"Then come on to Poulnaroe," said Mr. O'Conor. I trotted on quickly by his side, and before we reached the cover had managed to slip in something about Sir P— C—.

"What the deuce!" said he. "What! a friend of Sir P—'s? Why the deuce didn't you tell me so? What are you doing down here? Where are you staying?" &c., &c., &c.

At Poulnaroe we found a fox, but before we did so Mr. O'Conor had asked me over to Castle Conor. And this he did in such a way that there was no possibility of refusing him—or, I should rather say, of disobeying him. For his invitation came quite in the tone of a command.

"You'll come to us of course when the day is over—and let me see; we're near Ballyglass now, but the run will be right away in our direction. Just send word for them to send your things to Castle Conor."

"But they're all about, and unpacked," said I.

"Never mind. Write a note and say what you want now, and go and get the rest to-morrow yourself. Here, Patsey!—Patsey! run into Ballyglass for this gentleman at once. Now don't be long, for the chances are we shall find here." And then, after giving some further hurried instructions he left me to write a line in pencil to the innkeeper's wife on the bank of a ditch.

This I accordingly did. "Send my small portmanteau," I said, "and all my black dress clothes, and shirts, and socks, and all that, and above all my dressing things which are on the little table, and the satin neck-handkerchief, and whatever you do, mind you send my *pumps*"; and I underscored the latter word; for Jack O'Conor, when his father left me, went on pressing the invitation. "My sisters are going to get up a dance," said he; "and if you are fond of that kind of things perhaps we can amuse you." Now in those days I was very fond of dancing—and very fond of young ladies too, and therefore glad enough to learn that Tom O'Conor had daughters as well as sons. On this account I was very particular in underscoring the word pumps.

"And hurry, you young divil," Jack O'Conor said to Patsey.

"I have told him to take the portmanteau over on a car," said I.

"All right; then you'll find it there on our arrival."

We had an excellent run, in which I may make bold to say that I did not acquit myself badly. I stuck very close to the hounds, as did the whole of the O'Conor brood; and when the fellow contrived to earth himself, as he did, I received those compliments on my horse, which is the most approved praise which one fox-hunter ever gives to another.

"We'll buy that fellow of you before we let you go," said Peter, the youngest son.

"I advise you to look sharp after your money if you sell him to my brother," said Jack.

And then we trotted slowly off to Castle Conor, which, however, was by no means near to us. "We have ten miles to go;—good Irish miles," said the father. "I don't know that I ever remember a fox from Poulnaroe taking that line before."

"He wasn't a Poulnaroe fox," said Peter.

"I don't know that," said Jack; and then they debated that question hotly.

Our horses were very tired, and it was late before we reached Mr. O'Conor's house. That getting home from hunting with a thoroughly weary animal, who has no longer sympathy or example to carry him on, is very tedious work. In the present instance I had company with me; but when a man is alone, when his horse toes at every ten steps, when the night is dark and the rain pouring, and there are yet eight miles of road to be conquered,—at such times a man is almost apt to swear that he will give up hunting.

At last we were in the Castle Conor stable yard;—for we had approached the house by some back way; and as we entered the house by a door leading through a wilderness of back passages, Mr. O'Conor said out loud, "Now, boys, remember I sit down to dinner in twenty minutes." And then turning expressly to me, he laid his hand kindly upon my shoulder and said, "I hope you will make yourself quite at home at Castle Conor, and whatever you do, don't keep us waiting for dinner. You can dress in twenty minutes, I suppose?"

"In ten!" said I, glibly.

"That's well. Jack and Peter will show you your room," and so he turned away and left us.

My two young friends made their way into the great hall, and thence into the drawing-room, and I followed them. We were all dressed in pink, and had waded deep through bog and mud. I did not exactly know whither I was being led in this guise, but I soon found myself in the presence of two young ladies, and of a girl about thirteen years of age.

"My sisters," said Jack, introducing me very laconically; "Miss O'Conor, Miss Kate O'Conor, Miss Tizzy O'Conor."

"My name is not Tizzy," said the younger; "it's Eliza. How do you do, sir? I hope you had a fine hunt! Was papa well up, Jack?"

Jack did not condescend to answer this question, but asked one of the elder girls whether anything had come, and whether a room had been made ready for me.

"Oh yes!" said Miss O'Conor; "they came, I know, for I saw them brought into the house; and I hope Mr. Green will find everything comfortable." As she said this I thought I saw a slight smile steal across her remarkably pretty mouth.

They were both exceedingly pretty girls. Fanny the elder wore long glossy curls,—for I write, oh reader, of bygone days, as long ago as that, when ladies wore curls if it pleased them so to do, and gentlemen danced in pumps, with black handkerchiefs round their necks,—yes, long black, or nearly black silken curls; and then she had such eyes;—I never knew whether they were most wicked or most bright; and her face was all dimples, and each dimple was laden with laughter and laden with love. Kate was probably the prettier girl of the two, but on the whole not so attractive.

She was fairer than her sister, and wore her hair in braids; and was also somewhat more demure in her manner.

In spite of the special injunctions of Mr. O'Conor senior, it was impossible not to loiter for five minutes over the drawing-room fire talking to these houris—more especially as I seemed to know them intimately by intuition before half of the five minutes was over. They were so easy, so pretty, so graceful, so kind, they seemed to take it so much as a matter of course that I should stand there talking in my red coat and muddy boots.

"Well; do go and dress yourselves," at last said Fanny, pretending to speak to her brothers but looking more especially at me. "You know how mad papa will be. And remember, Mr. Green, we expect great things from your dancing to-night. Your coming just at this time is such a Godsend." And again that soupçon of a smile passed over her face.

I hurried up to my room, Peter and Jack coming with me to the door. "Is everything right?" said Peter, looking among the towels and water-jugs. "They've given you a decent fire for a wonder," said Jack, stirring up the red hot turf which blazed in the grate. "All right as a trivet," said I. "And look alive like a good fellow," said Jack. We had scowled at each other in the morning as very young men do when they are strangers; and now, after a few hours, we were intimate friends.

I immediately turned to my work, and was gratified to find that all my things were laid out ready for dressing; my portmanteau had of course come open, as my keys were in my pocket, and therefore some of the excellent servants of the house had been able to save me all the trouble of un-packing. There was my shirt hanging before the fire; my black clothes were spread upon the bed, my socks and collar and handkerchief beside them; my brushes were on the toilet table, and everything prepared exactly as though my own man had been there. How nice!

I immediately went to work at getting off my spurs and boots, and then proceeded to loosen the buttons at my knees. In doing this I sat down in the arm-chair which had been drawn up for me, opposite the fire. But what was the object on which my eyes then fell;—the objects I should rather say!

Immediately in front of my chair was placed, just ready for my feet, an enormous pair of shooting-boots—half-boots made to lace up round the ankles, with thick double leather soles, and each bearing half a stone of iron in the shape of nails and heel-pieces. I had superintended the making of these shoes in Burlington Arcade with the greatest diligence. I was never a good shot; and, like some other sportsmen, intended to make up for my deficiency in performance by the excellence of my shooting apparel. "Those nails are not large enough," I had said; "nor nearly large enough." But when the boots came home they struck even me as being too heavy, too metalsome. "He, he, he," laughed the boot boy as he turned them up for me to look at. It may therefore be imagined of what nature were the articles which were thus set out for the evening's dancing.

And then the way in which they were placed! When I saw this the conviction flew across my mind like a flash of lightning that the preparation had been made under other eyes than those of the servant. The heavy big boots were placed so prettily before the chair, and the strings of each were made to dangle down at the sides, as though just ready for tying! They seemed to say, the boots did, "Now, make haste. We at any rate are ready—you cannot say that you were kept waiting for us." No mere servant's hand had ever enabled a pair of boots to laugh at one so completely.

But what was I to do? I rushed at the small portmanteau, thinking that my pumps also might be there. The woman surely could not have been such a fool as to send me those tons of iron for my evening wear! But, alas, alas! no pumps were there. There was nothing else in the way of covering for my feet; not even a pair of slippers.

And now what was I to do? The absolute magnitude of my misfortune only loomed upon me by degrees. The twenty minutes allowed by that stern old paterfamilias were already gone and I had done nothing towards dressing. And indeed it was impossible that I should do anything that would be of avail. I could not go down to dinner in my stocking feet, nor could I put on my black dress trousers, over a pair of mud-painted top-boots. As for those iron-soled horrors—; and then I gave one of them a kick with the side of my bare foot which sent it half way under the bed.

But what was I to do? I began washing myself and brushing my hair with this horrid weight upon my mind. My first plan was to go to bed, and send down word that I had been taken suddenly ill in the stomach; then to rise early in the morning and get away unobserved. But by such a course of action I should lose all chance of any further acquaintance with those pretty girls! That they were already aware of the extent of my predicament, and were now enjoying it—of that I was quite sure.

What if I boldly put on the shooting-boots, and clattered down to dinner in them? What if I took the bull by the horns, and made myself the most of the joke? This might be very well for the dinner, but it would be a bad joke for me when the hour for dancing came. And, alas! I felt that I lacked the courage. It is not every man that can walk down to dinner, in a strange house full of ladies, wearing such boots as those I have described.

Should I not attempt to borrow a pair? This, all the world will say, should have been my first idea. But I have not yet mentioned that I am myself a large-boned man, and that my feet are especially well developed. I had never for a moment entertained a hope that I should find any one in that house whose boot I could wear. But at last I rang the bell. I would send for Jack, and if everything failed, I would communicate my grief to him.

I had to ring twice before anybody came. The servants, I well knew, were putting the dinner on the table. At last a man entered the room, dressed in rather shabby black, whom I afterwards learned to be the butler.

"What is your name, my friend?" said I, determined to make an ally of the man.

"My name? Why Larry sure, yer honer. And the masther is out of his sinses in a hurry, becase yer honer don't come down."

"Is he though? Well now, Larry; tell me this; which of all the gentlemen in the house has got the largest foot?"

"Is it the largest foot, yer honer?" said Larry, altogether surprised by my question.

"Yes; the largest foot," and then I proceeded to explain to him my misfortune. He took up first my top-boot, and then the shooting-boot—in looking at which he gazed with wonder at the nails;—and then he glanced at my feet, measuring them with his eye; and after this he pronounced his opinion.

"Yer honer couldn't wear a morsel of leather belonging to ere a one of 'em, young or ould. There niver was a foot like that yet among the O'Conors."

"But are there no strangers staying here?"

"There's three or four on 'em come in to dinner; but they'll be wanting their own boots I'm thinking. And there's young Misther Dillon; he's come to stay. But Lord love you—" and he again looked at the enormous extent which lay between the heel and the toe of the shooting apparatus which he still held in his hand. "I niver see such a foot as that in the whole barony," he said, "barring my own."

Now Larry was a large man, much larger altogether than myself, and as he said this I looked down involuntarily at his feet; or rather at his foot, for as he stood I could only see one. And then a sudden hope filled my heart. On that foot there glittered a shoe—not indeed such as were my own which were now resting ingloriously at Ballyglass while they were so sorely needed at Castle Conor; but one which I could wear before ladies, without shame—and in my present frame of mind with infinite contentment.

"Let me look at that one of your own," said I to the man,

as though it were merely a subject for experimental inquiry. Larry, accustomed to obedience, took off the shoe and handed it to me.

My own foot was immediately in it, and I found that it fitted me like a glove.

"And now the other," said I—not smiling, for a smile would have put him on his guard; but somewhat sternly, so that that habit of obedience should not desert him at this perilous moment. And then I stretched out my hand.

"But yer honer can't keep 'em, you know," said he. "I haven't the ghost of another shoe to my feet." But I only looked more sternly than before, and still held out my hand. Custom prevailed. Larry stooped down slowly, looking at me the while, and pulling off the other slipper handed it to me with much hesitation. Alas! as I put it to my foot I found that it was old, and worn, and irredeemably down at heel;—that it was in fact no counterpart at all to that other one which was to do duty as its fellow. But nevertheless I put my foot into it, and felt that a descent to the drawing-room was now possible.

"But yer honer will give 'em back to a poor man?" said Larry almost crying. "The masther's mad this minute because the dinner's not up. Glory to God, only listhen to that!" And as he spoke a tremendous peal rang out from some bell down stairs that had evidently been shaken by an angry hand.

"Larry," said I—and I endeavoured to assume a look of very grave importance as I spoke—"I look to you to assist me in this matter."

"Och—wirra sthrue then, and will you let me go? just listhen to that," and another angry peal rang out, loud and repeated.

"If you do as I ask you," I continued, "you shall be well rewarded. Look here; look at these boots," and I held up the shooting-shoes new from Burlington Arcade. "They cost thirty shillings—thirty shillings! and I will give them to you for the loan of this pair of slippers."

"They'd be no use at all to me, yer honer; not the laist use in life."

"You could do with them very well for to-night, and then you could sell them. And here are ten shillings besides," and I held out half a sovereign which the poor fellow took into his hand.

I waited no further parley but immediately walked out of the room. With one foot I was sufficiently pleased. As regarded that I felt that I had overcome my difficulty. But the other was not so satisfactory. Whenever I attempted to lift it from the ground the horrid slipper would fall off, or only just hang by the toe. As for dancing, that would be out of the question.

"Och, murther, murther," sang out Larry, as he heard me going down stairs. "What will I do at all? Tare and 'ounds; there, he's at it agin, as mad as blazes." This last exclamation had reference to another peal which was evidently the work of the master's hand.

I confess I was not quite comfortable as I walked down stairs. In the first place I was nearly half an hour late, and I knew from the vigour of the peals that had sounded that my slowness had already been made the subject of strong remarks. And then my left shoe went flop, flop, on every alternate step of the stairs. By no exertion of my foot in the drawing up of my toe could I induce it to remain permanently fixed upon my foot. But over and above and worse than all this was the conviction strong upon my mind that I should become a subject of merriment to the girls as soon as I entered the room. They would understand the cause of my distress, and probably at this moment were expecting to hear me clatter through the stone hall with those odious metal boots.

However, I hurried down and entered the drawing-room, determined to keep my position near the door, so that I might have as little as possible to do on entering and as little as possible in going out. But I had other difficulties in store for me. I had not as yet been introduced to Mrs. O'Conor; nor to Miss O'Conor, the squire's unmarried sister.

"Upon my word I thought you were never coming," said Mr. O'Conor as soon as he saw me. "It is just one hour since we entered the house. Jack, I wish you would find out what has come to that fellow Larry," and again he rang the bell. He was too angry, or it might be too impatient to go through the ceremony of introducing me to anybody.

I saw that the two girls looked at me very sharply, but I stood at the back of an arm-chair so that no one could see my feet. But that little imp Tizzy walked round deliberately, looked at my heels, and then walked back again. It was clear that she was in the secret.

There were eight or ten people in the room, but I was too much fluttered to notice well who they were.

"Mamma," said Miss O'Conor, "let me introduce Mr. Green to you."

It luckily happened that Mrs. O'Conor was on the same side of the fire as myself, and I was able to take the hand which she offered me without coming round into the middle of the circle. Mrs. O'Conor was a little woman, apparently not of much importance in the world, but, if one might judge from first appearance, very good-natured.

"And my aunt Die, Mr. Green," said Kate, pointing to a very straight-backed, grim-looking lady, who occupied a corner of a sofa, on the opposite side of the hearth. I knew that politeness required that I should walk across the room and make acquaintance with her. But under the existing circumstances how was I to obey the dictates of politeness? I was determined therefore to stand my ground, and merely bowed across the room at Miss O'Conor. In so doing I made an enemy who never deserted me during the whole of my intercourse with the family. But for her, who knows who might have been sitting opposite to me as I now write?

"Upon my word, Mr. Green, the ladies will expect much from an Adonis who takes so long over his toilet," said Tom O'Conor in that cruel tone of banter which he knew so well how to use.

"You forget, father, that men in London can't jump in and out of their clothes as quick as we wild Irishmen," said Jack.

"Mr. Green knows that we expect a great deal from him this evening. I hope you polk well, Mr. Green," said Kate.

I muttered something about never dancing, but I knew that that which I said was inaudible.

"I don't think Mr. Green will dance," said Tizzy; "at least not much." The impudence of that child was, I think, unparalleled by any that I have ever witnessed.

"But in the name of all that's holy, why don't we have dinner?" And Mr. O'Conor thundered at the door. "Larry, Larry, Larry!" he screamed.

"Yes, yer honer, it'll be all right in two seconds," answered Larry, from some bottomless abyss. "Tare an' ages; what'll I do at all," I heard him continuing, as he made his way into the hall. Oh what a clatter he made upon the pavement,—for it was all stone! And how the drops of perspiration stood upon my brow as I listened to him!

And then there was a pause, for the man had gone into the dining-room. I could see now that Mr. O'Conor was becoming very angry, and Jack the eldest son—oh, how often he and I have laughed over all this since—left the drawing-room for the second time. Immediately afterwards Larry's footsteps were again heard, hurrying across the hall, and then there was a great slither, and an exclamation, and the noise of a fall—and I could plainly hear poor Larry's head strike against the stone floor.

"Ochone, ochone!" he cried at the top of his voice— "I'm murthered with 'em now intirely; and d— 'em for boots—St. Peter be good to me."

There was a general rush into the hall, and I was carried with the stream. The poor fellow who had broken his head would be sure to tell how I had robbed him of his shoes. The coachman was already helping him up, and Peter good-naturedly lent a hand.

"What on earth is the matter?" said Mr. O'Conor.

"He must be tipsy," whispered Miss O'Conor, the maiden sister.

"I aint tipsy at all thin," said Larry, getting up and rubbing the back of his head, and sundry other parts of his body. "Tipsy indeed!" And then he added when he was quite upright, "The dinner is sarved—at last."

And he bore it all without telling! "I'll give that fellow a guinea to-morrow morning," said I to myself—"if it's the last that I have in the world."

I shall never forget the countenance of the Miss O'Conors as Larry scrambled up cursing the unfortunate boots— "What on earth has he got on?" said Mr. O'Conor.

"Sorrow take 'em for shoes," ejaculated Larry. But his spirit was good and he said not a word to betray me.

We all then went in to dinner how we best could. It was useless for us to go back into the drawing-room, that each might seek his own partner. Mr. O'Conor "the masther," not caring much for the girls who were around him, and being already half beside himself with the confusion and delay, led the way by himself. I as a stranger should have given my arm to Mrs. O'Conor; but as it was I took her eldest daughter instead, and contrived to shuffle along into the dining-room without exciting much attention, and when there I found myself happily placed between Kate and Fanny.

"I never knew anything so awkward," said Fanny; "I declare I can't conceive what has come to our old servant Larry. He's generally the most precise person in the world, and now he is nearly an hour late—and then he tumbles down in the hall."

"I am afraid I am responsible for the delay," said I.

"But not for the tumble I suppose," said Kate from the other side. I felt that I blushed up to the eyes, but I did not dare to enter into explanations.

"Tom," said Tizzy, addressing her father across the table, "I hope you had a good run to-day." It did seem odd to me that a young lady should call her father Tom, but such was the fact.

"Well; pretty well," said Mr. O'Conor.

"And I hope you were up with the hounds."

"You may ask Mr. Green that. He at any rate was with them, and therefore he can tell you."

"Oh, he wasn't before you, I know. No Englishman could get before you;—I am quite sure of that."

"Don't you be impertinent, miss," said Kate. "You can easily see, Mr. Green, that papa spoils my sister Eliza."

"Do you hunt in top-boots, Mr. Green?" said Tizzy.

To this I made no answer. She would have drawn me into a conversation about my feet in half a minute, and the slightest allusion to the subject threw me into a fit of perspiration.

"Are you fond of hunting, Miss O'Conor?" asked I, blindly hurrying into any other subject of conversation.

Miss O'Conor owned that she was fond of hunting—just a little; only papa would not allow it. When the hounds met anywhere within reach of Castle Conor, she and Kate would ride out to look at them; and if papa was not there that day—an omission of rare occurrence—they would ride a few fields with the hounds.

"But he lets Tizzy keep with them the whole day," said she, whispering.

"And has Tizzy a pony of her own?"

"Oh yes, Tizzy has everything. She's papa's pet, you know."

"And whose pet are you?" I asked.

"Oh—I am nobody's pet, unless sometimes Jack makes a pet of me when he's in a good humour. Do you make pets of your sisters, Mr. Green?"

"I have none. But if I had I should not make pets of them."

"Not of your own sisters?"

"No. As for myself, I'd sooner make a pet of my friend's sister; a great deal."

"How very unnatural," said Miss O'Conor, with the prettiest look of surprise imaginable.

"Not at all unnatural I think," said I, looking tenderly and lovingly into her face. Where does one find girls so pretty, so easy, so sweet, so talkative as the Irish girls? And then with all their talking and all their ease who ever hears of their misbehaving? They certainly love flirting, as they also love dancing. But they flirt without mischief and without malice.

I had now quite forgotten my misfortune, and was beginning to think how well I should like to have Fanny O'Conor for my wife. In this frame of mind I was bending over towards her as a servant took away a plate from the other side, when a sepulchral note sounded in my ear. It was like the memento mori of the old Roman—as though some one pointed in the midst of my bliss to the sword hung over my head by a thread. It was the voice of Larry, whispering in his agony just above my head—

"They's disthroying my poor feet intirely, intirely; so they is! I can't bear it much longer, yer honer." I had committed murder like Macbeth; and now my Banquo had come to disturb me at my feast.

"What is it he says to you?" asked Fanny.

"Oh nothing," I answered, once more in my misery.

"There seems to be some point of confidence between you and our Larry," she remarked.

"Oh no," said I, quite confused; "not at all."

"You need not be ashamed of it. Half the gentlemen in the county have their confidences with Larry—and some of the ladies too, I can tell you. He was born in this house, and never lived anywhere else; and I am sure he has a larger circle of acquaintance than any one else in it."

I could not recover my self-possession for the next ten minutes. Whenever Larry was on our side of the table I was afraid he was coming to me with another agonised whisper. When he was opposite, I could not but watch him as he hobbled in his misery. It was evident that the boots were too tight for him, and had they been made throughout of iron they could not have been less capable of yielding to the feet. I pitied him from the bottom of my heart. And I pitied myself also, wishing that I was well in bed upstairs with some feigned malady, so that Larry might have had his own again.

And then for a moment I missed him from the room. He had doubtless gone to relieve his tortured feet in the servants' hall, and as he did so was cursing my cruelty. But what mattered it? Let him curse. If he would only stay away and do that, I would appease his wrath when we were alone together with pecuniary satisfaction.

But there was no such rest in store for me. "Larry, Larry," shouted Mr. O'Conor, "where on earth has the fellow gone to?" They were all cousins at the table except myself, and Mr. O'Conor was not therefore restrained by any feeling of ceremony. "There is something wrong with that fellow to-day; what is it, Jack?"

"Upon my word, sir, I don't know," said Jack.

"I think he must be tipsy," whispered Miss O'Conor, the maiden sister, who always sat at her brother's left hand. But a whisper though it was, it was audible all down the table.

"No, ma'am; it aint dhrink at all," said the coachman. "It is his feet as does it."

"His feet!" shouted Tom O'Conor.

"Yes; I know it's his feet," said that horrid Tizzy. "He's got on great thick nailed shoes. It was that that made him tumble down in the hall."

I glanced at each side of me, and could see that there was a certain consciousness expressed in the face of each of my two neighbours;—on Kate's mouth there was decidedly a smile, or rather, perhaps, the slightest possible inclination that way; whereas on Fanny's part I thought I saw something like a rising sorrow at my distress. So at least I flattered myself.

"Send him back into the room immediately," said Tom, who looked at me as though he had some consciousness that I had introduced all this confusion into his household. What should I do? Would it not be best for me to make a clean breast of it before them all? But alas! I lacked the courage.

The coachman went out, and we were left for five minutes without any servant, and Mr. O'Conor the while became more and more savage. I attempted to say a word to Fanny, but failed. Vox faucibus haesit.

"I don't think he has got any others," said Tizzy—"at least none others left."

On the whole I am glad I did not marry into the family, as I could not have endured that girl to stay in my house as a sister-in-law.

"Where the d— has that other fellow gone to?" said Tom. "Jack, do go out and see what is the matter. If anybody is drunk send for me."

"Oh, there is nobody drunk," said Tizzy.

Jack went out, and the coachman returned; but what was done and said I hardly remember. The whole room seemed to swim round and round, and as far as I can recollect the company sat mute, neither eating nor drinking. Presently Jack returned.

"It's all right," said he. I always liked Jack. At the present moment he just looked towards me and laughed slightly.

"All right?" said Tom. "But is the fellow coming?"

"We can do with Richard, I suppose," said Jack.

"No—I can't do with Richard," said the father. "And I will know what it all means. Where is that fellow Larry?"

Larry had been standing just outside the door, and now he entered gently as a mouse. No sound came from his footfall, nor was there in his face that look of pain which it had worn for the last fifteen minutes. But he was not the less abashed, frightened and unhappy.

"What is all this about, Larry?" said his master, turning to him. "I insist upon knowing."

"Och thin, Mr. Green, yer honer, I wouldn't be afther telling agin yer honer; indeed I wouldn't thin, av' the masther would only let me hould my tongue." And he looked across at me, deprecating my anger.

"Mr. Green!" said Mr. O'Conor.

"Yes, yer honer. It's all along of his honer's thick shoes," and Larry, stepping backwards towards the door, lifted them up from some corner, and coming well forward, exposed them with the soles uppermost to the whole table.

"And that's not all, yer honer; but they've squoze the very toes of me into a jelly."

There was now a loud laugh, in which Jack and Peter and Fanny and Kate and Tizzy all joined; as too did Mr. O'Conor—and I also myself after a while.

"Whose boots are they?" demanded Miss O'Conor senior, with her severest tone and grimmest accent.

"'Deed then and the divil may have them for me, Miss," answered Larry. "They war Mr. Green's, but the likes of him won't wear them agin afther the likes of me—barring he wanted them very particular," added he, remembering his own pumps.

I began muttering something, feeling that the time had come when I must tell the tale. But Jack, with great good nature, took up the story and told it so well, that I hardly suffered in the telling.

"And that's it," said Tom O'Conor, laughing till I thought he would have fallen from his chair. "So you've got Larry's shoes on—"

"And very well he fills them," said Jack.

"And it's his honer that's welcome to 'em," said Larry,

grinning from ear to ear now that he saw that "the masther" was once more in a good humour.

"I hope they'll be nice shoes for dancing," said Kate.

"Only there's one down at the heel I know," said Tizzy.

"The servant's shoes!" This was an exclamation made by the maiden lady, and intended apparently only for her brother's ear. But it was clearly audible by all the party.

"Better that than no dinner," said Peter.

"But what are you to do about the dancing?" said Fanny, with an air of dismay on her face which flattered me with an idea that she did care whether I danced or no.

In the mean time Larry, now as happy as an emperor, was tripping round the room without any shoes to encumber him as he withdrew the plates from the table.

"And it's his honer that's welcome to 'em," said he again, as he pulled off the table-cloth with a flourish. "And why wouldn't he, and he able to folly the hounds betther nor any Englishman that iver war in these parts before,—anyways so Mick says!"

Now Mick was the huntsman, and this little tale of eulogy from Larry went far towards easing my grief. I had ridden well to the hounds that day, and I knew it.

There was nothing more said about the shoes, and I was soon again at my ease, although Miss O'Conor did say something about the impropriety of Larry walking about in his stocking feet. The ladies however soon withdrew—to my sorrow, for I was getting on swimmingly with Fanny; and then we gentlemen gathered round the fire and filled our glasses.

In about ten minutes a very light tap was heard, the door

was opened to the extent of three inches, and a female voice which I readily recognised called to Jack.

Jack went out, and in a second or two put his head back into the room and called to me—"Green," he said, "just step here a moment, there's a good fellow." I went out, and there I found Fanny standing with her brother.

"Here are the girls at their wits' ends," said he, "about your dancing. So Fanny has put a boy upon one of the horse and proposes that you should send another line to Mrs. Meehan at Ballyglass. It's only ten miles, and he'll be back in two hours."

I need hardly say that I acted in conformity with this advice, I went into Mr. O'Conor's book room, with Jack and his sister, and there scribbled a note. I was delightful to feel how intimate I was with them, and how anxious they were to make me happy.

"And we won't begin till they come," said Fanny.

"Oh, Miss O'Conor, pray don't wait," said I.

"Oh, but we will," she answered. "You have your wine to drink, and then there's the tea; and then we'll have a song or two. I'll spin it out; see if I don't." And so we went to the front door where the boy was already on his horse—her own nag as I afterwards found.

"And Patsey," said she, "ride for your life; and Patsey, whatever you do, don't come back without Mr. Green's pumps—his dancing-shoes you know."

And in about two hours the pumps did arrive; and I don't think I ever spent a pleasanter evening or got more satisfaction out of a pair of shoes. They had not been two minutes on my feet before Larry was carrying a tray of negus across the room in those which I had worn at dinner.

"The Dillon girls are going to stay here," said Fanny as I wished her good night at two o'clock. "And we'll have dancing every evening as long as you remain."

"But I shall leave to-morrow," said I.

"Indeed you won't. Papa will take care of that."

And so he did. "You had better go over to Ballyglass yourself to-morrow," said he, "and collect your own things. There's no knowing else what you may have to borrow of Larry."

I stayed there three weeks, and in the middle of the third I thought that everything would be arranged between me and Fanny. But the aunt interfered; and in about a twelve-month after my adventures she consented to make a more fortunate man happy for his life.

www.ingramcontent.com/pod-product-compliance
Lightning Source LLC
Chambersburg PA
CBHW021110190326
41524CB00009B/78